FIRST BLOOD

Owen glimpsed movement, silhouettes only a bit darker than the skyline, but clearly riders, six or seven of them.

They must have seen him at the same moment. A rifle boomed, but Owen had already whirled his mount to one side. His Winchester spoke once, and again.

He heard a bullet hit, heard a scream, and spotted a body drop to the ground. Owen shot once more, then spurred the mare and raced away. He wasn't fool enough to think he could handle that many attackers singlehandedly. Or was he fool enough to think they wouldn't be following him out to the range?

Soon the outlaw invaders were swarming around him like locusts. And the shots kept coming from all directions—in a war that would leave the range bloodsoaked and desolate. . . .

THE TERREL BRAND

E.Z. Woods

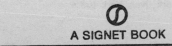

A SIGNET BOOK

NEW AMERICAN LIBRARY

PUBLISHER'S NOTE

This book is a work of fiction. Names, characters, places, and incidents either are the product of the author's imagination or are used fictitiously, and any resemblance to actual persons, living or dead, events, or locales is entirely coincidental.

Copyright © 1989 by Eva Zumwalt

 SIGNET TRADEMARK REG. U.S. PAT OFF., AND FOREIGN COUNTRIES REGISTERED TRADEMARK—MARCA REGISTRADA HECHO EN DRESDEN TN.

SIGNET, SIGNET CLASSIC, MENTOR, ONYX, PLUME, MERIDIAN and NAL BOOKS are published by NAL PENGUIN INC., 1633 Broadway, New York, New York 10019

First Printing, February, 1989

1 2 3 4 5 6 7 8 9

PRINTED IN THE UNITED STATES OF AMERICA

1

It was raining again, a heavy downpour that beat upon the already saturated ground and chilled the April air. As Owen Terrel reined his brown thoroughbred away from Houston's Capitol Hotel, his horse splashed through ankle-deep puddles that in places lay completely across the streets. The tall rider reined his horse to a stop for a moment to let a horse-drawn trolley pass.

There were few vehicles and fewer pedestrians out upon this wet evening. Earlier, wagons had rolled ponderously through the mud, farm wagons hauling goods to the docks, freighters bringing bolts of cloth, barrels of molasses, coffee, and sugar to the stores. Carriage and horseback traffic had kept the main streets of the big town lively. Although Houston had lost its status as capitol in '39, business was brisk since the war's end. Hub of trade between Galveston and the Brazos, Houston saw tons of cotton as well as other farm crops pass through, while the boats brought goods that moved out into the interior of the state.

Owen Terrel did not particularly enjoy town life, and his visits to Houston were few. But it was something to see the way the city was growing. And certainly when Owen married his betrothed, he would be expected to bring his bride in from the plantation often, for she took to town society like a hummingbird to honeysuckle.

Thinking of Julia Talbot, Terrel let his horse splash along the wet streets at a foxtrot, scarcely aware of the drum of rain on his coat and wide-brimmed felt hat. Owen had met Miss Talbot when he was eighteen, and she only fourteen, just months before the war. He had joined the army with all the enthusiasm of other young Texans longing to fight for the glorious cause, and served for a time with Hood's Texas Brigade. Both Owen and his older brother, Will, were at the Battle of Gaines' Mill,

and the Second Battle of Bull Run, and Antietam. Owen's
rank rose quickly to that of brevet captain.

Owen was decorated twice for outstanding bravery, but
he learned quickly that war was far from glorious. He
saw his share of blood and death and disease. In '64 he
was home with a severe leg wound. Will's wife, Amelia,
nursed him back to health, with the help of Jackson Dill,
once a Terrel slave and now the last worker left on the
Terrel plantation. During the two months of his conva-
lescence, Owen was privileged to spend time with Miss
Julia Talbot, now sixteen, beautiful and charming. Owen
courted Julia, and when he returned to battle, he carried
with him Miss Talbot's promise to become his wife.

This time Owen was sent to Brownsville and was
among those who fought at Palmito Ranch, in May 1865.
He and his comrades took captive some eight hundred
federal soldiers. But their victory turned to bitterness
upon learning from the captives that the South had sur-
rendered at Appomattox a month earlier.

Owen had long feared that the South could not win
against the North's superior resources, but he was unprepared for the sickening taste of defeat. Then, and on the
long and weary ride home, he had thought about Julia,
letting the memory of her fair beauty wash away a little
of the ugliness of war and defeat.

He had hoped that they might be married immediately.
Julia's father dashed that notion.

"Captain Terrel, suh," said Osbourne Talbot, "I cain't
but respect your fine war record. But I won't have my
daughter livin' in less than decent conditions. Terreland
is in bad shape, Terrel. You'll have to wait for Julia until
you are able to support her in comfort."

Owen fought down anger that day, bringing to bear the
control that the hardships and anguish of war had taught
him. He couldn't deny that the plantation he and Will
owned jointly was practically in ruins, the fields largely
unworked since the Terrels enlisted. Even with Jackson
Dill's help, Amelia had managed only to raise food for
those few still living at Terreland. Owen and William
would put the good land to work once more, but it would
be long before the Terrel family would know anything
resembling luxury.

Perhaps Owen had hoped that Julia, who managed to have her way in most things, would set her tiny foot down and demand to be married to Owen at once. But this time, though her blue eyes filled tragically, she agreed with her papa. "I'm not cut out for darkie work, dear Owen." She held out her camellia-white hands as if to beg Owen's forgiveness for their fragility. "I do admire darlin' Amelia's gumption, hoein' in her gardens alongside of her workers, but I simply couldn't do it. Why, I'd faint dead away in the heat!"

Owen could only accept the delay. He set himself to rebuild the Terrel family fortunes so that the house could be repaired, servants hired, and a genteel life provided at Terreland.

Nor did William, ten years older than Owen, spare himself. No one could have accused the Terrel men of laziness, and they were expert planters.

But they had not bargained for the carpetbaggers who moved hungrily into Texas and began to skim the cream from the state's bountiful resources. Heavy new taxes took up most of the profit from Terreland. Within two years the plantation was in full production, but there was still no money to enlarge the house. Once more Julia refused to ask her father to relent.

"Another year or so and we can have things nice, Owen," she said. "You know I hate waitin', but I do believe it's for the best. We'd be crowded to death, movin' in with Will and Amelia and little Melissa and Willy. They're such noisy children, aren't they?" She gave him a teasing look from under her lashes. "Why, we'd just never be alone!"

Owen agreed again to wait, but not for long. That fall the Terrel brothers began to build a new wing upon the house. Owen worked tirelessly on it. This would be his home, his and Julia's. "We'll discuss our wedding in the spring, Owen darlin'," Julia promised. "I fear it would be bad luck to wed in the winter, an' I must prepare poor Papa for our separation. You know how he dotes on me!"

But now the spring had come, and Owen's heart was light as he rode to Houston. He took a room at the Capitol Hotel and took pains with his appearance. His gray broadcloth suit was new, his boots well-polished. The collar of his shirt was starched uncomfortably stiff, and Will had loaned him his best cravat. Too bad he must ride through the rain, but his old overcoat would protect his clothing a bit.

Owen touched his tall horse lightly with the spurs as he rode past Miss Brown's Young Ladies' Seminary, a two-storied, galleried building. The lamplit windows turned the rain to golden curtains. Owen realized that he'd best hurry if he hoped to speak to Julia before dinner. This was to be a rather large party, judging from the invitation Julia had sent out to the plantation. He'd rather have approached her and Talbot when they were not entertaining, but the invitation had given him an excuse to leave the endless plantation work.

Deep in thought, Owen failed to notice a slight figure running from the gate of Miss Brown's seminary, until she practically collided with his horse. The girl slipped in the muddy street and fell under the thoroughbred's nose. Beau reared violently and spun to the side, shifting Owen hazardously in his saddle.

"Damn it, Beau!" Owen controlled the startled thoroughbred and blinked at the flurry of white petticoats that seemed to blossom from the mud. Beau was sidling uneasily. Owen quickly dismounted to assist the girl to her feet.

"Ma'am, are you hurt?" He caught her elbow, lifting her from a puddle six inches deep. It was too dark to see her face. She was muttering furiously in a low voice.

"Oh, how stupid! Can't even cross a street safely, run down by a reckless . . . Oh, look at my dress!"

"Ma'am—Miss," Owen said uncertainly, "did my horse step on you? Are you hurt?"

"My dress is ruined. Oh, what shall I do now?" It was a young voice, just now with a mournful tone.

"Did you come from the seminary, miss? Let me escort you back there. You're gettin' soaked to the skin."

Her arm stiffened under his hand. "No. I can't go back to Miss Brown's. They'd know I slipped out—" She cut her speech abruptly short.

Terrel saw a small portmanteau on its side in the mud, and grinned slightly. "Miss, I do believe you've run away. Well, you picked a fine night for it. They'll never be able to track you in this storm, not even with a pack of bloodhounds.''

She jerked free of his fingers, and her bonnet tilted up as she stared at him. Her face was a dim oval in the darkness, eyes wide pools of shadow. Indignantly she demanded, ''Are you makin' fun of me, sir?''

''Oh, no, miss,'' he assured her falsely. ''But it's still rainin' and I can't leave a lady standing in the street. If you don't care to return to the seminary, where may I escort you? It ain't safe for you to be out here alone.''

''Well, it's easy enough to see that,'' she exclaimed. ''I've scarcely taken five steps away from the walk and I've already been run down and shoved into the mud!'' She brushed uselessly at her muddy skirt. ''You needn't concern yourself, sir. Where is my bag . . . and my parasol? Oh, dear, your horse has crushed it.'' She lifted the bent and soiled object as if she had half a mind to punish Terrel with it.

''I feel responsible, miss. It was my horse who, er, destroyed your umbrella and knocked you down. I insist upon escortin' you to your destination. As a gentleman, I can't do less.''

She was quiet for a doubtful moment. ''Well, but how can I be sure you are a gentleman? I've heard that there are ruffians and riffraff in the streets.''

''And so you came out in a pourin' rain, in the dark, to see for yourself?'' Owen caught the sharp lift of her head and headed off the girl's retort. ''Beg your pardon, miss. Please, allow me to lift you onto my horse and take you wherever you were goin'. I am Owen Terrel, of Terreland Plantation. My brother is William Terrel.''

''Oh, yes, I've seen Mrs. Will Terrel in the stores, and she seemed quite nice.'' She hesitated a moment more, and Owen was ruefully conscious that his boots were getting coated with mud, and Julia was always protective of her pa's fine rugs.

''Oh, very well,'' sighed the young woman. ''Please take me to the west edge of town, where the three wagons are camped. I am going west with my uncle and aunt. They raised me, you see. My ma died when I was a baby, and Papa was killed at Antietam.''

Owen liked the quiet dignity of her words. ''I am truly

sorry, miss.'' He led his horse alongside the bedraggled figure. Beau seemed to accept the strange girl without nervousness, now that she was upright and the fluttering white white flounces of her petticoats were concealed.

Julia's dinner would be starting in a few minutes. Owen would be inexcusably late, but saw no help for it. The sooner he delivered this young lady to someone who could take charge of her, the better. Quickly he lifted her into the saddle, handed her the valise, and got on behind her. Beau was already in motion, hopeful, no doubt, of reaching a dry stable.

Fortunately Owen knew where the train in question was being fitted for the journey west, having passed the stout wagons on his way into town. He had felt a twinge of envy at sight of them. What wonders would those travelers see?

''What is your name, miss?'' Owen asked, conscious that her dress was soaked and she was shivering.

''Virginia Morgan,'' she murmured nervously.

''And your uncle? What is he called?''

''It—isn't important. You needn't meet him. Just let me off at the edge of the campground, Mr. Terrel.''

''That wouldn't be right, Miss Morgan. I'll take you to your family.''

''No, please, there is no need.''

''I will take you directly to your family,'' he repeated. She sighed and said no more.

Owen tried to calculate exactly how tardy he would be at the Talbot house. Twenty minutes to the campground, a few minutes at least to introduce himself to Virginia's family and assure himself that she was in safe hands. Then another twenty-five minutes to Julia's white-pillared mansion set grandly on expansive lawns with rose gardens endlessly tended by two gardeners.

A wry grin creased Terrel's thin, sun-browned face. Julia would not be best pleased to see him arrive nearly an hour past the time, spattered with mud to his boot tops. It would take some doing to smooth her ruffled feathers. She would scold, but surely she would be as happy as he to set the date of their wedding at last.

''We're almost there, Mr. Terrel,'' Virginia said with an odd quaver in her soft voice. ''It's that first wagon.

That's—that's my uncle, Joshua Morgan. And that's Aunt Faith, at the fire.'' She sounded as if she dreaded something.

Owen reined Beau nearer the campfire, protected under a canvas stretched out from the wagontop. A tall, angular woman was cooking a meal. In spite of the inclement weather, the scene was oddly pleasant, firelight making the white canvas rosy. Miss Morgan's uncle slogged through the mud toward the wagon, carrying firewood. He paused to watch the riders approach.

Terrel stopped the horse. "Mr. Morgan, may I speak with you, sir?''

Joshua Morgan peered at them. "Who might you be, sir?''

Owen slid off and lifted Virginia from the saddle. She dropped her valise. It splattered into the thick mud and further soiled both their clothing.

Owen swallowed his aggravation. "My name's Owen Terrel. I have brought your niece.''

"Captain Owen Terrel? I've heard of you, sir. What's this about my niece?''

Slowly the girl moved over to the fire and into the light. "Hello Aunt Faith, Uncle Josh.''

The woman stared at her. "Ginny, what in the world? My dear, you're soaked through and through. Here, stand to the fire, you're shaking.''

Mr. Morgan gestured to Terrel. "Come out of the wet, sir. Faith, pour the man some coffee.'' As Owen looped his reins to the wagon's tailgate, Mrs. Morgan hastened to do her husband's bidding. Owen stepped under the canvas. The rain drummed loudly upon the makeshift shelter.

Josh Morgan set his armload of wood down. "Now, then, Virginia,'' he said sternly, "you will explain why you are here, and not safe under Miss Brown's seminary's roof, enjoyin' a fine meal.''

The girl removed her wet bonnet. Long strands of chestnut hair had fallen out of the complicated knot pinned at the back of her head. Owen studied her curiously, for until this moment he had no clear idea what manner of person he had conveyed to this place.

She met Owen's look frankly with wide-set brown eyes

in the slim oval of her mud-smudged face. She was not beautiful in the popular style—taller than average, and slender of build. Her cheekbones were too pronounced, casting interesting shadows that slanted softly toward her mouth, which was vulnerable in expression but rather generous. Her nose was short and straight and her chin determined.

"Ginny, I asked you a question," Josh Morgan raised his voice to be heard over the rain. "What are you doing here, wet and muddy from head to toe?"

She drew herself up and turned to face her uncle. "I want to go west with you and Aunt Faith. Oh, I know you want me to stay in that stupid school for girls another year, but I've learned everything they know how to teach me, Uncle Josh, and I don't want you and Aunt Faith to leave me here alone." Abruptly tears overflowed her dark eyes, and Virginia whirled to fling her arms about her aunt, who made murmuring noises of concern.

"Now, Ginny, you know I promised your daddy I'd see to your education," Mr. Morgan said, patting her shoulder with a big hand.

"Josh," Faith Morgan said, "if she really wants to go . . ."

The girl sensed victory and lifted her head, turning back to her uncle. "It'll be safer for me to travel with my family than to come out later with strangers, Uncle Josh."

Owen realized he had no place in this family discussion. He set his cup down. "Sir, ma'am." He bowed to Faith. "I'm late for an engagement. If you'll excuse me . . ."

Josh Morgan turned. "Certainly, Captain Terrel. Sorry about this, sir. I don't know how you happened to bring our straying chick to us, but we're mighty obliged. As you can see, we're on the point of departure. Looks like we'll be taking our Ginny along."

"You're leavin' Texas?"

Morgan nodded. "Never thought I would. My ol' pappy was one of Austin's first colony here, I fought for Texas' independence from Mexico. But these danged carpetbaggers an' scalawags have taxed me to death. I lost my land. Reckon I could take up more, maybe in west

Texas, but I'm sick to death of the gov'ment we got now. They tell me things is freer in California, or Oregon.''

Owen nodded soberly. ''A lot of good men have made the same decision. Good luck to you, Mr. Morgan.''

''I thank you, Captain, and I hope our paths will cross again one day.'' He shook Owen's hand vigorously.

Virginia stepped forward. ''Thank you, Mr. Terrel,'' she said politely. Her smile made her unusual face quite beautiful for a moment. She seemed delighted that she was to have her way and move west with her family.

Terrel felt an odd twinge of misgiving. The trail was no place for a young, innocent girl. She could have no conception of the hardships of such a journey, into wilderness like nothing she—nor perhaps her people—could imagine. Aside from the normal hazards of the trail, such a small wagon train would be in danger from Indians and bandits. He hoped the Morgans had a competent guide.

But it was none of his business. Julia was often irritated at Owen for befriending those who had no claim upon him. His uneasiness at the thought of these good people crossing empty and hostile territory was likely proof that Julia was right, and he should mind his own business.

And he'd lingered here too long. Quickly he untied his horse and rode away from the wagon camp. He glanced back at the three people by the cook fire, silently wishing them well upon their trek. Even knowing the dangers they would face, he wondered momentarily—what would it be like to cut all ties and trek west?

He touched Beau with the spurs and galloped back toward town, and Julia.

2

When Osbourne Talbot and his daughter entertained, they took pride in lighting every room. Talbot was one of Houston's wealthiest citizens. He was instrumental in politics, an influence to be reckoned with. He got along with the carpetbaggers, as few Texans loyal to their southern roots could or would, and seemed unworried that these dealings lessened the respect of the Terrels and others who had fought for the Confederacy. Where power lay, there Talbot could be found. Perhaps that was satisfaction enough for the man.

But Julia would brook no criticism of her parent. If Owen expected to marry the belle of Houston, he must show Osbourne Talbot the semblance of respect.

Now, gazing up at the mansion, ablaze with lamplight, Terrel dismounted and handed the reins of his horse to a servant.

"I'll take him right to the stables. Cap'n, an' I'll tell Sam rub him down real good," the man assured him.

"Thanks, Jake." Owen took the steps to the broad portico two at a time. Inside the house, he handed his wet coat and hat to the butler and wiped his boot soles upon a doormat. But there was nothing he could do about the splashes of mud upon his boot tops and legs of his gray breeches.

"They's done wid supper, Cap'n Terrel," the bulter said. "Go into the drawin' room, suh."

Owen adjusted his cravat and turned along the corridor. He could hear music—Julia's sweet, childlike voice entertaining her guests with a romantic ballad.

As she finished singing, Owen stepped into a room too full of people and candles and flowers. Ladies and gentlemen were seated on pretty but not very comfortable little chairs Talbot had imported from Europe. Still at the piano Julia's softly rounded face was turned toward a man who stood beside her, a black-haired man in his forties, dressed in a dark suit and snowy shirt with a black string tie.

Recognizing him, Owen stiffened: Caleb Wardworth, almost girlishly handsome, with his pomaded black hair, thick-lashed, soulful brown eyes, carefully trimmed little mustache. A Northerner, Wardworth was shrewd, an opportunist, and fast becoming wealthy upon Texas's Reconstruction woes—in short, a carpetbagger. In spite of Talbot's willingness to deal with this galling element, Owen would not have expected to find this man in Talbot's house.

Julia's blue eyes moved to the group of guests and paused upon Owen's tall figure in the archway. Her smile faded. She riffled nervously through her music.

Osbourne Talbot had spotted Owen too. He stood, favoring the latecomer with an unsmiling stare before lifting Julia to her feet. She was magnificent tonight in ice-blue silk with festoons of lace draping the wide skirt, her shoulders provocatively bare. Her golden-blond hair was piled high, with little curls dangling at her temples.

"My dear, I think now is the perfect time for our special announcement." Osbourne turned to his guests, stroking his beard with a satisfied gesture. "My friends, I am mighty pleased to announce the betrothal of my Julia to a fine, upcomin' gentleman, Mr. Caleb Wardworth."

Owen froze, staring at the pretty tableau: doting father, exquisite daughter, triumphant suitor lifting Julia's delicate fingers to his lips in a dramatic gesture. Julia's face turned toward Owen. More than one of the guests followed her gaze, staring at Owen as if avidly awaiting his reaction. Would the young plantation owner call Wardworth out?

Owen ignored them, unaware of how he must appear, a tall man, dark hair falling over a weather-tanned forehead, gray eyes narrowed, wide mouth grim. The moment held tautly. Then Owen turned and left the room, striding along the corridor to the wide entrance hall.

Owen took his coat and hat and left the mansion, striding down the steps and around the house to the stables. The rain had stopped, but water still dripped from roofs and trees.

Word of Miss Julia's new betrothal must have reached the stable. Sam, the stableman, had known Owen for years, but tonight he kept his face closed and his eyes down.

"You be needin' your horse, suh?" Quickly he resaddled the gelding.

"Thanks, Sam." Owen took the reins and mounted. "Sam, when did Miss Julia start seein' Caleb Wardworth?"

"That Yankee been comin' around 'most ever' day all winter." Sam gave an eloquent shrug.

Owen drew a deep breath. "Well, reckon I won't be seein' you again real soon." He leaned to offer his hand, then urged Beau into a trot and left the lantern-lit stable. Julia came running along the wet drive, a shawl wrapped about her shoulders.

"Wait, please," she called breathlessly, holding her hand up to him.

He stopped the horse.

"Owen, dear, why did you run away? I wanted to talk to you, to explain—"

"I believe Mr. Talbot said about all that has to be said, Julia."

"Don't be like that, dear Owen. I know you were . . . taken by surprise tonight, but that wasn't my fault. If you hadn't been late for dinner, I could have told you before Papa made the announcement."

"Why didn't you tell me weeks ago, Julia? Did your promise to me mean nothing? All it took to change your mind was a slick scalawag, fawnin' around you and your pa."

She lifted her chin sharply. "Don't you dare insult my papa, Owen Terrel. He wants me to have the best life I can, not have to grub around in the fields. Caleb's doin' well, and he plans to enter politics. Why, he could be governor one of these days."

The flare of hope that had kindled when Owen saw her running out to stop him flickered and died. "Then this is what you want? This is your choice, Julia, not just Mr. Talbot's?"

She reached to play with his horse's mane with delicate fingers. "Don't be mad, Owen. I know you love me, and we can still see each other, sometimes." A tear flowed down her flawless cheek. "Part of my heart will always belong to you, Owen. Don't you want me to be happy?"

He straightened in the saddle. "I wish you every happiness, Julia."

He nudged Beau and left her standing there, beautiful in the moonlight that was breaking through the clouds.

Owen stopped at the hotel only long enough to get his gear and pay for his room. Within minutes he was riding out of town, headed for Terreland. It was midnight when he approached the old brick house, with its new wing built especially for Owen's bride. Owen felt a twisting ache in his chest, but he held a tight rein upon his emotion. That dream was gone, and no self-respecting Terrel would go into a damn-fool decline over a broken heart.

Owen turned Beau into a pasture. He was surprised to see lantern light in the kitchen window so late. Was one of the kids ailing? Concerned, Owen hurried toward the back porch, but before he set his boot upon the wooden step, the voices of his brother and Amelia made him pause.

"Owen loves this place, Will. I don't see how we can ask it of him."

"Joe Burdan's offerin' more than Terreland is worth, Melia. Damned if I don't believe we should take it an' pull up stakes, unless it would make you unhappy."

She was quiet for a moment. "I love you, Will Terrel, and I'll follow you anywhere. But would Owen consent to leave Texas? Julia would sink into a decline at the thought of movin' away from Houston an' her pa."

Will sighed so heavily it was clearly audible to Owen, outside the door. "Well, maybe I'd best forget the whole idea."

Owen chose that moment to step into the kitchen. "Before you forget it, Will, tell me what it's all about an' let me in on the decision."

Before tonight, with the shock of Julia's betrayal, Owen would have fought the idea of leaving Terreland. Now he could see the idea from Will's viewpoint, as a chance to sell out advantageously and leave behind the frustrations of working under the carpetbaggers.

"There's fine grazin' land for the taking, Owen," Will was saying. "I been talkin' to some men who hunted buffalo in New Mexico Territory, on the Llano Estacado. They say there's so much land an' so much grass a feller could run thousands of head."

"Where would we get all these cattle?" Owen asked.

Amelia poured coffee for them as William continued.

"Now, there's the fine part. There's a big spread near Brownsville, belongs to Richard King, the steamboat owner who ran the Union blockade for Texas. King's been runnin' longhorns since '53. His ranch is about the only one that far west that wasn't overrun by Indians durin' the war. I hear that a lot of cattle was let to run wild out there, ranches abandoned when the border forts were empty and the Comanche was raidin'. There's unbranded cattle thick as fleas on a hound's ear out there. In a few months we could round us up a herd and push 'em on to empty country and set up. Or we could buy a herd from King. That might be best, save us time to prepare for winter.''

Owen felt a flicker of interest. ''That don't sound half-bad, Will. Take a lot o' hard work to get set up, livin' quarters and the like, but I reckon the Terrels are no strangers to work. Jackson will help, if he wants to go, and one day little Willy will be big enough to help.''

Will grinned at the thought of his son working steers with horns longer than he was tall.

Amelia was not amused. ''I believe we'll just wait a few years for that.''

She sat down beside her husband. ''You'd best talk to Julia about it, Owen. Livin' would be mighty primitive for a while. There'd be no comforts, no fine furniture, no place to wear a pretty dress.''

Owen drew a deep breath. For a few minutes he'd almost forgotten. Well, now was as good a time as any to tell them.

''Julia don't figger into it. Seems she decided to marry a gent name of Caleb Wardworth.''

William's mouth dropped. ''That Yankee scoundrel? I don't believe it!''

Amelia's kind face displayed concern, but no surprise. ''Owen, I—I'm sorry.''

He ran long fingers over his chin, managed a slight grin. ''Reckon I'll live. Now, then, when do we leave?''

William regarded him soberly. ''Don't agree to this just for our sake, brother. Nor don't agree to it because you're hurtin'. It don't pay to run from problems.''

Owen leaned back, crossing his long, booted legs under the table. He looked around the comfortable kitchen, knowing that he was going to miss it, miss Texas and Terreland. He thought of the times he and Will had hunted, had fished in the bayou, worked these wide fields together.

"Don't pay a man to be afraid to step out to somethin' new, either," he said slowly. "Will, let's do it."

Will studied his younger brother for a moment, then stuck out a big, work-roughened hand. "Yessir, little brother. Let's do it."

They began preparations at once, closing the sale of the property, sending Jackson Dill ahead to purchase healthy young cows and bulls from Captain Richard King's overstocked Santa Gertrudis Ranch, selecting a few things they could take. Amelia packed only the most precious or necessary personal possessions: the Bible, her marriage certificate, clothing, and a favorite toy or two for the children. Wagon space must be reserved for food, bedding, medicines, garden seeds—the necessities of survival in a wild and untamed land. The men bought extra cartridges for their rifles and handguns and chose their best mules to pull the wagons.

The two Conestoga wagons pulled out in an April downpour, and the Terrels turned, their backs upon the wide, fertile acres that had been cleared and planted by the first Terrel to settle in Texas. Amelia wept as she held her tiny daughter protectively in her arms. Willy sat between his parents, his water-slicked hair already standing up, eyes round with excitement.

The men had hoped that two weeks of travel would put them northwest of San Antonio, where they would meet their herd, being driven up from Captain King's ranch. But rain had swollen every stream for the first hundred miles, and every road was deep in mud. They were forced to wait two days before being ferried over the Brazos. There was another wait at the Colorado. At last the skies cleared, but it was the first week in May before they spotted Jackson Dill riding to meet them, waving his hat, shouting greetings.

Owen and William rode forward at a gallop, weaving between the mesquites and other thorny growths.

Dill, once a Terrel slave, was near Owen's age. As boys, the two had been raised like brothers, and their bond of affection was firm. Will trusted him totally. Dill was a broad man with a finely sculptured face, and his loyalty and intelligence made him a valuable friend.

Jackson had proudly accepted the mission Will gave him, to negotiate with Richard King for the cattle, but he seemed delighted at being reunited with his own "family" once more. He yanked his long-headed, broom-tailed mustang to a stop near Owen's thoroughbred. Beau towered over Dill's mount.

"Jackson!" Owen slapped him on the shoulder. "Where'd you get that horse? Lordy, your boots are draggin' the ground."

"Well, sir, Cap'n, that black stud you sent me out on done went footsore. He's been grazin' with the Santa Gertrudis mares. Cap'n King promised that horse'll be fat and fit by the time you get to our herd. I s'pec he's figurin' to get him a few colts from that big black. He's mighty set on crossin' American blood on his Mexican-bred stock. Say, Mr. Will, I done bought a dozen cow-horses an' some mares."

Will grinned. "I hope they're a mite bigger an' better-lookin' than that thing you're settin' on." He tilted his head, grinning. "What the hell color *is* that?"

Dill patted the horse's neck. "Them Mexicans that works for Cap'n King call this mousie-gray color *grulla.*" He pronounced it "grooya." "This's one o' them wild horses the *vaqueros* catch an' break. They is tough as rawhide an' don't need more feed than a billygoat."

"Uh huh, I can see the resemblance," Owen said.

"How about the cattle?" William asked. "We send enough money with you?"

Jackson grinned proudly. "More'n enough, Mr. Will. Had plenty for the horses, too." He rummaged in a pocket and brought out a buckskin bag still half-full of gold coins. He tossed it to Will. "Seems cows is thick as jackrabbits since the war. Cap'n King's mighty glad to get shet o' some. He mighty near give 'em away."

"Let's hope they ain't quite so plentiful when we send our first steers to market, year or so from now."

"No, sir, them folks back East want beef. Cap'n King sends his herds to Abilene or Dodge City. He says they'll be markets north of the plains afore long, beef needed for railroad crews."

"That's what we been hearin' too." Will nodded with satisfaction. "This King sounds like a shrewd cowman. How'd he manage to hold his ground against the Comanche and Apache while the border forts were abandoned?"

"Well, sir, he moved a whole village out here from Mexico to work on his range. King's Ranch is their home now, an' they'd fight anythin' that come up the pike for Cap'n King."

"Jackson, how far to the herd? Can we make it before supper?"

"Jest about, Mr. Will."

"I'll ride back and help Amelia and Georgie get over that dry wash we came through," William said. "Owen, go with Jackson. If you see any game, get us some camp meat, will you?"

"We got the cows bedded near a li'l ol' crick," Jackson said. "Deer come down to drink, 'bout dark. We'll get a fine young one, wait'n see, Mr. Will."

The men parted, William spurring back to the two wagons. Owen held Beau down to a walk, more or less matching Jackson's mustang's rough trot. They passed the hours with the comfortable talk of old friends.

"What d'you think of this move, Jackson?" asked Owen at last. "You mind much, leavin' east Texas?"

Dill wiped his forehead with his shirtsleeve and resettled his hat. "Cap'n, things is mighty differ'nt out here. Takes gettin' used to. Air feels dry, don't it? An' Lordy it's big! They's so damn much country a man cain't hardly stand to think on it. They say on up into them Staked Plains, they's grass for a million cows."

Owen nodded. "That sounds like a real fine opportunity for us. If we can made our herd grow."

Jackson laughed. "I reckon that ain't no problem. Them critters jest natch'ly breed like rabbits."

Owen's grin lighted his lean face. "Well, then, reckon we're in business."

"Yessir, Cap'n." They topped a rise and overlooked a long meadow near a wide, slow-moving creek. Dill waved a powerful arm. "There's our herd, Cap'n!"

Owen halted his horse, whistled softly with amazement. "God A'mighty, just look at 'em!"

He hadn't imagined the sheer size of the herd, a thousand head of prime young cows, many with calves, and thirty or so brawny bulls, bellowing challenges at one another as *vaqueros* with wide *sombreros* circled the herd on sweating horses.

It was a scene filled with vitality. Yells of the herders mingled with the bawls of cattle and the pound of hooves as a horseman skillfully blocked a cow's dash for freedom and turned it back into the herd. Two bulls were squared off face to face, pawing the ground into powdered dust, hooking horns in a test of strength.

The cattle were marked in every combination of colors. They were long-legged and rangy, fiercer than the domestic stock Owen had been used to. Owen saw a herder step down from his horse to lift an injured calf. The little one's ma promptly charged the *vaquero*, barely missing him with sharp, forward-thrusting horns.

There were none of the enormously long horns Owen had heard about. The most magnificent horns were seen on longhorn steers, of which this herd had none. Nevertheless, the activity below set Owen's blood singing in his veins. Life on the plantation had never held this kind of excitement.

"Before we ride down there, Cap'n, they's somethin' you maybe oughta know," Jackson said. "I ain't rightly sure what it means. One of King's men rode in 'bout suppertime last night. He'd heard somethin' down to Galveston from some fellers who come in on a boat. It was about you, Cap'n."

"Me? Who were the men?"

"I don't know." Jackson's burly shoulders lifted in a shrug. "Thing is, they was askin' if anybody had seen you—an' a lady."

Terrel stared at him, one dark brow lifted. "What lady? Miz Amelia?"

"I don't rightly know, Cap'n. That *vaquero* couldn't recall her name. But he said she was a married lady."

Owen grinned and shook his head. "Sounds like somebody thinks I borrowed his wife. Well, if he catches up to me, reckon he'll be disappointed. Come on, let's ride on down."

"Yessir. Yonder's Cap'n King hisself."

3

They circled to ride down to the big man, who sat rather awkwardly upon a husky bay horse, upstream from the rowdy activity about the herd. But as they rode, Owen found himself turning again and again to look at the herd of longhorns he and Will owned.

Jackson introduced Owen to Richard King, the legendary man who had immeasurably aided the Confederacy, transporting Texas goods on his steamships.

The man was broad of jaw, powerfully built, and appeared fully as forceful as rumored. His greeting to Owen was hearty.

"Captain Terrel, it's a pleasure to meet you, sir. Does the herd meet with your approval? I asked my men to round up good stock for you and your brother."

Owen dismounted and came to shake King's big hand. "The cattle look fine, sir. Jackson here tells me he also purchased horses. I'm eager to see them."

King was looking over Owen's thoroughbred with the practiced eye of a horsebreeder. "That's a fine mount. Plenty o' stamina, I'd wager. Good, deep girth, powerful quarters as well. Reckon he could use a week or two on good grass, though. He's a mite drawed."

"He's carried me fur," Owen said.

"Well, mount up," King said, "an' I'll take you to the *remuda*."

"Don't believe I know that word, sir."

"Horse herd. They're grazin' about a half-mile beyond the creek."

"Cap'n, I'll find us a campsite an' git the fire goin'," Jackson said.

King led the way to the horses Jackson had chosen. For the next hour Owen looked at the mares, which would form the foundation of the future Terrel horse herd and the saddlestock they would need for working the cattle.

Some were Mexican-bred, not all beauties, but well-grown, sound, sturdy. The four younger mares were examples of King's own breeding plan, sired by his fine thoroughbred studs. These were handsome indeed, with neat heads, small ears, shorter cannon bones than their sires, and somewhat less height, but plenty of muscling in the hindquarters.

Owen eyed them with approval. "If this is the kind of horseflesh you're breedin' on the King spread, they'll soon be in demand across Texas."

King seemed gratified at the praise. "You'll soon be breedin' your own fine colts. Where do you plan to graze your stock, Mr. Terrel?"

"We've got a hankerin' to push on up into New Mexico Territory. Maybe the Staked Plains."

King nodded. "Ah, the Llano Estacado. The plains supported buffalo in the thousands, until they were slaughtered for their hides. No one will dispute your right to settle there. It's a vast, empty country. You can follow the Goodnight-Loving Trail and strike the Pecos about here." He bent to draw in the dust with a twig. "Push north along the Pecos River. If you need supplies, there's a little community west of the Pecos. It used to be called Rio Hondo—now I believe 'tis known as Roswell.

"Go east from there, maybe forty, fifty miles, climb the Caprock, and find yourself in a cattle paradise—if you don't mind open space. The main thing is to reach water. If it was me, I'd drive on fifty or a hundred mile, never be crowded. Now, then, here's the way to locate decent water. Some of my men been out that way."

Again he drew in the dust, showing that a line of widely scattered springs and small, shallow lakes could be found along an ancient trail used by Indians and later, Comancheros who sold weapons to the war parties.

He drew out a paper and gave it to Owen. "Here's your bill of sale for the livestock. Let's celebrate the transaction." He led Owen to an interesting vehicle, a red coach with black top and yellow wheels. "This is my common mode of travel," he explained. "Spent too many years on shipboard to be comfortable in the saddle." Reaching inside, he brought out a jug of whiskey and passed it to Owen, who took a swallow to toast a business deal satisfactory to all.

Dusk was falling. Owen mounted, to ride back to the Terrel camp. "We'd be mighty proud to have to share our evening meal, Captain King."

As they sat about the campfire that night, the Terrels' guest entertained them with many interesting tales, shipboard adventures, stories of devastating storms that sometimes struck the Texas coast. And he had everyone's attention when he spoke of the border bandits that often crossed the Rio Grande and stole cattle to drive into Mexico. "Them fellers hate Texans, for they believe that we drove 'em out of their own land. A lot of Texans treat Mexicans like dogs—makes for an almighty lot of resentment."

"You've been fair with the Mexicans," Will said. "Surely they leave your herds alone."

King's broad face creased in a wide grin. "My *kineros* have fought off their own cousins from across the border. I reckon I'll always lose a lot o' stock to the rustlers. The man who has organized the worst gangs is Juan Cortina. He's as set on revenge on the Texans as he is on thievery. Cortina's men have been known to drag men to death, mutilate . . . Well, but this ain't no fit talk in a lady's presence. Beg your pardon, Miz Terrel."

The next week was an education for the Terrels. The *vaqueros* helped them brand their herd. Watching them ride and rope, Will and Owen learned a great deal about handling the powerful, uneasy-tempered longhorns. For a brand they chose a diamond double T, the two attached letters enclosed within the diamond.

When the branding was done, they took leave of King and his men and started the cattle upon the long trek. Two of the *vaqueros* had agreed to hire on with the Terrels for the drive. Jackson had traveled with the herd long enough to see the methods used to keep this great, unwieldy caravan of cattle on the move and under control. Will and Owen took full advantage of his advice. The horses required as much attention, being faster and harder to round up if they managed to stray.

Fortunately, Victorio Sánchez was skilled at handling the *remuda*, and Juan Morales guided Amelia each day, driving one of the wagons, locating camping spots, helping her with the cooking—and guarding her and Melissa, the three-year-old. Soon the little girl toddled trustingly after the *vaquero*, and the kind, elderly man was unfailingly watchful of her safety. Once he killed a rattler with a thrown bowie knife only moments before the child might have been struck.

Owen and Will drove themselves to acquire the new skills. Owen was particularly interested in Victorio's methods of handling the horses. He struggled with Spanish in order to learn Victorio's secrets of breaking and training young stock and the reining techniques that could make a cowhorse fast and agile in turning, spinning, and backing.

Both of the Mexicans took their turns on nightwatch. William vowed that when the long trip was done he would award both men a substantial bonus.

The Terrels worked with a minimum of sleep, and Dill was no less diligent. The only one of the men who seemed inclined to be slack in his duty was Georgie, the sharecropper's son who had come with them from Houston. At nineteen, Georgie showed few signs of ambition. He got through the days with as little labor and as much complaining as he could manage. Owen and Will must often reprimand him for a job poorly done, or remind him of the duties he forgot completely. Once, when they were camped at a stream, Georgie was given the job of filling all the water kegs. He filled one, was distracted by the call to supper, and neglected to return to his chore.

Far into the next day's drive it was discovered that they were short of water. Will turned the air blue with a description of Georgie's shortcomings, while Georgie whined excuses.

After that, neither Will nor Owen trusted Georgie with an important job. Even a small mistake could cause endless trouble out here, so far away from help. Running out of water could condemn them all to death, as simple as that.

The Terrels pushed on, growing more skilled at handling the huge, cumbersome herd. Again and again the good cowhorses purchased from Richard King proved their worth. The well-trained horses could spot and out-run a bunchquitter faster than the men could react, heading the cattle and forcing them back into the herd. Each rider learned to stay alert lest his cowpony turn out from under him, leaving him afoot.

At night two riders must endlessly circle the bedded herd, watchful for the first movement that might portend a dreaded stampede. The Terrels had adopted the *vaqueros'* habit of lulling the cattle with sweet, dolorous ballads during these night guards. Owen favored the bovines with "Lorena" and "Dixie" and "Shall We Gather at the River." Will warned him that his singing was more likely to start a stampede than to prevent one.

The days were endless rounds of labor and dust, the men alert for signs of hostile strangers. In addition to the border ruffians King had warned of, the Terrels were grimly aware that Texas had her own lawless men, ready to sweep down upon a herd, kill the drovers, and steal cattle and horses alike. Rumors had it that there were still a few renegade Apache bands—and a more fearful enemy than these or the Comanche could scarcely be imagined.

Aside from these hazards, there was the heat and the dryness that seemed to stretch the skin of the travelers' faces tight across the bones, the sun scorching their skin until the men were as darkly tanned as their Mexican companions. Amelia and little Melissa must wear poke bonnets to protect their tender skin from the moment the sun rose until it set.

Then there were thunderstorms, terrifying with their gigantic spears of searing lightning that looked fit to split the earth in two or providing eerie electric displays, balls of fire that leapt among the horns of the cattle. Almost worse were the duststorms, when no travel was possible and mouths and noses must be covered with scarves to make breathing possible.

It was a red-letter day when they reached the Pecos, a wide, slow, muddy stream. The livestock had their fill of water for the first time in days, and the belt of cedars and cottonwoods alongside the river provided welcome shade. They drove the cattle along the east side of the river, watchful of quicksand. Owen learned to rope the horns of a bogged-down cow and drag her free with horses that did not particularly relish the duty. Once more the King stock horses Jackson Dill had chosen proved invaluable. Bred for working longhorns, they were less nervous in close situations than the Terrel thoroughbreds.

One night the family, Jackson, and Georgie gathered about the fire. Juan and Victorio had taken the first watch. Amelia was cleaning and putting away the tin pans and forks from supper. William poured himself a second tin cup of coffee.

"We should be near the town Captain King mentioned," Will remarked. "We better stock up on coffee and meal an' the like. What do you say, Melia?"

"A real town?" she asked, excited at the very thought. "Oh—but I need time to wash our clothes first. I never knew a body could get so mortal dirty."

Will grinned at his wife. "We'll camp about a half-day out."

As he had promised, Will halted the herd and *remuda* to give them all time to clean up. The Mexicans had guided them to a place they called the Bottomless Lakes. Amelia rejoiced over the wealth of clean water and began at once to wash clothing and bedding, much worn and grimed by travel.

She heated water to fill the wooden tub and bathed herself and the children, though Willy howled as he was scrubbed with Amelia's homemade lye soap. Inspired by her example, Will and Owen trimmed hair and beards that had been growning unchecked since the start of the journey. Both men behaved like boys again, splashing about in the blue water of the lakes.

Jackson avowed he liked his dirt, but must have accomplished his bath while the others slept, for he appeared in suspiciously glorious condition the morning the family set out for town. Amelia swore that she had forgotten he was black, so grayed by dust he'd been, and she complimented him upon his magnificent looks.

They left the herd in the care of the *vaqueros*, promising to bring them some treats from the town and give them time to enjoy the taste of civilization. Will's family rode in a wagon, the other men escorting them on horseback. The group felt very festive as they approached the little farms that heralded civilization and gardens irrigated from the *acequia* that the settlers had dug to bring water from the North Spring River. The town was little more than a scattering of crude, mud-brick dwellings and a few stores. But it was a community of people and, as such, a welcome sight to the Terrel family.

They bought coffee, sugar, and meal, and Will arranged to have lumber freighted in from a sawmill in the Sacramento Mountains, eighty miles west of Roswell. He bought a cookstove for Amelia and lashed it onto the wagon. The general-store proprietor advised them that they might find the other supplies they would need before winter at Fort Griffin, Texas, some two hundred miles east of the area they planned to settle.

Owen turned to William. "Maybe I ought to ride to Fort Griffin in a day or two and bring back the goods. The sooner the better."

"Good idea. I could spare Georgie to go with you."

Owen glanced at the pimply-faced young man who was selecting a bright calico shirt. He grinned at Will and shook his head. "Do me a favor an' keep him."

Before dark they returned to camp and relieved Juan and Victorio from duty, so that they could enjoy the town for a few hours.

The two *vaqueros* rode back into camp after midnight, harmonizing a Mexican ballad. And next day at dawn the cattle, the wagons, and the *remuda* were on the move again, east, toward the great, empty Llano Estacado.

4

Now they left all evidence of human habitation quickly behind. Every day beyond Horsehead Crossing, on the Pecos, it seemed they were moving farther and farther into a land never meant for people. There were salt cedars and willows and cottonwoods along the Pecos. Beyond that, only low brush—shinnery oak, mesquite, greasewood. Red sand baked underfoot, sending up waves of heat.

The great escarpment rose in the distance before them, the boundary of the Llano Estacado, a bluff that reared up out of the earth, running for hundreds of miles north and south. Known as the Caprock, this abrupt lift of rugged, uneven, eroded rock and earth was like nothing seen in all their traveling. It was as if an immense section of the earth had simply been lifted hundreds of feet above the adjoining land.

They camped at a spring under the Caprock, and at dawn the mules strained to bring the wagons up the steep, curving trail to the top of the escarpment. The riders had already choused the herd and the *remuda* up onto the plain the night before.

Owen rode near the wagons, in case of trouble. Georgie carelessly let a wheel of the first wagon slide off the edge of the trail, nearly upsetting it.

"Keep your mind on your business, Georgie," Owen shouted. It was doubtful that Georgie paid the least mind. He was impervious to reprimand.

Amelia guided her team safely up the narrow, sidling trail. When they were safe on top, she halted her two span of mules to let them catch their wind.

Owen sat his horse nearby. "The trail will be easier from here," he said.

Amelia's eyes scanned the surrounding landscape. Except for the dust cloud east of their position, where the herd moved at its slow pace, there was little to see save an immense flat grassland that seemed to stretch on, featureless, forever. The largest growth was mesquite—they could see nothing that could be called a tree. The passage of the herd was the only sign of movement, save for the wind-bent grass. Totally cloudless, the sky was a gigantic, overwhelming bowl that made the mind shiver, that seemed to reduce men and livestock to the size of ants.

Owen was startled to see tears running down Amelia's face, marking the skin that was no longer fine and white. She wiped the moisture away with a thin hand.

"Melia . . ." he began, helplessly.

"Owen, I—I miss the trees!" she gasped. But immediately she brought herself under control. "Oh, would you listen to me! Don't you tell Will I was blubberin' like a baby." She sniffed and wiped her face dry. "Well, we must get 'round the herd and find the next campin' place so I can get some food on to cook."

"Will said he'd send Juan with you when you pass the herd."

She nodded and clucked to her mules. Georgie had already driven the other wagon away from the edge of the Caprock. Without looking back, Amelia followed. A little worried about her, Owen rode alongside until she shooed him away. "I'm fine now. Go help Will with the cattle."

Owen found Will at the point of the herd.

Will reached to punch him on the shoulder. "You ever see a better grazing country, Owen? And we can take our pick of just about any part of it, wherever there's water for the cattle."

Owen had to admit that William was right. The grass brushed gently against his stirrups as Beau trotted. There was enough, it seemed, for a unimaginable number of cattle. The land all about the riders seemed endless.

But he was still disturbed by the rare sight of Amelia in tears, and he saw how this huge, unpeopled space might seem to a woman, a nightmare of sameness, without trees or streams or landmarks. "Will, how long you reckon until we find a good site to settle down?"

"I'd guess four, five days."

"Mind if I make a suggestion?"

"We're partners, ain't we?"

"Put someone to work on a place to live, right away."

Will seemed puzzled. "I figured we could camp a little while, work on a water supply an' some pens for the saddle stock."

Owen studied over the right thing to say, without interfering too much in his brother's business. "Woman needs a house that don't move around," he said at last. "An' trees. We got to get some trees started soon as we can."

Will nodded slowly. "Reckon you're right. This could be a hard go for a woman. Melia deserves whatever comfort we can manage."

Owen grinned. "I remember Pa used to say, 'Always keep the cook happy.' " He was silent for a few minutes, turning plans over in his head. "I believe if you can spare me now, I'll get on my way to Fort Griffin, buy the supplies we need. You got that list we made last night?"

Will rummaged in a pocket, brought out a folded bit of paper. "You have enough money, Owen?"

"More'n enough. I'll be back as soon as I can." He grinned. "If I can find my way back! Ain't a lot o' landmarks out here!"

"I'd as soon you didn't joke about that." Will studied him for a moment. "Don't hurry too much. Have some fun, little brother. Get some beans and bacon an' coffee from the wagons and take extry ammunition. Never can tell what you might run into. Keep an eye on the stars ever' night to be sure of your direction. Be might easy to get lost out here or stray too far from water."

Owen gave his brother a smart salute and galloped back toward the wagons.

Funny how different it was, riding alone across this strange, unearthly country, leaving the herd and his family far behind. It required a mite of resolution to keep going, farther and farther into godforsaken emptiness. All that damned space had a way of sapping a man's courage and bringing on a sense of confusion.

The first night on his own, Owen made a dry camp, hoping to find water for Beau the next day. And he was fortunate, for midmorning found him nearing a shallow, alkali-rimmed pond. He knew better than to use the water until he found the spring that fed the pond, where it came from the earth, clean and pure.

Beau buried his black nose in the spring, and Owen filled his canteens, pausing to splash the cool water on his face and neck. Then he mounted and rode on. The sun seemed hotter here than anyplace he'd been, but there was not a trace of that steamy dampness that marked warm weather in east Texas. He was learning to like the dry air. It seemed to fill the lungs more easily, and it smelled good, of mesquite and grass and sunlight.

He let Beau move at a steady trot, alternating with a walk. No need to push the big horse unduly.

Owen had ridden several miles past the lake when an object, clearly foreign to this wild, empty environment, appeared in the distance. It was a little off Owen's direction, but anything out of the ordinary here was something that should be examined. The survival of a traveler could depend upon his alertness to what went on about him. Owen took his rifle from the saddle and levered a shell into it, then held it across his thighs, ready for anything.

The object grew, its shape becoming defined. Wagons, two of them, parked at an awkward angle. There were no animals, oxen or mules, and no sign of life. Owen slowed Beau to a walk and circled the wagons at a little distance. A tragedy had taken place here, and people had lost their lives. That much was clear, even before Beau shied away from a shallow grave overlaid with slabs of rock.

Satisfied that there was no danger, Owen rode closer. "Hello," he called. "Anyone here?"

At first it seemed that he would find nothing living. Then there was a slow movement from underneath one of the wagons, and an emaciated dog, white with a black eye patch and comically bent ears, crawled out, whining a pathetic welcome as he cringed at Beau's feet.

Owen dismounted, but he kept his rifle. "Well, now, boy," he murmured to the dog. You all alone?"

The dog wagged joyfully and rushed to the wagon he'd left. He continued to whine, wriggling underneath where there was a tangle of blankets. He emerged again to frisk about Owen's feet despite his starved, weakened condition, then dived under once more.

"What you got there, boy?" Owen bent to pull back

the blanket to reveal a white face, eyes closed, dark hair matted, skin drawn tight over delicate bones. One small hand emerged from the dusty wraps.

"Lordy, it's a woman!" Owen lifted her wrist, felt for a pulse. It was there, but faint.

He rushed to his saddle, brought his canteen. Very gently he eased the unconscious girl out from under the wagon. She was disturbingly light. Owen tried to wake her, but she only moaned, a mere breath of sound.

He lifted her head, held the water to her lips, carefully poured a bit between her teeth, waiting to see that she swallowed before trying another drop or two.

Then he laid her back upon her blanket and made a fire from dry mesquite twigs, starting water to boil in the small coffeepot he carried in his saddlebag. He opened a can of beans and set it to warm, started salt pork frying. The girl was starved nearly to death, and the water kegs on both wagons were bone-dry. If she wasn't too far gone to swallow some food, she might have a chance.

He left his cooking long enough to unsaddle Beau, hobble him, and turn him loose to graze.

Returning to the girl, he saw that she was still asleep, or unconscious. Her face was gray with dust, and her dark hair was tangled and dirty.

Cursing under his breath, Owen decided to look into the wagons, see if he could figger out what had happened here. He started with the one she had sheltered under, wondering why she had not simply climbed inside. Perhaps she had been too weak to do so, or disoriented by hunger and the shock of her predicament.

The wagon was surprisingly tidy. A trunk and some furniture stood to one side. The cooking things were in their proper place. But there was no food. He found a good Henry rifle but no cartridges. Owen opened a little, hidebound trunk that looked as if it might contain papers, and indeed it was so. On top of everything lay an ornate family Bible.

Owen opened the Bible, found the family records, and idly read the beautifully written names: Adelaide and Conrad Morgan, their wedding recorded, fifty odd years ago. Under their names, two sons, Barnabas and Joshua, and then Joshua's bride, Faith. And Barnabas had married Anna, and a daughter had been born to them: Virginia. Owen frowned. Where had he heard these names? But of course! The girl he'd taken to the wagon train at the edge of Houston.

With a muttered oath, Owen left the wagon, to study the girl's unconscious face intently. Could this be the same young woman he'd lifted into Beau's saddle that rainy night? This frail girl was much thinner than he remembered. But it was Virginia Morgan. His heart twisted with pity. What tragedy she must have lived through!

Owen went to move the food from the fire. He mashed beans with hot water and chipped up a bit of bacon into the resulting mush. Then he lifted the girl's shoulders so that he could support her head against his chest. She stirred, murmured something, like a sleepy child.

"Miss Morgan!" Owen shook her gently. "Virginia, try to wake up. I have some food here. You'd best eat."

She sighed and her eyes opened, closed, opened again, dazed and unfocused.

"That's the way," he encouraged. "Now open your mouth and see if you can swallow some o' this." He spooned the soupy stuff into her mouth. After the first spoonful she opened her mouth automatically, though she still seemed half-unconscious. Owen fed her only a small amount at first, afraid that her starved body might react with nausea. He gave her water. She drank that more easily now. Her body, if not her mind, was becoming more aware.

When he stopped feeding her, she sank back into slumber once more. Owen found cleaner blankets, shook them hard to rid them of sand and dust, and made a bed within the wagon. He lifted Virginia inside and left her to sleep.

Owen sat down to eat, leaving a generous portion for the dog, who had returned unsuccessful from his hunt. The poor creature swallowed the food in two gulps and drank thirstily, wagging his tail so hard that he moved his entire body. Owen built up the fire and set the coffee to warm again, then went to examine the second wagon. Immediately he was sorry he had eaten. There was the body of a woman inside the canvas walls. She must have died only in recent hours.

After the initial unpleasant surprise, Owen was touched

by the effort that had been made to lay out the corpse properly. Someone had smoothed the graying dark hair, and the hands were folded upon the covering blanket. The woman's eyelids were weighted with gold coins from a little metal box that had been left open at her side. There were other coins in the box, an amount that looked to be several hundred dollars. But the money had been of no value at all to a starving girl hundreds of miles from anyone who could help her, faced with the death of her last human companion. Owen thought that the dead woman was Faith Morgan, Virginia's aunt, though she looked older than he remembered.

He sighed and went to find a shovel and prepare a grave near the one he had found earlier. He wrapped the body in blankets and carried it to its final resting place.

When he'd covered the grave, Owen removed his hat and bent his head for a respectful moment, then returned to camp and a welcome tin cup of coffee.

He stood by the fire, deciding what he ought to do next. His trip to Fort Griffin would have to be postponed, of course. Miss Morgan was far too weak and ill to be taken that distance, and it would be rough on Beau to carry them both so far. Best to turn back to the alkali lake until Virginia was stronger.

He rummaged in the wagons, gathering a few things he thought belonged to Virginia. She should have her uncle's money, of course; that would be vital to her future, when she was well enough to return to Texas. He stowed the small metal box in the saddlebag, along with the Bible and some trifling bits of jewelry he found. He would need extra blankets and a change of clothing for the girl. He hesitated over the Henry rifle, decided to take it. Will had ammunition for it, and it could be useful later. He could carry nothing more. Perhaps later he and Will could bring a team to haul in anything else of value. Likely these things were all that the girl could call her own.

Owen made another meal, boiling a handful of cornmeal to make a gruel. At dusk, he went to the girl's wagon to bring her out. He was startled to find large dark eyes regarding him with a kind of resigned terror.

"Well, now, you're awake," he said. "Ready for your supper?"

"Wh-what?" she gasped, weakly.

"You've slept the whole day. Even slept through your dinner. I got supper ready, though maybe not the tastiest thing you ever ate. Let me help you out of here."

But she was staring at him with a different expression now, a gladness and relief that made her look like a creature not of this world, those wide dark eyes blazing in her thin white face. "It's you! It's . . . But how?" Suddenly her eyes were aswim with tears and she tried to sit up. Instinctively Owen held her against his chest, as he would have a child in need of comforting. Awkwardly, he rocked her back and forth, patting her back. Her bones felt pitifully prominent.

"Don't cry," he murmured. "I'm here, and you'll be all right."

She seemed not to hear him. Her whole body shook as she cried and gasped out her story.

"They're all dead! The Paynes' wagon turned over in a river—they both drowned, and Mr. Kelp, a rattlesnake bit him." She shuddered. "Mrs. Kelp, she—she wouldn't leave his grave, and when we m-made her, she got her husband's gun and . . . Sh-she was all bloody, Mr. Terrel. And we buried her and drove on, but we got lost, and we went on and on. We couldn't find w-water anywhere, and the oxen ran off." She gulped and quivered so that Owen was alarmed and tried to hush her, but she seemed to be compelled to spill it all out.

"Uncle went to find the teams, and he just never came back. That—that was a week or more past. Aunt Faith, she was dying. I walked a long way, trying to find my uncle, but . . . Aunt Faith was dead last night when I—" She let out a wail of sheer anguish.

"All right, all right, I know," Owen said. "I buried your aunt. Who's in the other grave?"

She gulped, swallowed. "Little Billy Kelp. He—he was only three, and he wasn't ever strong. It was so hot, and we gave him the last of the water, but—"

Owen rocked her gently. "I understand. You did all you could, Virginia. Now I'll carry you out and give you something to eat."

She stared up at him with drowned eyes, eyes that had beheld almost more horror than her soul could bear. "Mr.

Terrel,'' she asked hoarsely, ''do you know where we can find water?''

His throat constricted with pity. ''We'll be riding tonight to where there's all the water we would ever need. Don't be afraid. You're safe now.''

Quickly, seeing how desperately pale she was, he lifted her out, made her eat. The food and coffee brought a hint of color into her face. After they had eaten, Owen told her to rest and went to catch and saddle Beau. Then he lifted the thin, weak young woman into the saddle and, as once before, got on behind.

''We'll be riding for several hours, but we'll go slow. You sleep if you feel like it.''

She glanced around anxiously. ''Wait. Where is Whiskey?''

''Whiskey? I don't—''

''The dog. I can't leave him.''

''No, no, we won't leave him. He was eating what was left from supper a few minutes ago.'' Owen whistled, and the white-and-black dog came trotting from behind the wagons.

''We're goin' now, boy, see that you keep up.'' The bedraggled white tail waved agreeably, and the dog fell in behind the horse.

Virginia Morgan relaxed against Owen's chest with a little sigh. In minutes, rocked by Beau's easy walk, she was asleep, her head drooping against Owen's arm. As they rode, the night deepened, moonless. Stars, amazingly close in the ultraclear sky, began to appear. Owen looked for the north star, made sure he was headed due west.

It was an odd experience, moving in the starlit dimness, trusting to the horse's sure sight to make his way. There was almost no sensation of progress, for the little that could be seen was without landmark. They might have been moving in some dark dream, with no progress whatsoever.

Owen shifted, moving Virginia to a more comfortable position. She must have been dreaming—she moaned, a sound full of fear. He drew her closer, hoping to comfort her.

5

The horse picked up his pace eagerly when he scented water, and Owen knew they were near the alkali lake. He steadied the sleeping girl within his arms. Twenty minutes later they stopped at the edge of the still, blackly gleaming water. Stiffly, Terrel slid off and lifted the girl down. She stirred and woke as he carried her to a place where he could put her down. She seemed confused as to Owen's identity.

"Uncle Joshua?" she murmured.

"No, Miss Morgan. It's Owen Terrel. I found you at your wagons, remember?"

There was a moment of silence, and then Owen heard her gasp as memory flooded in. He returned to his horse and brought the blankets to make a bed for her. "You rest now," he said.

He built a fire, comfortingly near Virginia's bed. The dog crept near her, and she drew the animal close with one arm. The emaciated girl was silent, tearless. She stared into the flames, and their golden flickers were reflected in her wide dark eyes.

When Terrel had started coffee boiling, he tended to the horse. He brought coffee to the girl, and she drank it eagerly, although her fingers trembled and she held her cup in both hands. "Mr. Terrel, how do you happen to be out here, so far from Houston? And where are we going?"

"We're going to camp here a day or two until you feel able to ride, then we'll go to my family. We brought a herd of cows out of Texas, my brother and I. We're fixin' to start a ranch out here."

He saw her wide dark eyes turn nervously upon the darkness and distance. The two of them might have been the last people upon the face of the earth. "Is it only just you and your brother?"

He thought he knew what worried her. "And my

brother's wife, Amelia, and their children. Willy is five, and little Melissa is three.''

He heard her long-drawn, slightly unsteady breath, and he felt pity for the horrors her young mind had faced. What must she have felt, the lone survivor of her family and their traveling companions in this huge, empty land? The hope of seeing another woman must be the most pleasant prospect in many weeks.

"When you're well enough, we'll see you get back to Texas. Or wherever you have family.''

She shook her head. "I have no family left.'' But she did not lapse into tears again. "I think I will sleep now, Mr. Terrel," she said.

"That's just what you need. Be dawn soon, but you rest as long as you can.''

She lay down, turned so that the firelight fell upon her face, and sighed like a tired child. Dark lashes rested upon her cheeks. She kept one hand on the dog's back, fingers twined in his long fur.

Owen studied her for a moment, thinking how fragile she looked, how out of place in this wilderness.

He rolled out his own blanket across the fire from Virginia's. Whiskey thumped his tail and curled closer to the sleeping girl. Owen was glad of the clever animal's presence. He would warn them of anything that came near.

The heat of the midmorning sun woke him. Swallowing dryly, he flung back his blankets and stood. Miss Morgan still slept, the sun full upon the tender skin of her face. Quickly Owen cut and bound together stout branches of mesquite and fashioned a shade by draping one of the blankets over the makeshift frame.

As he went to bring the horse to the spring, a cottontail rabbit bounced from under a mesquite. Owen snapped a shot at it with his Colt, missed, downed it with the second shot. He had to beat the dog to it. Whiskey, with his black eye patch and half-mast ear, looked comically grieved when Owen took the rabbit away from him.

"We'll share," Terrel promised. "Let's get this varmint skinned and cooked.''

He built up the fire and began the breakfast, eager to have his first cup of coffee. His shots had not disturbed

Virginia, sleeping heavily. He woke her when the food was ready.

Miss Morgan seemed much stronger today. She ate hungrily, then got up, unsteady on her feet but not giving in to weakness. She washed her face at the spring and walked slowly about the area.

"Would you be all right here alone for an hour?" Owen asked. "There were antelope tracks by the water this morning. Might be I could spot one, if you wouldn't mind staying by yourself for a while."

He saw the quick tensing of fear, but she surprised him by agreeing at once. "Yes. I'll keep Whiskey with me."

"I won't go far, or be away long. Stay in the shade. And keep this nearby." He took his Colt Peacemaker out and handed it to her. "Do you know how to shoot?"

She took the gun. "My uncle made me learn. I'm fairly accurate, but I don't like guns much."

"It's just a precaution, in case you see a snake or skunk."

She nodded and placed the weapon on her blankets.

Owen saddled Beau, rode out to make a mile-wide circle about the water hole, but though once in the far distance he thought he saw a flash of white that might have been a pronghorn, it was too far for a shot, and he had been gone as long as he dared. No sense in making Miss Morgan suffer more loneliness than was necessary.

When he rode back to the little camp, he found Virginia patiently feeding shinnery twigs into the fire. She'd made fresh coffee, hot and black.

"I'd have done that," Owen protested. He dismounted and unsaddled Beau. "You should rest, gather your strength."

"I'm feeling much better," she said. "I know you need to get back to your family. We could start in the morning—or tonight, if you'd rather."

Owen felt a stirring of admiration. When he had met her, Virginia Morgan had seemed a pampered, willful child. Now, as she faced him, her thinned face white under its tan, her steady eyes were far from childish. Virginia Morgan was definitely a woman, one who had suffered, and tried to deal with the illness and pain of her family, and had been drawn back from the very brink of death.

"Best to travel at night, I reckon," Owen said.

"I shall be ready whenever you say."

"I believe we'll wait another day or so, to be sure."

And so, three days later, just at dawn, the brown gelding carried his two riders into camp at the spot Will Terrel had selected for the headquarters of the ranch. Amelia was working at the cook fire and she shaded her eyes with her hand, trying to see who was approaching. Will was coming at a gallop from the herd, a half-mile south of the camp.

"Owen, what on earth," Amelia cried. "We thought you were halfway to Fort Griffin! And who is this? Oh, you poor dear! Owen, put her there by the wagon wheel." Quickly she poured coffee for the two weary travelers.

By this time Will had dismounted and signaled to Georgie, who was shambling along with a basket of buffalo chips for the fire. "Here, come see to Owen's horse, Georgie."

"Howdy, Will." Owen grinned crookedly. "Hope you can wait a little on that load o' supplies." Amelia was bending over Virginia, who seemed faint and had not yet spoken.

"Where'd you find her?" Amelia demanded. "Where are her people?"

"All dead," Owen said quietly. "She was alone, except for the dog, there, and half-starved. Thought I should bring her to you, Melia."

"You did exactly right," his sister-in-law exclaimed. "Georgie, bring me water, put it to heat. I'll help her bathe and put her to bed in the wagon. Will, is that beef still good? I'll make a broth—"

"Please, ma'am," Virginia protested faintly, "give Mr. Terrel something to eat. He gave me most of his food."

"Dear God! Owen, sit down, and I'll—"

"I'll get it. You tend to Miss Morgan, Amelia." He bent to fill plates for Virginia and himself. "After breakfast I'll ride out with you, Will."

"No, sir, you get some sleep. I'll send Victorio and Juan to Fort Griffin. They can hire us some men an' send out the stuff we need. I s'pect they'd like to get back to Texas."

"Will's right, Owen," Amelia said briskly. "You'd best get some sleep. But you'll have to spread your blankets yonder where the men are digging the well. I aim to skin these filthy clothes off this poor child and get her cleaned up, so you men can just make yourselves scarce as hen's teeth, you hear?''

Owen nodded and glanced at Virginia. The girl's eyes followed Amelia worshipfully, as if she were the most beautiful sight ever encountered. Owen felt a foolish twinge of envy and laughed at himself. He supposed it was more than enough to get a man thinking he was something special, having a pretty young woman dependent upon him for her very life. And enough to deflate his pride very suddenly, when she turned to another source of comfort.

Owen swallow the last of his coffee and went to find a place to catch some sleep. There was a good-sized mesquite bush near the spot where the men had begun to dig, hoping to add to their source of water. He checked under the branches for a lurking snake, scorpion, or centipede, then rolled his blankets out and was asleep almost before he relaxed.

He woke at dusk, ashamed to realize he had wasted an entire day. Hurriedly he crawled out, shook his blankets, and rolled them up. Then he spent the next half-hour making shift to clean himself up a bit.

When he'd washed and changed into a clean shirt, he walked back to the wagon, enjoying the aroma of supper cooking, and the little breeze that had sprung up as the sun descended. Dust rose in small bursts under his boots. He passed by the site Will had apparently chosen for the family dugout, marked by pegs driven into the ground. Only a few shovelsful of earth had been removed from the square of ground. Owen decided to put himself to that particular job for an hour or so after supper.

Will's favorite horse was ground-tied near the wagons, and Will was hunkered down with a plate of food in one hand, a fork in the other.

Will glanced over Amelia's shoulder. "Hey, little brother! About time you came back to life. Grab a plate an' get some of Amelia's good stew."

"Sit down. I'll bring it, Mr. Terrel."

Owen turned quickly and for a moment was dumbfounded. Who was the lovely young woman smiling at him across the buffalo-chip fire? Rich chestnut hair, clean and shining, was caught at the nape of her neck with a ribbon, and fell nearly to her waist. Amelia must have cut some of the unmanageable knots from it, shortening the hair near Virginia's face, for it was loose and softly waving about temples and cheeks. Virginia's face, thinned by her tragic experiences, was made beautiful by the wide dark eyes that sparkled with returning vitality. She wore one of Amelia's neat calico dresses, too large for her, but belted in about the waist and falling gracefully to her small feet.

"Miss Morgan!" Owen heard Will chuckling at his reaction, and brought his amazement under control. "Should you be up?"

"Oh, yes. I rested all afternoon."

Owen could scarcely take his eyes off the girl he had brought in, grimy and nearly too weak to stand, only hours before. The transformation was astonishing.

As he ate, he listened to Will's plans for the ranch. "We've already found moist soil in the well. I think we'll hit water pretty quick. There's a spring a quarter-mile south we can use until then. Jackson's building some rock troughs there for the stock."

"I'll work on the dugout," Owen offered. "Unless you want me to ride out again for Fort Griffin."

"Already sent Juan and Victorio. Say, one good thing, Juan wants to come back an' work for us. He'll bring back our freight. I wrote a letter to King, told him how helpful his men have been to us."

Owen's mind wandered. He found himself staring at Virginia once more, still astonished at the change a bath and change of clothing had wrought. She was eagerly conversing with Amelia, who said something that made the girl laugh. It was a rare, sweet sound, warmed a man's heart to hear it.

Owen helped himself to more coffee, bent to pat Whiskey, who lay happily between Willy and Melissa. His waving tail stirred the dust.

"Has anyone fed this dog?" Owen asked.

Amelia turned, snorted. "Only everyone who passes by him. And the children have nearly petted the fur off him."

"He's a good dog," Virginia said softly. "He caught a big lizard when I had nothing to eat, and he let me take it, even though he was starving, too. I cooked it."

"Oh, my dear!" Shocked at the thought of being obliged to eat such a thing, Amelia hugged Virginia fiercely. "Don't you worry, as long as you are with us, you will never go hungry again."

Owen stood. "I'll work on the dugout a bit before dark. Then I'll take first watch with the herd, Will."

"You can relieve Jackson, little brother. I been keepin' one man on watch at a time, at least until we know more about this country. I sent Georgie out to check the *remuda*. The horse herd's been stayin' near the water, pretty good. I keep a few saddle horses picketed, just in case the loose stock takes a notion to move farther out onto the prairie. I'll feel better when we get some pens built. Keep your eyes open, little brother. Cain't never tell what's out there."

Owen saw Amelia's little, involuntary shiver. Again he realized how frightening this country must be for a woman, for there was not even the illusion of shelter or refuge here, only a sense of helpless exposure. At times it would make any human long for trees and hills and buildings—anything to break the flat, immense openness.

Owen picked up a shovel, walked across to the dugout. After a moment Will joined him, and the two men worked companionably as the long summer evening deepened into darkness. They had dug the dwelling site out to a depth of three feet by the time they stopped for the night.

Owen rode Will's horse to the *remuda*, turned him loose as Georgie brought him a fresh mount. "Hey, Owen," snickered the kid, "if you'll tell me where you found that there purty gal, reckon I'll go round me up one."

"Careful how you speak of Miss Morgan," Terrel said. "Did Will put you on second watch?"

"Yeah."

"Spell me about one, then. An' take a fresh horse back to camp for Will."

Owen mounted and touched spurs to his mount. He let the bay buck for a few minutes, just for the hell of it, then galloped to the loosely grouped herd. He sent Jackson Dill to the wagon for supper and spurred the bay toward the herd. The cattle were mostly bedded down now.

Making his first circuit, Owen felt better than he had in a long time, his spirits lighter. It was a relief to get Virginia safely here, where Amelia could look after her. And it was good to be moving easily about the cattle, drinking in the sounds and scents of the prairie night. The plains were harsh, unforgiving of mistakes, but they had much to offer, a clean, uncrowded expanse, a sky that hung the stars almost close enough to touch.

His bay shied at something real or imaginary. Owen caught his balance, controlled his mount. Time to stop woolgathering and pay attention to the job at hand.

The next days were filled with steady work. When the men were not on watch with the peacefully grazing herd, they stacked rock to use for pens and the upper walls of the dugout. The first dugout pit was finished. The lumber they had ordered at Roswell arrived, and the family dugout was quickly finished—low rock walls, a stout door, roof, and window shutters made from the new boards.

"This damned stuff is so green it's sure to warp," Will complained. But when the roof was covered with the planks and then with sod, the dim, cool shelter smelled pleasantly of the resin in the pine wood, and of the moist earth.

There was only one room. The window had a rawhide flap that could be let down in case of storm. Rawhide was used to hinge the thick shutters and door, which could be barred securely. The earth floor was packed hard, and Will lined the inner walls with the remaining planks, something of a luxury.

If Amelia minded moving into the odd little dwelling, she hid her feelings. Will set up the cast-iron cook stove he'd bought in Roswell. Soon the stovepipe merrily belched smoke, and Amelia began baking bread and pans of corn bread in her oven.

Owen built bunks on two of the dugout walls; they would serve for both sleeping and sitting. Amelia aired the feather ticks she had brought from Texas, and soon there were comfortable beds for each of the women and one bunk for the children.

The men were already digging a second room for the dugout, a near necessity, since Virginia would need a separate place to sleep soon, so that Will could rejoin his wife. In addition, Owen, Jackson, and George had their own bunkhouse to build. Winter would make shelter for everyone imperative.

The men took time to lead a team of mules to the spot where Owen had found Virginia and retrieve the best of the goods there, and the best wagon. There was a cane-bottomed rocking chair and a cedar chest and Faith Morgan's good china. Virginia insisted upon sharing household goods with Amelia.

The men were jubilant when the well exceeded their expectations, a plentiful supply of water at a shallow depth. They began another well, to supply the cattle as they grazed farther afield.

Owen often worked fourteen hours a day, yet he scarcely felt weary each evening as they enjoyed a good meal on the long plank table Will had set up in the front yard of the main dugout. As long as the weather held good, they would not be cramped within the dwelling's one finished room.

On a late June evening, they sat enjoying their supper. Whiskey prowled happily beneath the table, brushing against the knees of the diners, waiting for the bits of meat and bread that more than one slipped to him. Suddenly the dog bolted from under the planks, barking loudly.

Will and Owen stood and hurried out to meet two freight wagons, approaching slowly, drawn by ox teams. Will had been wondering what had become of his order of supplies from Fort Griffin.

On the first wagon, Juan waved his sombrero and loosed a flood of excited shouting as Owen lifted an arm in welcome.

Owen struggled to follow the rapid Spanish mixed with English, puzzling over the words he caught. "I bring *esta mujer—la señora—para usted—*"

"What's he saying?" Will asked, frowning.

But the wagon was nearer now and Owen's mouth fell open as he saw clearly the second figure upon the wagon seat. She was wearing a wide, very feminine hat, tied firmly under a small, determined chin. The flounces of her skirt fluttered in the breeze, displaying ruffled petticoats.

"What in the—"

"Who is that?" Will muttered.

Owen felt a whirlwind of emotions—disbelief, excitement, dismay. "Damn it, Will. That's Julia!"

6

Juan was still waving and shouting. Julia was leaning away from him, frowning, as if offended. But when the wagon pulled to a stop near the men, she became all smiles.

"Owen . . . Will! It's so wonderful to see you. The trip has been horrible, you can't imagine. We were stuck in sand a dozen times. Why, I was beginnin' to think I'd never, never find you."

She was weeping as she began to clamber down from the wagon. Owen moved to help her, but as his hands clasped her tiny waist, she seemed to faint, her pliant body relaxing into Owen's arms.

"Julia, what the devil!" He tried uselessly to stand her on her feet. At last he was forced to lift her in both arms. Her wide hat fell off and her golden head nestled into the hollow of his shoulder.

Will stared at their unexpected guest. "Juan, where in hell did you find her?"

Juan was grinning with the delight of a man who had presented a friend with a marvelous surprise. *"No, no, la señora,* she finds me, in Fort Griffin. She asks for Señor Terrel—she wishes to come *aquí."* He shrugged, lifted his hands, palms upward. *"Está bien, no?"*

"Sí, Juan," Will said, but his voice was dry. "It's okay." He turned to Owen, and his eyes were amused. "Well, what now, little brother?"

Owen glanced down at his very attractive burden. "Damned if I know."

"I suggest we take her to Melia." Will grinned. "Reckon she never expected so many lady callers to drop in, way out here."

The others were still at the table. Amelia rose and came to meet Owen, her round face a picture of astonishment. Virginia was clearing the supper things. She paused, watching curiously.

"Why, it's Julia Talbot! How in the world—" Amelia gave Owen a quick, concerned glance. "Take her inside."

He gingerly placed Julia upon one of the beds within the dugout. Amelia covered her with a blanket, fresh-washed and sun-dried, and then moved hurriedly to light a lamp. Owen stepped back and Amelia stood quietly at his side, studying the blond girl, whose cheeks were quite healthily pink. Amelia's eyes narrowed.

"Go outside, Owen." He wondered why she spoke as if he were hard-of-hearing. "I'll tend to Julia. She's fainted. I'll just dash a dipperful of cold water in her face and bring her out of it."

At once Julia's golden lashes quivered and lifted. One fragile hand lifted, pressed against her forehead. "Oh, where am I?" she whispered. She moved weakly to sit up.

Owen started forward to help, but Amelia's suddenly outthrust arm barred his way. He gave her a puzzled glance.

"You're in my house, Julia," Amelia said.

Julia stared at her, then about the small, square room. "This is your house?" She seemed horrified. "Where's the rest of it?"

"Julia," Owen broke in, "what are you doing out here? Where is your pa, and Caleb Wardworth?"

Julia sat up suddenly, swinging her feet to the floor. "Don't speak that man's name in my presence! I never want to see him or hear of him again. That snivelin' worm. He killed my pa, Owen. He claimed Papa insulted him, an' he challenged him to a duel, but you know Papa never could shoot. He hated guns, never touched one unless he had to." Tears were flowing down her cheeks again, but now they were accompanied by harsh, desperate sobbing, as she babbled out her story.

Amelia came and put an arm about her, but Julia jerked away and jumped to her feet, to rush into Owen's arms.

Virginia, who had stepped inside, gazed at the scene for a moment, then turned and left the house.

"You sayin' Caleb shot your pa?" Owen asked. "Did you report it to the authorities?"

Julia lifted a wet, reddened face. "You know how it is in Texas nowadays, Owen. Sometimes I think the outlaws are runnin' the place. There was nobody to help me. And

I—I wanted to be with you! So I packed my things and got on a boat—''

Abruptly Owen remembered the message Jackson Dill had passed on to him before the Terrels took delivery of the herd, that men were looking for him—and a woman. Julia! They were looking for Julia, figuring she had come to the Terrels. And if they were looking then, they would likely still be looking.

Abruptly he released himself from Julia's clinging arms. "Take care of her, Amelia," he said. "I need to talk to Will about this."

Owen's brother had ridden out to the herd. Owen was saddling a stout roan he'd left hobbled near the house when Virginia came quietly up to him.

"She's very pretty, Owen. Is she the girl you were betrothed to?"

He looked down at her. "Now how'd you hear about that?"

She blushed, but stood her ground. "Women have to have something to talk about. I asked Amelia why you sometimes seem sad. She told me about Julia Talbot."

He shrugged. "Well, reckon it was no secret."

The last glow of the sunset gilded the ends of her hair, lifting in the light breeze. Her slender face was grave, questioning. Owen was aware of a kind of easing of his heart and mind as he studied the gentle angles and curves of her face. Her eyes were deep and shadowy with thought. "Amelia said you loved her very much. I can see why."

Owen sighed. "Yeah. Julia was a real belle, back home."

"She'd be a belle anywhere. Did she break your heart, Owen?"

He was startled by her directness. Turning away, he pulled up the cinch of his saddle, kneed the roan to make him deflate his belly, tightened the cinch a bit more. "Melia tell you that too, or does it show?" He chuckled. She did not smile in response.

"She's traveled so far to find you, she must regret whatever happened between you." There was an odd little catch in her voice. "I'm glad for you, Owen." She turned and started away toward the dugout, but he called her back.

"Ginny, do you know how to shoot that Henry rifle we brought from your wagons?"

She frowned, but nodded. "A little. It's heavy for me, but I have fired it."

"Good. Come with me."

She followed him to one of the wagons. He rummaged within, came out with the Henry and a box of cartridges. "Now, then, I want you to load it. Go ahead, I want to see if you know how."

Puzzled, she took the rifle, carefully keeping it pointing groundward. He nodded his approval. "I'm not sure I remember . . . Oh, yes, like this."

"That's fine. Why don't you practice that, later? Now, see that rock, over there, that white outcropping? There's still enough light, I think. See if you can hit that."

She looked up at him worriedly. "Owen, I can hit much better with a handgun than this big ol' rifle."

"Try it anyway. For me, honey."

Her wide dark eyes flew to his. Color rose in her slim face. Owen felt a slow surge of pleasure, a feeling like nothing he had ever known before. In that moment, he would unhesitatingly have fought a corral full of Mexican bulls for this girl. He hadn't consciously meant to touch her. Somehow, his hands found their way to her shoulders. He felt the warmth of her skin through the cotton of her dress. It was as if they two were alone, miles from anyone.

Her lips parted. She started to speak, but he stopped the words with a kiss that was simply the most urgent impulse he'd ever experienced. He heard her soft sound of surprise and protest. But it seemed so right to be holding Ginny that he merely drew her closer, wrapping her about with strong arms.

Her slender body trembled against him. In that moment Owen Terrel became a whole person, and it was strange, because he'd never known that he was not complete and sufficient within himself.

After a long moment he stepped back, smiling down at her. "Now, blow the hell out of that rock!"

But she stood very still for a long moment, gazing at him with that intent, questioning look that made her seem to be searching a man's very soul. Then, with a long, unsteady breath, she rather awkwardly levered a shell into the chamber, turned, and lifted the rifle. She took her time, aimed carefully, pulled the trigger. The big rifle boomed. There was a puff of dust a few inches to the right of her target. Nervously, she glanced at him.

"Not bad. Try again."

Again she shot—chipped the edge of the rock. Owen had her shoot a few more times, then reload the gun. Amelia had run out to see who was shooting, and Owen heard distant hoofbeats, Will or one of the boys coming to investigate the ruckus. For the moment he ignored them.

"Keep that gun within reach at all times, Virginia," he instructed soberly. "We may be in for some trouble, and I want you to shoot fast three times to signal the men if you ever need help, if anything threatens you or Amelia or the children—" He hesitated. "Could you shoot at a man if you had to, Ginny?"

She swallowed hard. "Owen, I don't know."

"If the children were in danger? If someone threatened your life, or Amelia's?"

"If the children were in danger, yes, I think so."

"Good girl." He turned, went to his horse, and mounted. "It's all right," he called to Amelia, who had stopped near the dugout, one hand shading her eyes against the last light. "Just teaching Ginny to shoot." He spurred the roan. The sturdy horse sprang roughly into a run as Owen rode to meet Will.

Owen's brother listened quietly to the story of Julia's flight from Texas, his dark brows drawing sharply as Owen repeated the rumor Dill had heard, of men in Galveston looking for the Terrels.

"Sounds like this Wardworth is figurin' to track Julia down. Sure determined to have her, ain't he? Looks like he'd know Julia thought more of her pa than just about anyone. Once Wardworth dueled with ol' Talbot, Julia would never have nothin' to do with him."

"I wonder how that came about?" Owen mused. "Talbot never was a brave man. It would take a heap of insult to make him try to outshoot that slick dude. And when Julia lit out, why would Wardworth bother to chase after her? Be easier to sweet talk another heiress, seems like."

Will nodded slowly. "Seems there's things we ain't bein' told." His glance was penetrating. "Could Julia be lyin' to us?"

Owen lifted his hat, wiped sweat from his forehead. The

last light of sunset painted a distant line of cloud in astonishing colors, but the day's heat lingered. "No, surely not, Will. We been friends a long time. And maybe that ain't important now. Thing is, if Caleb Wardworth is still followin' Julia, we'd better be on the lookout. No way I could turn Julia over to a man she don't want to go with."

Will stilled his restive horse, stared down at the ground for a moment. Then he looked up, met Owen's eyes steadily. "You still in love with her?"

If Will had asked the question a day earlier, Owen's answer might have been a quick yes. All through the last terrible year of the war, the thought of Julia had been for Owen the essence of loving. Her decision to marry another, her failure to inform Owen that she was allowing Caleb Wardworth to court her, had shaken the illusion of perfection he'd built about her. Still, grieving over the death of those dreams, he had expected the fact of his own love to hold steady, though he might wish it otherwise. He simply had not considered that he would ever be able to stop loving Julia Talbot.

But then he had found a helpless girl, on the brink of death. He had struggled to save her, and providence had rewarded his efforts. And he'd gotten used to her presence, her quiet voice, her unexpected moments of infectious laughter.

Still, it had not occurred to him that anything at all had happened to tear down the shrine he kept in his heart and mind. Strangely, it was the unexpected sight of Julia that first rocked the devotion he'd believed unshakable.

And then, that moment with Virginia, a moment unplanned, catching him by surprise . . .

He shook his head, and his smile was rueful. "Things are mixed up right now."

Will nodded, accepting that. "Would you take a word of warnin'? Ain't nothing harder to stop than a woman bound and determined to lay hands on a man's freedom. If you ain't truly in love with Julia, you might oughta make that clear right off."

Owen grinned. "Oh, I doubt she came away out here just to corral this refugee Texan. No way I can compare to that shiny carpetbagger, Wardworth. It might have been different if this had happened when we still had Terreland. I don't even have so much as a shack to offer her now. Reckon she'd get to pinin' for her pa's mansion right soon."

"You regrettin' the move?"

"No, sir, big brother. Terreland sure would seem small and cramped after all this." He waved an arm at the unbroken horizon.

"Reckon you're right. Well, if there's a chance Caleb Wardworth is cookin' up some sort o' party for us, we'd best do some planning."

"We ain't exactly an army. Five of us—if you can even count Georgie. Wish we still had Victorio. He was a dead shot."

"Juan says he hired a new hand at Griffin. Feller's horse got down with colic at the town stables. Juan gave him twenty dollars to get a decent horse. He'll be along soon as he tends to some personal business."

Owen lifted an eyebrow. "Seems he shoulda been here by now. Reckon he lit out with our twenty dollars?"

Will laughed. "Well, if he turns up, let's hope he can shoot. Meanwhile, I'll pass the word to Jackson and Juan to keep their eyes open. Georgie too, but he wouldn't notice if the sun went down at noon."

He paused thoughtfully. "I think I'd better let Amelia in on all this too. I'll leave my old shotgun with her, in case of need. And I believe we'd be smart to have one man at the house all the time."

"Virginia can shoot enough to make a man dodge, anyhow." Owen smiled.

Will studied his change of expression with a little smile of his own. "You should have warned us you were about to conduct artillery practice. We thought it was somethin' serious. I'd best get back to tell the others there's no alarm—at least not yet."

"I'll do that, Will, you go talk with Amelia."

The brothers spurred their mounts in opposite directions. Owen was wondering if it was overcautious to be worrying about Wardworth. It was possible that the man had given up by now and returned to Houston to take up his political aspirations, perhaps to court the daughter of some other influential Texas citizen.

But neither Owen nor Will Terrel had risen in the ranks

during military service by being careless. Best to take a few precautions.

Owen located Jackson Dill a few miles from the dugout. He had been working on a well, taking turns with Georgie, digging for two hours, then checking the herd while Georgie took over in the deepening trench. It was likely that Georgie used his turn at the digging for a quick nap, but short of the satisfaction of kicking his skinny rump halfway to the headquarters, there was little that could be done about Georgie.

Not so with Dill. Dirt and rocks and clods landed with regular thuds outside the pit. Jackson was a mighty worker, and the Terrels had never had occasion to doubt he'd finish any job he started, nor lag in the doing of it.

"Jackson," Owen called as he dismounted. The dirt ceased to fly and Dill clambered up out of the hole.

"Howdy, Cap'n. We gotta rig a windlass purty quick here."

"I'll bring some stuff out in the mornin' and I'll help you and Georgie. Jackson, you got plenty of rifle cartridges?"

Dill eyed him curiously. "Shot at a couple coyotes this mornin'—reckon I could use a few." Dill moved to his ground-tied horse, lifted the Winchester from the saddle to check.

Owen handed him some of his own. "Get more at the headquarters. An' keep that gun in the hole with you when you're workin'. Might be wise to take a look about now and again, too."

"Somethin' wrong, Cap'n?"

"Remember the talk King's man brought from Galveston? Some men lookin for me and a woman?"

"Yessir, I surely do."

"Julia Talbot came in on the freight wagon from Fort Griffin, hour or so ago. Seems she's been traipsin' over half o' Texas looking for us."

Jackson grinned widely. "Lookin' for us, you say? I opine that lady's been lookin' for *you*, Cap'n."

Owen ignored his friend's gibe. "Seems she's running from trouble," he said, and explained.

Jackson whistled softly. "They was talk back home that this Wardworth was in with the Wilkins gang. Why,

I myself seen Wardworth and some of them fellers in one o' them saloons down by the bayou, an' they was *mighty* brotherly.''

Owen's gray eyes narrowed. Jim Wilkins was a familiar and hated name across half of Texas. A huge man, sandy-haired, splotch-freckled, he was credited with any number of crimes. Sometimes he was called Comanche Jim, for his habit of slipping into Indian territory if the law got too close.

Wilkins was said to be one of the most ruthless of the lawless men who were making life dangerous and miserable for honest folk across Texas. Oddly enough, he had never been convicted of a crime. Brought before judge and jury three times—twice for killings so gory folks shuddered at the telling—witnesses against him had been frightened off by Comanche Jim's border scum.

"What's your thought, Jackson?" Owen asked. "Am I spookin' at shadows here? Seems pretty drastic for a man to chase us way out here, even for a woman like Julia.''

Jackson shrugged. "Would you foller a woman that far, Cap'n? Would you foller Miss Julia a way out here?''

Owen sighed. "Sure, at one time. If I'd thought there was a chance she still cared for me. This ain't the same. She seems scared to death of Wardworth. Would a woman be so afraid of a man who loves her?''

"Cap'n, you have to ask a woman 'bout that. Maybe he wants her no matter if she wants him or not. Or maybe they's more to it—somethin' she ain't told you yet.''

Owen dismounted, tied his horse. "Well, go get your supper, Jackson. An' I wish you'd help Will unload that hired freight wagon, so the driver can get an early start back to Griffin tomorrow.''

"I'll be happy to he'p Mr. Will.'' The broad black man mounted his horse and rode away.

Owen dropped into the well, taking up the pick. Georgie should have relieved Jackson some time ago. Evidently he preferred riding lazily about the herd to digging.

An hour later, Georgie's paint horse at last ambled to the well site. Owen was just leaving his work, preparing to go look for the hired hand.

"Little late, ain't you, Georgie?" Owen asked coolly. Doubtless Georgie hadn't expected Owen, rather than

Dill, to be waiting at the well. Owen could not see his expression, but the pimply-faced youth seemed at a loss for words. Owen jammed his shovel upright in the dump of earth.

"Georgie, you gotta start pullin' your weight around here, or we'll hire someone who will. You should have spelled Jackson hours past."

Georgie's bony shoulders lifted in a shrug. "Aw, don't worry 'bout that nigger—"

Owen cut him off with icy contempt. "I hear you speak of Mr. Dill that way just once more an' you can draw your pay and hightail it back to Texas. Jackson Dill is twice the man you'll ever be, unless you commence to mend your ways."

"Sorry, boss," Georgie mumbled after a sullen moment. "I didn't know it was you workin' here."

"It don't matter whether it's me or Dill or whoever! You were told what to do. See that you do it, from now on."

Owen's anger ebbed. Perhaps he was too harsh with the young man. Maybe all he needed was a good lesson. "Listen, Georgie, we all share the work. You climb down right now and do your two hours' diggin'."

"Well, hell, no," yelled Georgie. "It's past time for supper an' it's too dark to be down in that damn hole."

"I'll bring you out a couple o' lanterns. And somethin' to eat—when you're through. I plan to check if you actually move some dirt, too, so don't think you can get away with havin' yourself a nap."

"No, sir! I won't do it, it ain't fair."

"You do it or you come get your pay. It don't matter to me, because if you can't do the work you were hired for, you ain't worth a whole lot to us."

As Owen got on his horse and rode away from the well, Georgie was getting down from the paint, shouting cuss words like an angry little boy. Owen couldn't have served him up a more stinging punishment than to make him wait for supper, for Georgie had a huge appetite. But it was time to put a stop to his laziness.

7

Will was watering a couple of saddle horses when Owen rode up. Lamplight glowed from the dugout window, fifty yards away. Smoke lifted from the stove pipe, and Owen could smell coffee.

"I need a couple of lanterns, Will."

"Look in the wagon, there."

"Could you send someone out with some food for Georgie in a couple of hours? I left him diggin' at the new well."

"What's got into Georgie? Never knowed him to miss his supper!"

"He's been lettin' Jackson do all the dirty work. I hinted that somebody else might make a better showin' at his job, if he don't look alive."

Will chuckled. "I'll take the food out myself."

Owen took the lanterns from the back of one of the wagons and remounted. "See you later."

Back at the well, Owen lighted the lanterns for the furiously silent digger, saw that a reasonable amount of earth was being moved, then left Georgie to his reluctant labor.

The herd was quiet, some of the animals grazing slowly on the tall grass, others bedded down. Owen rode slowly about the herd. In the distance he could see the tiny glow from the dugout window. Strange to think that Julia was there with the others tonight, when he'd never expected to see her again. It should have been a happy surprise. But somehow the thought of Julia set up an uneasiness in his mind. He sighed, clucked to the roan, made yet another wide, easy circle about the herd.

Juan relieved Owen at midnight. The well site was deserted now, the lanterns dark, and all was quiet at the headquarters. Tired, Owen rolled into his blankets.

Whiskey, evidently banished from the dugout, lay down companionably nearby.

"Keep one eye open, boy," Owen told him, and was quickly asleep.

He was up long before daylight, braving the dawn chill to wash in the stone trough. "You get any cleaner we won't know you," Will warned him, approaching the trough with a tall, loose-limbed man whose yellow hair hung raggedly about his ears, under his worn hat.

"You should try it sometime, big brother." Owen grinned. "Make life pleasanter for us all."

"Owen, this here's Olaf Jones, the man Juan hired. He rode in last night. He can work livestock, an' he's done some buildin'. Believe we'll start them pens as soon as that load of cedar posts gets here. We can use cedar pickets for the bronc corral."

Owen stuck out a wet hand. "Pleased to meet you, Mr. Jones."

"I also am pleased, Mr. Terrel." Jones' face was broadly constructed, eyes a bright, merry blue. He had a little difficulty shaping his words and a swinging upward lilt to his sentences. Owen thought Jones was likely not the name his pa had given him.

"Are you Swedish, Mr. Jones?"

"Ya, Svedish. How do you know this?"

"Oh, Owen's a mind-reader." Will grinned. "Come on, Owen, let's all go eat."

As the men approached the dugout, Owen's eyes were searching for one slender form, but he saw only Amelia, setting a pan of biscuits on the table.

"About time, you men. Jackson was the only one on time, and when he found himself alone with three women, he bolted. Oh, there he comes now. Willy, stop that!" She slapped at two small hands as her son tried to snatch some bacon from a platter. "Will, please take this child off my hands today. Let him chase a calf or somethin'. Sit down, we'll eat in a minute."

Owen turned to Dill, who had apparently been working a bit on his own appearance. His dark face gleamed with scrubbing and he wore his second-best shirt. His glance at Will and Owen was nervous, as if he dreaded their laughter.

Will punched him lightly upon the shoulder. "My, how you shine, Jackson! After you eat, take some food out to Georgie. I sent him out to the herd early. Take your bed-rolls too—I want you two to camp out there. Take turns with the well, again, an' see to it that Georgie does his share. Keep a sharp eye for trouble. The rest of us will start puttin' up the corrals."

"I'll take the first watch tonight," Owen said. And more quietly, "We'll need someone to watch here too."

"You need somebody stand guard?" rumbled the Swede. "I sleep not so gude." Again, the upward inflection upon the last word. "I will stand guard."

Will glanced at him in approval. "Owen, you wanta see if you can scare up an antelope today? We could use a change from beef."

"Right. I'll get started right away."

Saddling a fresh horse, he rode out from camp several miles, then began to move south. The day was fine, and Owen's sorrel horse was lively, shying at wind shadows in the tall waving grass. As he rode, he studied the horizon on every side and gave attention to the ground about his mount, alert for sign of whatever had been moving about the area.

He found antelope tracks about noon, but they were not fresh. He rode farther south, but before he found game, he discovered something of greater interest: someone had camped in a shallow swale, some fifteen miles southeast of the Terrel headquarters. There were tracks of three shod horses about the area. Quickly Owen scanned the distances. He could see nothing moving.

Satisfied that no one was nearby, Owen climbed down, felt the dead coals. They were slightly warm. The riders had left early this morning, likely before dawn. He remounted, circling the camp until he found tracks leading west. Owen eased his rifle free, checked the load, kept his eyes moving, searching for anything out of the ordinary.

Perhaps there was no need for the chill edge of alarm he felt. These riders could have been simply travelers on their way to the Pecos Valley. Yet, such travelers were extremely rare in this area and it might pay to be alert to all possibilities.

By midafternoon the tracks had led Owen within sight of the Terrel herd. A trampled area in an arroyo, horse droppings, and cigarette butts told him the riders had rested here for some time, out of sight of the Terrel riders. Now his suspicions were fully alert. Could be these men had simply stopped for a meal. But why hadn't they openly approached the headquarters or the men with the herd?

There was another suspicious circumstance: when the strangers rode away, they had used the arroyo for cover until out of sight of the Terrel holdings. Owen followed them for a mile or so farther before turning back. He'd best head back home, mention what he'd found to Will and the others.

He let his mount move out at a brisk trot. Like all horses, the sorrel knew where "home" lay, and traveled more eagerly in that direction. Owen was so engrossed in his thoughts that he almost failed to note the flicker of white and golden tan as a resting antelope buck leapt up and turned to gaze at him, poised for the swift flight that would take him out of range in seconds.

Swiftly Owen lifted his rifle, sighted, leading the graceful creature as it bounded away. The Winchester slammed into Owen's shoulder and the pronghorn went down. Half an hour later he had bled and gutted his antelope and tied it behind the saddle, though the sorrel was decidedly reluctant to carry the game. Owen had barely set his boot toe in the stirrup when the horse reared and bounded forward. But his rider was on, finding the off stirrup, discouraging the uncontrolled run before it got fairly started. The horse danced, head high and ears back, for a mile before settling down.

There was praise from Amelia when Owen brought in the tender young buck just at dark. "Will, if you dress that out tonight, I'll fry some steaks for breakfast," she offered.

"Patience, woman. Let me sharpen my bowie knife, an' I'll get at it. I can already taste those steaks."

Jones and Jackson Dill arrived, and Dill took Owen's horse.

"I'll see to him, Cap'n. Git you some coffee."

"Owen, dear," called a light voice.

Owen turned to see Julia coming out of the dugout.
Virginia was behind her, carrying Melissa, as they
crossed to the lantern-lit table. The light fell flatteringly
upon Julia. She was wearing a gown that would have
graced the finest home in Houston, rose silk with deep
lace flounces, and a pink velvet sash. Her hair gleamed
palely in the warm light, dressed high upon her head.
She seemed fully aware that each of the men stood riv-
eted by the vision she presented.

She stepped forward, holding out her hands to Owen.
"Amelia's been so wonderful to me. She kept the children quiet so I could sleep the day away."

"You can thank Ginny for that," Amelia commented.
"She took Willy and Melissa for a walk to pick wildflowers. Melissa brought me a posy." She took her little
daughter and kissed her on both plump cheeks, making
her giggle.

Owen gave Julia a light, formal bow. "You're dressed
mighty fine tonight," he commented.

She glanced down at her dress. "Oh, this ol' thing? I
left home in such a hurry I could only pack a few dresses.
When I think what I had to leave, it just makes me sick."

Her face was enchantingly wistful. Will snorted softly.
Owen turned away from Julia and moved to the table.
"Amelia, that smells mighty good."

As they sat down and began to pass the platter of beef
and a bowl of turnip greens, Virginia moved around the
table, filling coffeecups.

When she reached Owen's shoulder, he caught her free
hand and pulled her onto the end of the bench beside
him. "Amelia, pass a plate over here before this girl
fades to nothin'."

Julia heard and turned her head sharply, a frown mar-
ring her prettiness. "Virginia, bring the coffeepot around
here, please."

Ginny started to obey, but Owen kept a firm grip upon
her hand.

"We'll pass it down." He handed the big, granite-
ware pot to Olaf, who courteously tipped it to fill Julia's
cup. She gave a sharp shrug and drew her expensive silk
shawl up about her shoulders.

Owen slid a generous slice of meat into Ginny's plate.

Little Melissa trotted around the table and squeezed her soft little body between Owen and Virginia. "Hungry," she announced.

Virginia hugged her and offered the child a sliver of meat.

When Owen had finished his meal, he went to the picketed saddle horses. Olaf Jones followed. "I generally throw down my bedroll out here." Terrel indicated the clean, grassy area at one end of the partially finished pens. "I keep a horse saddled, just in case." He moved to a bay mare he liked to ride and began to saddle her.

"Which horse I may use?" asked Jones.

"Take your pick. I like that big roan there. He looks like an outlaw, but he ain't bad an' he won't give out on you."

He half-expected the Swede to think twice before approaching the horse. Olaf did not have the look of a natural-born rider. But Jones moved calmly to the roan, ignoring the indications of ill will, the animal's white-rimmed eye, the threateningly laid back ears. Olaf quickly saddled the horse. So far, Olaf Jones was making a good impression upon Owen.

"You wish me to help guard cattle?" Jones asked.

"Watch here, until Juan can take over, about midnight. Then get some sleep. I'll wake you at dawn to take a turn with the herd."

"Mr. Terrel, I may ask question?"

"Sure."

"I am to be alert for"—he hesitated, apparently seeking the correct words—"for somet'ing especial?"

"Yes. There are some men that we believe mean us harm."

Olaf nodded. "It is not the men of the law?"

Owen laughed. "No, these fellers are mighty allergic to the law, Jones. They ain't what you might call good folks. Even the women and children ain't safe from the likes of them. See that you watch well."

"I will do so," Jones promised soberly, and Owen believed him.

Owen swung into his saddle. He liked the bay for night work. She was not apt to get nervous when faced with the unexpected, and her night vision was excellent. He rode over to the dugout, where Will was resting, enjoying his pipe, seated at the plank table.

"Need to have a word with you—away from the house," Owen said softly.

At once Will stood and followed Owen a little distance away. "What is it, Owen?"

"We're bein' watched. I found plenty of signs today."

Will lifted his head sharply. "You spot anyone?"

"No. I saw tracks of three riders, but I wouldn't bet that's the crop."

Will sighed and Owen thought he knew what his older brother was thinking. Even out here it seemed they were not to be allowed to settle down and live in peace.

"All right," he said at last. "You want some company on first watch?"

Owen considered. "No. I don't reckon they're ready yet. But warn the women not to venture far from the dugout. I don't want Ginny out pickin' wildflowers with the kids anymore."

For answer Will slapped his brother's shoulder and headed back to the house. Owen touched the bay mare with his spurs. She lifted into an easy, slow lope.

Fifteen minutes later he reached the herd. It occurred to Owen that they would not be able to keep up this constant guarding of the herd. Sooner or later the cattle would have to be allowed to roam pretty much at will, limited only by their accustomed watering places. But with strangers watching the herd—strangers who did not announce themselves to the Terrels—there was no choice but to continue their night watches.

After an hour or so, Owen halted the mare, dismounted, and slipped the bit from her mouth so she could graze and rest. He moved fifty feet away, listening to the night, examining every sound for anything out of the ordinary. He filtered out the normal herd noises, the rustlings of grass stirred by the intermittent breeze. He bent and placed an ear to the ground, listening for the regular beats that would mean something or someone approaching from the surrounding country.

There was nothing. For a space of time Owen hunkered down on his heels, cataloguing the various sounds: the mare cropping the tough grass a few yards away, a bird ruffling its feathers for a moment in a clump of shinnery, the rattling of a dry yucca bloom when the wind gusted.

He kept his Winchester in his hands. There was something uncomfortably familiar about this lonely watch in the darkness. How many nights had he kept watch thus during the war years while his comrades slept?

A half-hour slid by. Owen had learned to rest without sleeping, letting tension dissolve from muscle and bone. The silence deepened. The moon was down. Nothing seemed to be moving on the face of this vast expanse of level land, at least nothing that would not normally be about. Owen could imagine rabbits, coyotes, and badgers going about their nocturnal business. No doubt there were burrowing owls and bull bats scouting the night. At a distance there would be wild horses and burros and perhaps antelope sampling the water holes of the plains.

All this was right and natural, nothing to cause the underlying uneasiness that suddenly gripped Owen. He stood, moved to the mare and found her with head up, ears pointed as she studied something Terrel could neither hear nor see, to the east. It might only be some wild thing moving about. Then again, it might not.

Owen quickly replaced the bit in the mare's mouth, pulled the headstall over her ears. Suddenly the bay nickered. Owen stiffened. There were horses moving in the distance. Now the picketed cowponies were making a ruckus.

Owen tugged the cinch strap snug and mounted. He let the mare trot eastward, peering into the darkness. He was leaving the herd behind, and perhaps that was a risk. But whatever disturbed the mare was certainly approaching from the east. Owen spurred the mare to a lope.

He passed near the dugout and gave a sharp whistle to alert Olaf and Will. Jones must have been ready; Owen heard a mounted horse moving out to join him at a hard run.

The Swede caught up quickly. "Somet'ing is about?" the big man called softly.

"Riders, east of here. Go back and tell the others, then help me patrol. Got your rifle? Forgot to ask, can you shoot?"

"I shoot very gude." The man chuckled and expertly wheeled the feisty roan back to the dugout.

The mare kept her ears tipped forward. Owen let her choose her own direction. She knew better than he where to find the intruders, whoever they might be.

He had ridden only a few yards farther when the bay stopped and flung up her head. Owen glimpsed movement, silhouettes only a bit darker than the skyline, but clearly riders. He could not at once determine how many, perhaps as many as six or seven.

They must have seen him almost at the same moment. A rifle boomed, blasting apart the peace of the night. But Owen had already whirled his mount and spurred her leaping to one side. His Winchester spoke once, and again. Another shot whined by his head. He whirled the mare again, sent her back toward the strange riders. Apparently his unexpected return confused the intruders. Someone let out a shout of warning just as Owen levered another shell into the chamber and shot at one of the dimly seen targets.

He heard the bullet hit, heard a scream, and a body thudded to the ground. Hooves pounded as a loose horse cut away in panic. Owen shot once more, then jerked the mare aside and back toward the headquarters. He wasn't fool enough to think he could handle this many attackers singlehandedly.

They were following, running their horses recklessly.

Owen trusted to his own surefooted mare. The men behind him smelled an easy prey now. He let them gain upon him just a bit. Then, hearing what he had expected to hear, horses approaching from the dugout, he pulled his mount to a sliding stop, was off before she halted, crouching as he fired three quick shots into the approaching horsemen.

A horse went down; the dislodged rider yelled, but scrambled up to fling himself behind a mesquite. Then there was firing from behind Owen. He smiled grimly, hoping his brother did not mistake him or his mare for a target. As one of the Terrel riders approached at a run, Owen stood and shouted, "Will, here!"

He was shooting all the while, but his targets had scattered now. Off to the right, Olaf's Sharps boomed menacingly, further discouraging the attackers.

In a moment, there was nothing left of the gang but the sound of horses racing eastward.

Will reined in practically on top of his brother, dust rising about them both. "Damn it, Owen, you could've hollered quicker. I nearly shot you."

"Well, you didn't," Owen said mildly. "Tell the men to spread out, Will. I think there's still one out there, on foot." Olaf and Jackson Dill joined the Terrel brothers. Owen heard another horse to the left of them, probably Juan. Georgie would not be riding so daringly into trouble.

"One on the ground and lively, men," Will said. "Look sharp. Try to take him in one piece."

Owen set his toe into his stirrup, lifted his long body into the saddle. The four riders spread out, walking their horses forward, holding their guns ready.

"You, out there," Owen called. "Drop your gun and step out!"

There was no reply for a moment and the horsemen moved forward menacingly. Then there was a muffled shout ahead of them. "Hold it, men," Owen called. The line of Terrel riders halted.

"Come out, mister. Your buddies have left you behind."

"Is that Mr. Terrel?" A clump of shinnery trembled.

"Owen Terrel. I'm listenin'."

"Here's my weapon." Something hit the ground to one side of the brush. "I'm comin' out. You figurin' on shootin' me?"

"Up to you. Step out with your hands up."

After a long moment, the man came out of the brush, hands high. Olaf rode behind him, prodded him forward with the long barrel of his Sharps. The captive walked up to the others, stood quiet. Owen dismounted, took a rawhide strap from his saddle, and tied the outlaw's hands behind him. He remounted and drove him ahead of his mare like a roped calf.

Owen dismounted within the angle formed by the two parked, covered wagons, and lighted a lantern.

"Let's see what manner o' varmint we've caught here.

Olaf, you mind to ride out to the herd and take over? Where's Georgie? Anyone seen him? Damn! Little weasel didn't bother to come in from where you camped. Jackson, go with Jones. Kick that kid out of his blankets, make him help guard the herd. You men keep your eyes open. I doubt they'll try anything more tonight, but don't be caught off guard."

Without comment, Jones and Dill rode into the darkness.

The lantern light disclosed their captive as a short, sturdy, bowlegged man, bearded, dressed in grimy buckskin. He'd apparently lost his hat when his horse went down. Greasy dark hair hung lankly down his shoulders.

"Now, then, friend. Who are you and who you ridin' for?" Will asked grimly.

The man seemed to be studying the brothers as intently as they studied him, apparently deciding whether to answer. Casually, Will lifted his rifle barrel . . . just enough to suggest something to the defiant captive.

The man blew his breath out, defeated. "They call me Crow. I'm a buff-hunter, or was, till we run outta anythin' to shoot."

"What are you doin' with that bunch of bushwhackers?"

Crow shrugged.

"Just who is it you're workin' for?" Owen asked.

"Calls hisself Comanche Jim." He seemed to enjoy dropping this bit of information, as if he hoped to see a start of fear. If so, he was disappointed.

"You see a dude with this Wilkins? City feller name of Caleb Wardworth?"

But now the outlaw seemed to have lost interest in conversation. He gave an elaborate yawn. "You fellers got some coffee made? I sure could use a cup."

Owen felt inclined to grin at the man's audacity, but he kept his face expressionless. "Mister, we don't bring out tea and cookies for just any ol' gang that rides in shootin' up the place."

"What you gonna do with me?" Crow kept a defiant grin on his face, but Owen saw the flicker of anxiety in his eyes.

"I reckon we'll decide that tomorrow," Will said.

"For now, make yourself comfortable here by this wheel."

"You leavin' me tied up?" The man seemed honestly shocked.

"You expect to be left free?" Will spat contemptuously into the dirt. "You came out of the night, hopin' to murder my family. Reckon you better count yourself lucky we don't practice a little Comanche justice on your filthy hide!"

Crow seemed to wilt a bit. "All right, Mr. Terrel. I'll set here an' keep my mouth shut. But you got nothin' to fear from me anymore. I—I swear!"

"Save it," Owen advised coldly. He tied Crow to the wheel, wondering what they could do with the man. There was no law within two hundred miles, nor could they spare a man to escort this owlhoot to the nearest town.

Owen tossed a blanket over Crow. They left the silent captive staring into the darkness, and walked toward the dugout.

"What do you think, men?" Will asked. "No trees handy to hang the varmint. Shoulda shot him."

Owen shook his head. "I never shot an unarmed man. Can't bring myself to do that."

Will sighed, an impatient sound. "No, reckon I cain't either, much as I'm tempted. But neither will I deal soft with night riders that menace my family."

"Señor Will is right," Juan put in. *"Los kineros* would not let this man to live."

Owen replied mildly. "Shootin' a man down when he's riding at you, meanin' to kill, is one thing. Blowin' his head off while he stands helpless, tied, that's different."

For a moment there was only the sound of their boots in the sand. "I cain't argue with you, little brother," Will said. "But we'll have to deal with him someway."

"Tomorrow I'll take him twenty miles or so south, give him a canteen, and a horse. If he can make it out of the Llano without weapons, reckon he won't come back."

"If he does come back—"

"If he does, he's a dead man," Owen said.

8

There was a short bark from Whiskey as the men approached the dark dugout. Amelia was too wise to target their home with a lighted window. Will called out to her and she came immediately from the dark doorway and up the earthen steps to the yard. Virginia was immediately behind her, carrying the Henry rifle, and a figure in white hovered in the doorway: Julia, peering out nervously.

"Will, are you all right?" Amelia cried.

"We're all fine, sweetheart."

She ran to him and was caught close. Her voice was unsteady. "We heard shooting."

"Yeah, had us a little ol' ruckus. Don't you fret now."

Julia came rushing up the steps, past Virginia, who stood quietly. Miss Talbot, in a fine cambric gown and wrapper, stumbled and almost fell into Owen's arms.

"Owen, I was so scared. Darlin', are you hurt? We were afraid any minute terrible men would burst in on us." She began to weep hysterically, her soft, slender body trembling in Owen's arms.

Embarrassed, he set her away and moved back. She drooped as if she would fall.

Amelia turned and caught Julia firmly about the waist. "There's nothin' to cry about, Julia. Come back to your bed now."

Julia suddenly stiffened, and her chin lifted angrily. "Bed? A rawhide bunk in a room full of children? My papa's horses had a better home."

"Well, do forgive us, Julia. Maybe you'd rather sleep out of doors?" Amelia's voice held just a hint of acid.

Julia let out a moan of sheer rage, but she returned to the dugout with Amelia.

Will turned. "Get some sleep, Owen.

"I need to speak to Virginia," Owen said.

She came toward him hesitantly. The dog frisked about her ankles, delighted to have her company at this unusual hour.

"Let's walk out away from the house," Owen suggested, and she moved quietly beside him, still holding the Henry rifle. A little way out onto the prairie, Owen halted. All was quiet again now, but Virginia gazed into the dark distance, and she shivered as the wind lifted, briefly.

Quickly Owen put an arm around her. "Cold?"

She sighed. "No. Julia was right, Owen. We were afraid when we heard the shooting. Who was out there?"

"No one for you to worry about, Ginny. They're gone now, likely won't be back."

She pulled away, faced him in the dim starlight. Her wide dark eyes were deep shadows, the shape of her face was delicate, yet somehow strong, and Owen had an impulse to cradle that face within his big hands. But he sensed that his touch would not be welcome just now.

"Don't treat me like a little child, Owen Terrel. I'm holding a gun, ready to try to protect your little niece and nephew. I'm—I'm a part of whatever it is, whether you like it or not, and I have a right to know who I'm goin' to be shooting at."

This was a new side of the girl who had seemed so fragile, so helpless when he lifted her from a mud puddle in a Houston street. Standing before him, right hand gripping the big rifle, her long dark hair lifting in the early-morning wind, she seemed very much a woman, and not at all helpless.

She stamped a small, booted foot under the edge of her plain flannel wrapper. "Do you hear me? I want to know what's happening. Does it have anything to do with Miss Talbot?"

"Take it easy. I'll tell you what I know—or guess." He hesitated, ordering his thoughts. "You already know I planned at one time to marry Julia."

Her head bent sharply, but he saw her nod.

"The same evenin' I met you, Julia announced she would marry a man called Caleb Wardworth. When my family and I left Houston, I believed their wedding would take place any day. Now Julia says Wardworth killed her pa in a duel, and she ran away, hopin' to find us."

"To marry you?" Her voice was muffled and she did not lift her face.

"No, ma'am. She's said nothin' of the kind."

But Virginia was shaking her head. "I'm sorry, Owen. That was none of my business, and I shouldn't have asked."

"Well, that ain't important now. The thing is, Julia's scared of Wardworth, and we think he and some other men are followin' her."

"Why?"

It was the same question he and Will had pondered uselessly. Julia had promised to marry Wardworth, but changed her mind after her pa's death—and that was certainly no surprise to anyone who knew her almost fanatic devotion to her father. But why had she felt it necessary to leave her home? And why indeed had Caleb Wardworth followed her eight hundred miles across Texas and into New Mexico Territory. Was it simply that the man was loath to give up a beautiful woman? Unless he intended to force her to marry him—and heaven help the man who tried to force Julia to anything—what did he expect to gain from such a pursuit? And whatever his reason, why did he bring a small army?

"Of course," Virginia went on, "anyone can see that Julia is beautiful enough for a dozen men to follow her around the world." Did her grave tone cover a hint of mockery? "But I still wonder, what does he plan to do when he finds her? And why would he come at night, with other men, and guns?"

"Seems he's already found her. As for his plans—that's anybody's guess. I reckon the guns have something to do with me. He may mistake the reason she's followed us."

"I don't think there's any mistake about it," she said. "She's made no bones about it, talking with Amelia, an' she doesn't care a bit when I hear what she says. She came to you because she knows she made the wrong choice, back in Houston. And if that man Wardworth is jealous . . ." She drew a worried breath. "Owen, you're in danger. This man is dangerous." She lifted her hand and he caught it, warming it within his own.

"He'll find we ain't helpless here." Owen said.

"You . . ." Now her voice sounded again like that

young girl he'd lifted from a muddy Houston street. "I don't suppose you could just give Julia back to him?"

Startled, Owen laughed. "That's a little bit hard on poor Julia, don't you think? Judgin' from that little foray tonight, Wardworth is not an easygoin' kind of feller."

She sighed. "No, I guess you can't let him just take her away." Nevertheless, she sounded regretful. "I suppose the rest of us will just have to protect her."

"I can't see another choice right now, can you?"

Her face lifted. "You said it wasn't likely those men would come back. I don't think that's true, Owen. This Wardworth must have had a good reason to come this far, so they won't just stop now, will they?"

He wanted to give her a reassuring lie, but she was too smart to believe it. "No, Ginny. They likely won't stop until they see they're gettin' no place. But they won't be back tonight. They know they can't surprise us. So you go back and go to sleep now."

"How about you? You can't stay awake day and night."

"I'll rest," he promised. "But don't worry, I sleep light. And that dog of yours would warn us of anything moving within a quarter-mile around the dugout."

She seemed reassured and obediently went back inside the dugout. Owen studied the night for a short time, then rolled out blankets—shaking them briskly just in case a scorpion might have taken refuge within their folds—and stretched out. He was quickly asleep and did not rouse until daylight.

But he found that his promise that Whiskey would alert them to anything unusual proved false. The captive, Crow, had managed to free himself and had crept away in the darkness. Julia, nervous in spite of the others in the dugout and Will asleep just outside, had taken it upon herself to call the dog inside. She had let him sleep near her bunk, although she had been incensed by his presence until now, worried about fleas.

Annoyed, Owen instructed her to leave Whiskey outside from now on, where he could perform his duties as a watchdog.

Her face, pale in the early sunlight, was remorseful. "I'm sorry, Owen darlin'. I just didn't think—and I did feel so much safer with the dog inside. If only you could always be nearby, I would never worry."

Owen turned away and ate a hurried breakfast—antelope steaks, water gravy, flapjacks, and sorghum, washed down with coffee the color of stove blacking. Will followed him when he went to turn out the mare he'd kept picketed the night before. He saddled a rawboned dun gelding.

"Let's track that buff-hunter a ways," Will said. "I'm inclined not to let him get back to his gang."

"I was about to suggest it myself," Owen agreed.

Will flung his saddle on a short-coupled mustang with a Roman nose and a white-ringed eye. It was no surprise to either man when Will had to endure a brief spell of bucking from the mouse-brown horse. The dun was inspired to emulate Will's mount, and ordinarily Owen would have enjoyed the challenge and let him do his worst. Today he was in no mood. He wheeled the dun in a tight, dizzying circle, spurring him to the effort, until the horse lost the urge to throw his rider.

When the cloud of dust began to settle and Will's horse was down to halfhearted crow-hopping, the brothers gigged their mounts into a lope to the east, watching the ground for the marks of Crow's boots. Will was an excellent tracker, able to spot the tiniest mark upon the earth, grass pressed down, or a shinnery twig bent by the passage of animal or man.

"You sure our man will try to catch up to the gang? After all, they left him behind last night. Seems he might resent it," Owen said.

"Don't reckon he's got much choice, since he didn't try to steal a horse from us. He's afoot out there, without food, and only that half-canteen o' water I left on the wagon. Far as I could tell, that's all he took before he lit out. Guess he figured we'd hear him if he rummaged around lookin' for a weapon or tried for a horse with Juan sleepin' practically under the picket rope."

Owen nodded. "That figures. Will, I believe I hit someone out there last night when I first spotted them." Owen waved an arm. "If he's alive an' the others didn't stop to pick him up, might be we could find him, see what he knows."

"Worth a try. Let's split up and have a look. Crow will

be headed straight east. We can pick up his tracks again later.''

They began to search for the fallen outlaw, rifles ready just in case. But when they located the man Owen had hit, they saw that he'd doubtless been dead even as he hit the ground. There were no signs that he had even moved, no marks that he had dragged himself more than an inch or so.

While Will kept watch on the apparently empty distances around them, Owen climbed down and turned the facedown body over. Neither he nor Will recognized the man.

''Jackson's comin','' Will commented.

Owen examined the dead man's pockets for a clue to his name or the names of family the Terrels could write to with word of his demise. But there was nothing save a bowie knife upon the belt, a few coins, and a half-sack of tobacco in his shirt pocket. Will spotted the dead man's rifle several feet away in a greasewood bush. As Owen straightened from his distasteful job, Jackson Dill reined his horse to a stop and stepped down.

''One of them bushwhackers?'' he asked.

''Yeah. Ever see him?'' Will asked.

Jackson tilted his head, studying the unpleasantly staring face. ''No, sir, I don't know 'im. Likely one of Jim Wilkins' men.''

''Keep that stuff from his pockets,'' Will advised. ''We ever hear his name, we'll send his things and money back to his folks.''

Owen nodded, dropped the things in a saddlebag. He felt the familiar depression, more than once experienced during the war, of knowing that a man had died at his hand. Even in defense of his own life and the lives of his family, dealing out death was not something he enjoyed, nor could he feel pride in the accomplishment.

''I'll go get a shovel.'' Jackson climbed on his horse, hunched his shoulders as he peered down at the dead man. ''Anyplace special you wanta put 'im?''

''I'll bury him,'' Owen said, somewhat sharply.

Will gave him a quick, knowing glance. ''Owen, this feller was a sidewinder. He asked for what he got. Don't go feelin' guilty. Had he elected to stay to home, makin' a honest living, he'd be alive today."

Owen managed a grin. "Yeah. But I clean up my own messes, when I can."

"Whatever you say. Jackson, bring the shovel and give Owen a hand while I scout a little, try to cut the trail of the other one."

"Right." Jackson wheeled his horse, galloped back to the wagons, and returned shortly. He brought a blanket as well and took turns with Owen, digging in the sand and loose rock until they had a grave of decent depth. They wrapped the dead outlaw, laid him in, and covered him.

Will trotted his mustang back to the grave, got down to fashion a rude cross with pieces of mesquite limb bound together with a bit of rawhide. He planted it firmly at the head of the grave.

"Gettin' sentimental, Mr. Will?" Dill grinned.

"Not much. I'm thinkin' this'll make a nice little reminder if his buddies ride this way again."

They resumed looking for the trail of the escaped captive. Within the hour, they struck the deep hoof marks of five shod horses, and bootmarks of a man afoot. The Terrels and Dill followed the trail for ten miles before Will signaled a halt.

"Don't think we'd best follow farther," he said. "The trail is circling to the south a little. Makes me think someone might be leadin' us away."

Owen nodded, uneasy at the thought that the headquarters was defended only by Juan, unless Georgie had ridden in for food. That was likely, but not much comfort.

They were turning their horses when Owen spotted something dark alongside the trail about a quarter-mile farther.

"Think I'll take a look at that. I'll follow you back," he told the others.

"We'll wait," Will said.

Owen spurred his horse to the spot. When he was closer, he could see that it was a man, lying still, crumpled. There was dried blood on the side of his head. It was the man who called himself Crow.

Alert to ambush Owen studied the area nearby, but could see no cover where anyone might lie concealed. The horse tracks were all over the place at that point as if the group had halted for a couple of hours. Farther on, the hoofmarks lined out southeast as far as he could see.

He dismounted, levering a shell into his rifle, for one of the prone outlaw's hands was tucked under his chest, though the other was outflung and relaxed. He was not dead. His ribs moved shallowly. Could be he held a knife or gun, and waited for someone to approach . . .

Owen laid the rifle barrel gently on the man's neck. "Crow, looks like you need a little help, man."

There was no slightest flutter of Crow's eyelids. His mouth was open—dust coated his tongue and a column of ants busily crossed it and moved down his chin. Satisfied that the outlaw was unconscious, Owen lifted the rifle, toed the relaxed body over. The right hand was revealed, empty, the palm bloodstained as if he had touched his injured head before he passed out. But who had inflicted this wound? The man had been unharmed when the Terrels left him tied last night.

Will and Jackson rode up. "Damn, it's the feller we caught last night," Will muttered. "What's wrong with him?"

"Somebody used a rifle butt on him, looks like," Owen said. "Reckon he found his friends an' they had a fallin'-out."

"Not enough mounts," Dill guessed. "An' maybe short of water. Them fellers don't like to share."

"Or maybe they thought he'd made a deal with us."

"Damned skunks, ain't even loyal to their own," Will rasped. "Okay, who wants to walk back?"

"Ol' Coyote will carry double. I'll hold him on," Owen said. They lifted the unconscious man across the saddle. Owen mounted behind, steadying Crow's limp body.

"Jackson, ride along with Owen," Will said. "I think I'll get back, see if the family's all right."

He spurred away and the other men came along at a slower pace. By the time they reached the ranch yard, Amelia was ready with hot water and bandages to help the injured man. They laid him on the table and Ginny helped as Amelia bathed the head wound, bandaged it with strips of cloth. Julia stood back, knuckles pressed to her lips as she watched. It was clear that the sight of the outlaw frightened her, perhaps making her situation more real and immediate to her mind.

Owen moved to stand near her. "Julia, have you ever seen this man?"

She shook her head violently, and she was so white that Owen feared she might faint. He placed a supporting arm about her drooping shoulders. "Steady now, he can't hurt you. He's helpless."

She shuddered and shrank closer to Owen, turning her face into his shoulder, murmuring something. He bent his head. "What did you say?"

"Let him die!"

Startled, he drew back. Her blue eyes were hard, defiant.

"You don't mean that, Julia. We can't leave a helpless man to die."

"He came here to do us harm. Why are you helpin' him? If he don't die, he'll try again to do what Caleb wants and kill me."

"What makes you believe Wardworth would want to harm you, Julia? The man wants to marry you. He thinks I've coaxed you away from him, an' he's mighty jealous. Reckon it's me he wants to lay in a grave. Damned fool should have known you wouldn't marry a man would duel with your pa."

She stared at him, seemed on the point of saying something, then turned on her heel and rushed back into the dugout. Perplexed, Owen turned to find Ginny's wide, grave gaze upon him. She seemed to be thinking hard about something, and there was a sadness in the depths of her dark eyes.

"Will, best make this man a bed in the shade," Amelia said. "I won't have him in my house, mind you!"

"No, ma'am," Will grinned slightly, winking at Owen. "We'll put him under a wagon. Ginny, think you ladies could keep an eye on him, in case he takes an urge to wander off again?"

"We'll watch him," she said steadily.

"I'll tell Willy to watch him, too." Amelia gave a last brisk tug on the bandage tie. "Willy," she called. The towheaded little boy ceased his game of mumblety-peg and came running to his mother. He stared at the unconscious man stretched out upon the table where he had, an hour past, eaten his cornmeal mush.

Amelia gave him instructions to play within sight—but never within reach—of Crow. "If he starts to move or says anything, you come get one of us, you hear me, Willy?"

"Yes'm," the little boy said. "Can I hold Pa's pistol on 'im?"

"No, sir, you can't." Will ruffled his son's hair. "I'll be teachin' you to shoot any day now. You stay away from the guns until I do."

"Will you really learn me to shoot, Pa?" Willy asked, round eyes sliding around to Crow as if he feared the man might suddenly rise and grab him.

"Just as quick as I have a little time. Now you do as your ma says, an' don't you forget to watch this feller. You let out a yell if he twitches an ear." Will turned to his wife. "Amelia, you women keep a sharp eye out," his tone underlining the importance of his command. "Don't just watch this sorry *hombre* you just patched up, but the prairie too. From now on, we got to expect trouble."

Her nod was matter-of-fact. "We'll handle it. An' don't you men get careless, you hear me, Will Terrel? Those scoundrels might try to steal our cattle."

"You're right, Amelia. They likely will. We'll be ready if they try it."

He kissed her cheek. Jackson Dill and Owen moved the injured outlaw under the nearest wagon. Willy took up his mumblety-peg game at a little distance.

After they settled Crow on blankets, Owen moved to his horse and mounted. "I'll hitch up the mules to a wagon and haul the stuff for the windlass. Jackson, see can you help me head ol' Steamboat. That damned mule gets harder to catch ever' day. Hobbles don't even slow him down."

He waited for Jackson to get mounted. "Will, you care if I use those twelve-foot beams there? The windlass crank and rope's already on the wagon. I see Georgie coming, yonder. Soon as he eats, send him out to help at the stock well.''

So the work of the homestead began once more. Even with the threat of attack hanging over them, the cook fire required fuel, the livestock would need a reliable water supply before winter, the horses must be tended.

Nevertheless, vigilance was the order of each day. The women were never left at the headquarters without at least one man near enough to come running at the slightest alarm. Will kept his word to teach his young son the proper use of a gun, though he was strictly forbidden to touch a weapon unless Will or Owen were with him.

Still concerned with the safety of the women and children, Owen offered to help Julia learn to shoot, but she became nearly hysterical at the thought of having to handle a rifle or even Owen's Peacemaker. Amelia did manage to persuade her to carry a little derringer. The sleeve gun had belonged to Amelia's grandfather, who once had pursued the profession of riverboat gambler. But no one had much hope that Julia would ever muster the nerve to use the derringer. The best use the women managed to put Julia to was that of watching for approaching riders. Even at that, she was so much inclined to hide within the dugout that she could not be relied upon.

The injured Crow regained his senses the second day after he was found and brought back to the headquarters. He was weak and dazed, and seemed scarcely to understand where he was. The blow to his head had been severe, and his understanding was limited at first to remembering how to chew and swallow and obey the very simplest commands of those who cared for him.

Nevertheless, with his return to consciousness, Owen and Will made sure that there was always a man within reach to help the women, should Crow attempt to do them harm. There was no question, in his present condition, of turning him loose upon the prairie to make his way to a town. It would have been condemning the man to sure death.

9

After the night attack, the Terrel family and crew worked with the feeling that violence might erupt again at any moment. Julia was so fearful that she would scarcely leave the dugout, even to visit the outhouse, unless someone was with her. Virginia often drew this duty, carrying the Henry rifle. If she resented the necessity of guarding the nervous Miss Talbot, she kept it to herself.

Further, she proved herself a competent guard when she was called upon to shoot a rattler that had invaded the shade of the outhouse. Julia's shrieks brought her running. It required two shots, but the snake lay bloody and writhing in its death throes within the outbuilding. Owen had just returned to headquarters when he heard the shots. In moments he jerked his horse to a stop at the scene of the ruckus.

Virginia stood gazing silently at her victim, beginning to reload the heavy rifle from the cartridges she kept in her apron pocket. Julia was fleeing back to the dugout, feet tripping and tangling within the lace-trimmed drawers she had not paused to replace. The blond girl was still uttering choked yelps as she ran. In moments, only the white undergarment, kicked out of her way, was visible upon the path.

Owen tilted his head, grinning at Virginia. "Lordy, ma'am, I would not want to exchange shots with you."

"I missed the first time," she mourned.

"An' you had your target cornered, too. Still an' all, it wasn't bad for your first battle."

Her eyes glowed as she smiled at him. "Thanks, Owen. Would you mind gettin' that thing out of there for me?"

Owen obligingly dismounted, found a dried yucca stalk nearby, and dragged the dying snake out into the dust.

Virginia gave a peculiar little sigh. Owen saw that there was a tinge of white under her suntanned cheek.

"Hey, you been workin' too hard, girl. Let's go for a ride."

"What?" She gave him a startled glance. "Oh, I can't, Owen. I've got to take in the dry wash before dark. If it comes up a little wind, those sheets will blow off the mesquites and halfway to Texas."

"Never mind that. Julia can do it. Reckon she owes you a favor. Come on." He took the rifle out of her hands, leaned it against the wall, caught her slim waist in both hands, and boosted her onto his dun gelding. He handed up the gun and climbed on behind the saddle. His arm went around her waist so naturally that he had to restrain the urge to pull her back against him. Lifting the rein, he sent the gelding trotting smartly to the dugout. Circling to the front, they found Amelia standing outside, turning meat in a large skillet over the fire. She grinned at the two of them.

"What's this about Julia bein' attacked by a regiment of serpents?"

"It was one undersized sidewinder, an' our Ginny dispatched it without help. I'm about to take her for a little ride before supper. Okay with you?"

"That's a fine idea. She's been workin' like a slave and Julia runs her ragged."

"Speakin' of Julia, it wouldn't hurt her to take over a chore or two. Make her bring in that dried wash out back. Oh, and tell her she left somethin' of hers in the path."

"I may have to drag her out of doors, but I'll try. Go ahead, Ginny, and have a good time."

"Thanks, Amelia. I won't stay long. I promised to read Melissa a story." She handed her rifle to Amelia.

Owen sent the horse galloping toward the new corral Olaf and Jackson Dill had finished only yesterday, which now held the saddle stock caught up for the day's use. He roped out a quiet mare for Virginia and quickly cinched Amelia's sidesaddle on. Ginny mounted gracefully as Owen held the rein. In a few minutes the two of them headed their mounts west onto the empty prairie.

The evening was deepening toward dusk, and the sunset flamed orange and gold above a low band of purple cloud.

"Hope that brings us some rain," Owen commented. "It's gettin' mighty dry."

"How is the stock well going?" Virginia asked.

"We hit a little bit o' water today. Give us a week an' we'll be able to fill a trough couple o' times a day for the livestock."

Virginia reached to pat her mare's neck. The little mustang took this as an encouragement and lifted into a gallop. Ginny slowed her without trouble and laughed happily. Owen, watching her, noticed that the sunset light, sending shimmering waves of pink-gold across the grassland, lighted her slim, delicately boned face, gilded strands of hair that had worked loose from the lustrous dark knot pinned at the nape of her neck.

"If it doesn't rain right away, will there be enough feed for the cattle and horses?"

Owen smiled, thinking of the hundreds of miles of grass all about them, virtually unused except for the herds of wild burros and horses and perhaps a few buffalo.

"Plenty of grass. Water's the main thing. Makes a man uneasy to see so little rain. Reckon we'll get used to it."

Ginny looked about her thoughtfully. "You know, I think I like it out here. At first I thought I'd never seen anything so desolate. But I've learned to love the way the light changes the color of everything from hour to hour, and the way the shadows of clouds race over the grass." She turned to Owen, her wide dark eyes thoughtful. "And the air is wonderful, so light and dry. There's never any mould on the linens or dishes. And the sky! I never knew it could be so blue, or the stars so bright and close."

Owen nodded. "I like that too. The bigness of it doesn't bother you?"

She seemed to give serious thought to his question before answering. He waited, content to watch her. Somehow she seemed to grow more attractive with every passing day, in spite of the fact that she worked from dawn to dark and had little or no time for primping. Virginia would never have Julia's prettiness, but there was something unique about her. Maybe it was the transparent way her expression altered from moment to moment with the quick and intuitive workings of her mind. She was sensitive and intelligent, and these qualities were reflected in the depths of her dark eyes. Yet she had a sense of humor and her mouth was made for smiling.

"Well?" he prompted. "Does all this space worry you?"

"Yes, sometimes," she admitted. "Sometimes, like after the raid—those men trying to sneak down on us like savages in the night—I feel helpless and scared. We're so far from other people who could help us. Suppose Willy or Melissa get sick, or one of you men should get hurt. It would take days to reach a doctor."

He kneed his gelding closer and caught her left hand. "I know. It's harder for a woman, I expect. When you're used to neighbors and stores and churches and schools for the young 'uns, it's mighty strange to find yourself away out in the middle of nowhere, neighborin' with rattlers in the outhouse."

Her laugh was as sweet a sound as a mockingbird at dawn. "Oh, I think I've forgotten what stores and churches and schools are like. I do miss them, I think. But this is not so bad."

"But you'll be wantin' to go back, I reckon, soon as we can spare someone to take you."

He was watching her closely, and he saw her responsive face reflect surprise and something else. Her merriment vanished. She seemed suddenly older, a self-possessed young woman, no longer the relaxed, engaging companion of a moment before.

Owen was dismayed. He'd said something that displeased her . . . but what?

"Yes, of course," she said, so formally that it increased his puzzlement. "Whenever you can spare time for one of your men to escort me to the nearest town, I'll start to make my own way." She kicked the sorrel mare and let her run, bending gracefully in the saddle.

For a moment Owen watched her, bemused, before his own restlessly dancing mount was allowed to follow.

She had a head start and the sorrel mare was faster than she appeared. Owen, still not sure how he had offended, spurred his horse to catch up.

Ahead, the girl disappeared in her following dust cloud as her mare slid down into a dry arroyo that wandered across the plain. Owen's dun was yards away when something triggered an alarm within his mind. Virginia's horse should have topped the opposite side of the gully moments ago . . .

Obeying instinct, Owen wheeled his horse to the right, spurred him thirty yards parallel to the gully, and leapt from the saddle even as he pulled the horse to a stop that set the dun back on its haunches. He left the mount ground-tied. Moving with the hunting silence that Will had taught him years ago, he found a way down into the arroyo, rifle in his left hand, Colt ready in his right. He reached the rocky bottom of the wide, deep cut in the dry earth. Swiftly, for his heart thudded with fear for Ginny, he made his way back toward the point where she had disappeared into the gully.

Then, nearing that place, Owen slowed and went more cautiously to the last bend in the gully. He pressed his back to a steep clay wall, removed his hat, and peered around the obstruction.

He was not really surprised to see the back of a man, Ginny clamped before him within the bend of his left arm, his left hand brutally covering her mouth. Owen did not have to see the right hand to know that it held a gun, covering the trail where he evidently expected Owen to appear. Nearby, the mare Virginia had been riding stood, head up, her ears swiveled toward Ginny and her captor—and thus toward Owen. If the gunman had been paying attention to the mare, he might have realized that there was a threat behind him.

But, Owen reminded himself grimly, there could well be more men nearby. If so, Owen would have to have all the luck to get Ginny safely away. He raged within himself. He never should have taken her so far from the headquarters. At least he should have been alert to possible danger, instead of lollygagging like a moonstruck calf. All that was beside the point now. He must act quickly, before the outlaw harmed Ginny.

Owen glanced behind him—he saw no one. That did not mean that the man who held Ginny was alone. Yet he might well be a solitary spy posted here by Wardworth or Jim Wilkins to keep an eye on Terrel headquarters, clearly visible a half-mile to the east.

Owen stepped softly away from the arroyo wall, moved

toward the gunman who held Ginny. His boot heel grated upon a stone and he expected the outlaw to turn. Fortunately, Ginny chose that moment to struggle fiercely within the man's grip, and Owen could hear muffled squeaks of rage as she squirmed, kicking wildly with both feet, thus placing the entire weight on her tormentor's left arm. The man staggered, almost losing his grip upon the slender girl.

And at that moment, Owen steadied his pistol barrel, aiming at the back of the outlaw's neck.

"Let her go," he advised softly.

The man froze, not daring even to look at Owen. Slowly, he relaxed the tension of his left arm and Virginia was loose.

"Ginny, run for your horse," Owen said. But first, with a sob of sheer fury, she whirled and favored her captor with a slap that rocked his head, dislodging his hat. The man grunted and brought up the pistol he held in his left hand, striking viciously at her. The blow caught her shoulder, near the neck, and she let out a cry of pain.

Owen's fury seemed to sharpen his vision and to slow the events of the next moments to a crawl, when in reality they occurred very swiftly.

Virginia staggered back, tripped over a boulder, and fell. The man turned. For the first time Owen realized that it was Caleb Wardworth himself, though the man's best friend might have been forgiven for not recognizing him. The dandified carpetbagger who had strutted about Houston was no longer so well-groomed. He wore travel-stained clothing. His untrimmed hair was greasy, his pasty skin reddened and peeling from days in the sun.

Wardworth loosed a shot at Terrel. Owen felt its impact in his upper left arm, causing him to drop the rifle he held, even as his own finger tightened upon the trigger of the Peacemaker. His aim had been spoiled and the outlaw was not hit. Wardworth whirled, caught Ginny's wrist, and was jerking her to her feet when Owen's second shot burned a path at the nape of the outlaw's neck.

With a strangled yell, Wardworth released Ginny and ran. He flung himself upon her mare and was narrowly missed as Owen fired once more. But Wardworth was out of sight now, out of the arroyo. Owen ran past Ginny and

scrambled up the steep west slope, reaching the top in
time to see Wardworth whipping the mare to her utmost
speed to the northwest. Hampered by Ginny's sidesaddle,
he bounced, but managed to stay on the running animal.
If Owen had still held the Winchester, he might have
managed a shot at the fleeing man. The Colt was useless
at this rapidly increasing range.

And he was aware that he and Virginia were in danger
here. One of their mounts was gone, Owen was bleeding
severely, and Ginny must be taken back to the dugout at
once, in case Wardworth's cronies were about.

He turned back, found Ginny holding his rifle, gazing
anxiously at him.

"Is he gone?" Her voice broke, then steadied.

"Yes. Come with me. We have to get to my horse."

"That awful man," she cried. "He stole that dear little
mare. Why didn't you shoot him?"

Owen was feeling a growing weakness from the loss
of blood, but he had to grin at that. "I was tryin', girl.
Reckon you could have shot straighter." He jerked his
bandanna loose. "Could you tie this around my arm?
Quick! We need to get out of here."

Belatedly, Ginny realized that Owen had been shot.
"Dear God," she gasped, running to him. "You're hurt.
Oh, Owen!"

"Gotta slow the bleeding."

She knotted the bandanna about his upper arm with
trembling fingers.

The moment she finished, he hurried her along the floor
of the arroyo to the spot where he had climbed down.
They scrambled up the steep slope, but before they left
the dubious shelter of the gully, Owen surveyed the surrounding ground. His heart sank. The dun was gone. The
shots must have spooked him.

Behind him, Ginny called softly. "What's wrong,
Owen?"

"My horse is gone."

"We can walk back. Unless your wound . . . ?"

He could hear the strain and worry in her low tones,
and he reached back to touch her shoulder reassuringly.

"I'm all right. But I ain't at all sure we ought to start
across the open until dark."

''You think—you think he'll come back with his friends?''

''Could be,'' he said. ''But when my horse gets home, our men will know there's something wrong. They'll come lookin'.''

''Owen, I think I hear horses.''

He turned his head. Her hearing was keener than his. In the distance he could see horsemen—four, or perhaps five, hard to tell in the deepening dusk and the dust stirred up by the racing horses. ''Damn!'' he muttered. ''Good ol' Caleb had his buddies stashed away—maybe in this same arroyo couple of miles farther on.''

He glanced down at Ginny, smiled into her frightened dark eyes. ''Reckon Will better hustle on out here.''

''Owen, what shall we do?''

He saw her draw a deep breath, striving to control fear as the running horses drew closer.

He thought for a moment. ''Can't stay here, no cover. It won't be much better in the cut, but it's the best we can do. Let's see if we can get some help.''

He lifted his rifle, fired three shots quickly, hoping that someone at the ranch would hear and start this way. Then he and Ginny slid back into the deep arroyo and hurried along it toward the north. There was a chance that Wardworth had left a mount along here—surely he hadn't been stationed here on foot. Yet there was just as much chance that his horse had been left beyond the trail Ginny had taken into the cut.

Beside him, Ginny stumbled. He caught her elbow firmly, ignoring the nausea and slightly swimming head caused by his loss of blood.

''I think we'd best find a place to wait,'' he said. ''Will and Jackson and the others will be coming.''

''There!'' Ginny pointed to a little side wash that notched the high walls of the arroyo.

''Wait. Let me check for snakes.''

He tramped into the narrow, angled gully, probing into its farther reaches with his gun butt. He was hardly startled when a hissing rattle sounded, and he spotted a coiled shape several feet away. Rather than shoot again, advertising their position, he handed Ginny his rifle, lifted a large rock, and slammed it down upon the snake's ugly head. He fished it out and flung it away, then made sure there was no other menace lurking in the narrow slot.

"All right. Give me the rifle and slide in there." He checked his Colt, handed it to her. "Ginny . . ." he hesitated.

"Yes?"

He moved in beside her, lowering his long body until he could just see over the jutting, red-earth wall in front of them. "Can you stand to shoot?"

"You know I can shoot!"

He turned to her, so close that he need only breathe the words, for they could both hear the outlaws' horses on the opposite bank of the arroyo, pounding past their position, heading for the place Caleb Wardworth had left the two of them earlier.

"Ginny, I know you can shoot a snake. Can you shoot a man? Shoot to kill?"

He heard her breathing still for a long moment, then begin again, unsteadily. Still she did not reply.

"Ginny?"

"Owen, do I—do I have to?"

His heart constricted with concern for her. He reached to grip her hand. "You might. To save your life—and mine."

Again a little silence, then, "I'll shoot."

"Good girl. Now stay still. It'll be dark in a half-hour. Maybe they won't find us right away."

But he knew that was false hope. His tracks and Ginny's were still visible in the sandy areas of the dry arroyo, nor would the outlaws fail to spot the dark splotches of blood he'd lost. These men were born hunters, and they would very swiftly trace their human quarry. He readied his Winchester. Then there was nothing to do but wait.

He could hear rough voices, the words muffled by the bends of the gully. He heard shod horses moving about, the steel shoes clinking against stone. Wardworth's men must be spreading out, one or more riding each bank of the arroyo, others tracking along the floor.

Damn it, Will, get out here, Owen thought urgently. He felt desperate at the thought of Ginny's danger. If those devils got past him, took her alive . . . He clenched his jaw at the thought.

There was a shout, only yards away, and the clatter of hooves along the rock-strewn gully. Owen shrank a bit lower, pushed Ginny down. A thin clump of shinnery overhung the inadequate shelter where they crouched. He slid his rifle barrel gently under the thin branches, sighted grimly at the spot where the first horseman would appear.

"Ginny," he whispered, "they'll be behind us, and maybe at the top of the banks. Keep your eyes open."

He felt her turn, slowly, careful not to make a sound, and he felt pleased by her quick intelligence. He found himself smiling a bit, in spite of their hazardous position.

And then, the first of their trackers appeared, bent over his saddle, studying the marks the two of them had left, in the arroyo floor.

"Hold it right there," Owen shouted, unable to take the easy way: send a bullet into the man until he was aware of Terrel's presence.

The outlaw had no such inhibition. His rifle boomed even as he straightened, and the shot round plowed into the top of the eroded slab of soil between him and his intended prey.

10

Owen's forefinger tightened on the Winchester's trigger. The rifle jerked in his hands, its boom unnaturally loud in this narrow earthen slot. Quickly he levered in another cartridge. The outlaw's next shot went wild as he pitched backward, a silent yell opening his mouth. The body toppled onto the earth. A frightened, sweated horse dashed past. And beside Owen, the Colt sounded, simultaneous with Ginny's cry of alarm.

Owen whirled, snapped a shot at a bulky silhouette above them on the edge of the gully. He missed. The target wheeled his horse away. Owen turned again to the gully itself, but the next fire came from the opposite bank, and Owen swore grimly as the pistol shots came perilously close to him and sent dirt into Ginny's eyes. She gasped and tried to wipe her vision clear, even as Owen shot and apparently nicked the rider upon the back. It was a huge man with a fleshy, heavily freckled face—Comanche Jim Wilkins himself. The outlaw let out a shout of rage and leveled his pistol at them.

But another shout sounded nearby—and gunfire from the east, rapid, menacing.

"Wardworth, look out," yelled Wilkins, and brutally reined his horse about. The pound of hooves vibrated through the earth beneath Owen and Virginia as the attackers were driven off.

"About time, brother," murmured Owen thankfully. But he did not let Ginny leave their bit of shelter until he heard Will shouting for them.

As the two of them moved unsteadily out of their cramped refuge, Will's horse plunged to a dust-clouded stop a few feet away.

"My God, Owen! Are you two all right? What in hell happened here? Damn it, Owen, are you bleedin'?"

Owen managed a grin. "Will, you keep talkin' that-

91

away, Amelia's bound to wash out your mouth with lye soap."

Ginny was pale and one hand was pressed against her neck, where Wardworth had struck her. Owen gave her a worried glance. "We need to get Ginny back to the house quick as we can."

"Reckon we need to get you both back."

Will turned and bellowed, "Jackson, we need that horse over here."

Dill appeared, leading the dun that had fled for home. Owen helped Ginny mount, climbed on behind her. Her shoulders were drooping. Owen placed an arm about her, steadied her against his chest, clenching his jaw with anger at the man who had hurt her and at himself for missing his chance to kill Wardworth.

"Mr. Will, you want me'n Jones to chase after them bushwhackers?" Dill asked.

"Not now. We'll study on it a little," Will said.

"I got one of 'em," Owen said.

"We found him. Jackson, catch that loose horse and heave the dead man on. We'll bury him after we get back. I don't want to leave the homestead and herd too long."

They made their way back, watchful in case of renewed attack. It was nearly full dark, and conceivable the outlaws would try to hit the Terrel group before they reached the headquarters.

But they reached home without further incident. Owen rode directly to the dugout, handed Ginny down.

"She's got a bad bruise on her shoulder, Melia. You got any of that liniment you used to make?"

"Never mind about me," Ginny said. "Owen's been shot."

Amelia drew in a harsh breath. "Get down, Owen," she ordered. She turned to the dugout, where Julia hovered fearfully in the doorway. "Bring me hot water and bandages, Julia."

She made Ginny sit and began to remove Owen's shirt, then shook her head distressfully. "I'll have to cut the sleeve." She ordered Julia peremptorily back to fetch her sewing scissors.

Then Amelia went to work upon his wound, and Owen could spare little thought for much besides pain. The bullet had gone through, but Amelia was ruthless in disinfecting the wound and in picking shreds of cloth from the entrance site, while Will, who had set Olaf and Jackson to digging a grave for the dead outlaw, held a lamp high.

Amelia had advised Virginia to go inside and lie down, but she insisted on staying, watching the proceedings anxiously as Owen's wound was disinfected with whiskey and carefully bandaged.

"That's gonna be stiff and sore as the devil for a few days," Will observed.

"Could be worse," Owen said with a breath of relief when Amelia was finished. "Think we could have some of that coffee?"

The cook fire had burned low, the supper preparations forgotten in the excitement. But the coffee was hot and black and restorative. As Amelia took Ginny into the dugout to examine her injury, Julia bent to dip stew into a tin plate for Owen and brought it to him with a thick slice of the bread Virginia had baked earlier.

"Can you eat, Owen dear?" she asked softly, touching his hand with slender fingers.

"When I can't eat, you can shovel me under," he said. "Will, you'd better get some of this before the men smell it and come arunnin'. You too, Julia."

"Oh, no, I couldn't, my heart's just flutterin' so. Feel it?" She lifted his hand, to demonstrate.

He pulled away, conscious of Will's badly concealed grin. "Beg pardon, Julia," Owen said hastily. "Could I have another cup o' coffee?"

She moved reluctantly to get it for him, a frown of temper on her pretty face.

Will ate quickly, set his plate in the tin tub where water was being heated to clean the dishes and pots. "I'd best ride out to the herd. I'll have Dill take first watch here. You women best finish out here and go inside soon as you can."

"I'm goin' with you." Owen stood, waited for a slight dizziness to pass.

"No, sir, you ain't. You rest, take the second watch here if you want."

"I'm goin' with you," Owen insisted quietly. "They'll

be more likely to hit the herd tonight, figurin' we'll be huddlin' at home. Tomorrow we got to talk about all this. We don't have enough men to keep up a twenty-four watch much longer.''

Will nodded, face stone-chiseled in the lantern light. ''The same thought crossed my mind. Sooner or later they'll wear us down or pick us off one by one.''

Ignoring the pain of his wound as best he could, Owen went to get a fresh horse while Will stepped to the dugout door to tell Amelia where he was headed. Owen heard slow hoofbeats, unlimbered his gun, and stepped into the shadow of one of the wagons until he heard Olaf Jones' deep tones. ''Hallo! It is Olaf!''

''Ride on in, Olaf.''

''We have buried that man. Mr. Dill is coming soon.''

''Thank you. Ask Jackson to take first watch here, until I get back. You get something to eat, then turn in. Will and I are headed out to the herd.''

''Yes, Mr. Terrel.'' Jones nodded.

''Another thing, Olaf. Saddle some of the horses, in case of trouble. If we hear shots, we'll come arunnin', but I want the women and kids to have a chance to ride out, if need be.''

''I will do it,'' Jones said.

Owen had his own and Will's mounts saddled by the time his brother was ready to go. His bandaged wound slowed him somewhat, and he had to pause for a moment, feeling weak, when he had finished. Will shook his head when he saw the saddled horses. ''What would it take to slow you down, little brother?''

''Let's hope we don't find out,'' Owen replied. He mounted, barely caught his balance when the fresh horse danced.

Will moved his horse alongside. ''I hear you lost a good mare an' Amelia's saddle today.''

''Yeah.'' Owen grinned ruefully. ''But think how Caleb Wardworth felt, havin' to show up in front of his friends ridin' a lady's sidesaddle.''

Will laughed softly. ''That would've been somethin' to see.''

Both men gave attention to the plains about them, dimly visible in the starlight. Without being conscious of it, both men were using senses honed keen by years of experience, noting the very sound and scent of the sand under their horses' hooves, the direction and intensity of the wind. Thus the faint trace of smoke teasing his nostrils made Owen draw his horse to a stop for a moment.

"Somebody's cookin' supper over yonder. Wish we had time to drop in for a little visit, unexpected-like."

Owen could tell from Will's thoughtful silence that he was almighty tempted, too. But it wasn't a good idea. There was no way to tell how far that smoke was, or even if they would find there the men they wished grimly to meet. It could be a neat decoy, a way to draw men away from the herd or from Terrel headquarters.

"Best hold on here tonight," Will said at last.

Owen sighed, but did not argue. His bay horse swiveled his ears forward. They were approaching the herd. The men reined in.

"Georgie! Juan! We're coming in."

"*Bienvenidos, compadres,*" came Juan's low call.

Owen spurred his horse to a gallop, Will close behind. They found the Mexican on the north side of the herd, *cigarrillo* glowing in the dark, his *sombrero* making a broad shadow in the dark.

"Go in an' eat, Juan," Will said. "Get Georgie and take him with you. Rest a couple of hours and come back. We may have trouble tonight."

But Juan, in his rapid mix of Spanish and English, explained that he did not know where Georgie might be. "I cannot find him. He has gone *muchas horas.*" He gestured widely.

"When did you see Georgie?" Will asked.

The Mexican said that it was after Señor Will had left the herd at noon to dig in the new well that Georgie went away.

"You saw him go?" Owen broke in, leaning forward.

Juan shrugged. "*Sí, señor.*"

"Now, what the hell would Georgie ride off for?" Will puzzled.

"Maybe he spotted something he wanted to see closer. I hope he didn't run into Wardworth's men. I'll make a circle or two, see if I can find his tracks."

"Owen, you be mighty watchful," his brother warned.

"Them Wardworth coyotes would be plumb tickled to catch you alone."

Owen grinned. "Will, is that all the faith you got in me? They catch me alone, I'll invite 'em to breakfast."

Owen rode for two hours, circling and recircling the Terrel headquarters, casting farther and farther afield, but he saw nothing of Georgie or of the outlaw gang. At last he brought his tired horse back to the herd.

"No use," he said as Will joined him.

"Well, maybe he'll be back by mornin'," Will sighed.

They rode in opposite directions about the widely scattered bunches of cattle. Owen wondered if they should have gathered them into a tighter herd. Will felt that nightly gathering would only make it easier for cattle thieves to run the herd off if they were together. Thus the men simply patrolled, depending upon their horses' night vision and ability to scent other horses to warn them of the approach of riders.

Aside from the dark, flattened shape of a badger gliding away under a stone slab that roofed its den, nothing unusual came near the cattle. When the moon rose, the prairie expanse was softly lighted. Anything larger than a rabbit would have loomed dark against the skyline. Only a Comanche or Apache brave, with the endless patience of his race, could have crept close without being discovered.

Juan returned at midnight. Will insisted on staying with him. "You keep watch at the dugout," he told Owen. "After Jackson has slept, send him out to take my place."

All was quiet as Owen approached the headquarters and called out to Dill, identifying himself. Whiskey romped out to meet him. Dismounting, Owen patted the dog.

Jackson appeared from the darkness beside one of the wagons. "Ever'thing's quiet, Cap'n."

"Thanks, Jackson. Get some sleep. Will needs you with the herd at dawn."

He unsaddled his tired horse and turned him loose, then settled himself to watching, the dog lying quietly nearby, now and then lifting a white nose to taste the night wind. There was no disturbance. At dawn Owen

woke Jones, then tended the horses in the pens before
rolling into his blankets for an hour's sleep.

The growing heat of the sun woke him. He rose, noted
that Will was sleeping hard under one wagon. Crow
snored comfortably under the other. It crossed Owen's
mind that they were all growing used to their tame captive and hardly bothered to worry about any danger he
might represent. Whether that was good or bad, it could
scarcely be changed now. They had little time and energy
to spare for keeping an eye on Crow, who was recovering
rapidly though he still occasionally seemed confused.

Owen reached under the wagon where the recovering
outlaw slept and shook Crow's shoulder. Ginny approached, carrying a tray for Crow. Julia was terrified of
having him join them at the table, so the others carried
his food to him.

"Time to roll out, Crow," Owen said, and the man
blinked and flung back his blankets. He stood, still a
trifle unsteady. The men had debated over whether to
try to keep him tied. There seemed little reason to trust
him. Yet Amelia and Ginny had judged it inhuman to
keep him tethered like an animal. And it was true that
he had thus far offered no harm to the family that had
saved his life. Now his black eyes lighted at the sight of
Ginny and he smiled like a bashful boy.

"Here's your breakfast, Mr. Crow," she said. It made
Owen nervous for her to be so near the outlaw. He
watched narrowly as Crow took the food and hunkered
down against the wagon wheel to enjoy the plate of
floured and fried salt pork and biscuits and coffee.

"This is mighty good, Miss Virginia," Crow said.

"If you want more, you just come and ask," she said.
"Does you head still hurt, Mr. Crow? I wish we had
some willow bark to boil for a tea. My granny used to
swear by it."

Crow swallowed and looked up. "I feel better today,
thank you, miss."

Virginia walked over to Owen, head tilted. "Owen,
come and eat while it's hot," she said.

They started toward the dugout. "Ginny, I wish you'd
let one of the men tend to Crow. He could be dangerous."

"It's all right." She patted her skirt pocket. "I have the pistol Amelia gave Julia. Since yesterday, I'm an old hand at shootin' at people." She grinned and lifted a hand unconsciously to the bruise where her neck and shoulder joined.

Owen regarded her with amused exasperation. "Ginny, Crow could overpower you before you could begin to drag that derringer out. Now, you listen to me, you mustn't trust this man. It worries me that we have to give him the run of the camp."

She shrugged, wincing at the soreness in her neck. "I don't believe Mr. Crow is really a very bad man. Besides, what else can we do?"

Owen sighed. "Danged if I know. Still it bothers me, havin' him underfoot. We're shorthanded, and havin' to watch the herd night and day—"

"And the women and children," she put in.

"Can't think of anything more worth watchin'." His steady look brought a flush of color to her tanned cheeks.

"Of course you must protect Julia," she pretended to misunderstand.

"I wasn't thinkin' of Julia, particularly," was his mild reply. He caught her arm and halted her. "Ginny, I need to ask something. What made you so mad at me yesterday when we were riding?"

She tried to turn away, but he made her look at him. "It was when I mentioned that you might want to leave us. I was hopin' you'd say you wouldn't want to find better company than the Terrels." He smiled crookedly.

She stared at him, startled. "Well, why didn't you say so? It sounded as if you were in a hurry for me to go."

He frowned. "Damn it, Ginny, I've been scared to death you'd ask to leave us."

She held his gaze for a long, tense instant, her face a study of conflicting emotions. There was something very unsettling in her wide dark eyes. At last she smiled. "Well, and maybe I will go away. I guess it depends on—" Abruptly she started toward the house again. He had to take a quick step or two to catch up.

"Depends on what?" he demanded, both charmed and puzzled by her low laugh.

"On a lot of things." She seemed to struggle to suppress the smile that made her so lovely, and at last gave in to it. "Hurry, Owen. I'm starved, aren't you?"

They walked together to the plank table. Owen was as aware of Virginia as if he'd held her hand, though there was a decorous distance between the two of them.

Julia was nibbling disinterestedly at her breakfast. She watched them with narrowed eyes as they approached, and her mouth had a sulky look.

"Sit down, Owen. I'll get your food," Virginia offered. Perhaps from a mischievous impulse, she leaned quickly to place a light kiss on his cheek. Mischief or not, Owen felt an odd lurch of his heart, and in that little, insignificant moment a dream that had been growing in his mind became totally dependent upon one slender, chestnut-haired girl.

Before Owen had finished eating, Will was up and about. He sat down on a bench at the table, hugged Amelia as he set coffee in front of him, and rubbed a hand over his beard. He looked tired. Owen supposed his own lack of sleep must be showing, too.

Will took a cautious sip of the hot coffee. "We gotta do some figurin', Owen."

11

"Amelia, you and Ginny come an' sit," Will said. "Willy, hush your noise now. If you're through eatin', sit still and listen." He turned to Owen. "We got to make some decisions. I've called all the men in for this."

Juan and Jackson Dill had already been at the table. Now Olaf joined them, smiling his appreciation as Virginia provided him with a plate of food and coffee. Georgie still had not turned up, Owen noted rather belatedly. It was one of the sad things about Georgie. He was seldom missed.

"What is it, Will?" Amelia gave Melissa a bite of biscuit.

He sighed and stood. It made what he had to say seem the more important, and even the children watched him, large-eyed.

"We all know we've got a big problem," he said. "For some reason, Caleb Wardworth, who was Miss Julia's betrothed, has chased her clean out here, an' he seems ready to kill any or maybe all of us, to get her back."

Owen glanced at Julia, saw her bow her head sharply, her cheek reddening. He felt a quick sympathy for her. She must be imagining what it would be like to be dragged back to Houston, forced to wed a man she abhorred. She need not fear. The Terrels would not allow that to happen.

"Now, then," Will continued, "we been fightin' off this gang's attacks pretty well. But I reckon even Willy here could prob'ly see that they got the advantage over us. We're outnumbered. We ain't even sure how many men they got, while they can surely count us, 'thout much trouble. We don't know where they are at any given time, while our herd an' our homestead has us tied in place. They can hit us at any hour, day or night."

Julia gave a muffled sob and pressed her linen handkerchief to her eyes. "We'll all be killed," she cried.

"It's all my fault. Oh, I beg you all to forgive me." She lifted tear-wet eyes and gave them a piteous look. "If you want to send me out to them, I—I'll go!" Then she burst into a storm of weeping. Virginia stood and went to her, putting a consoling arm about her shoulder.

"Nonsense, there'll be no more such talk," Will said severely. "Now, then, we need to make plans. The women and even the little children have a deadly stake in this. That's why I'm talkin' to all of you."

Amelia's chin lifted. "It's about time, Will Terrel. Believe me, I'd rather know the worst an' try to be prepared."

Ginny nodded her agreement. Owen could see that she was frightened. Frightened or not, she would hold steady in the face of danger. He had ample proof of that already.

"All right." Will nodded. "Now, then, Owen, let's have your thoughts on this."

Owen leaned his elbows on the table. "I think you spelled it out clear, Will. We're easy targets. We got this home here—an' God knows we're all proud of the start we've made. Someday we'll have a fine house standin' out here, and barns an' stables, all the things we hope to build. And we got the herd. That's our livin'. It'd be bad to lose the cattle or the horses. On the other hand, cattle an' horses ain't worth much to us if we lose our lives."

Will nodded. "Right. And we've already lost one man, maybe."

Amelia lifted her face sharply. "What?"

"Georgie rode out yesterday sometime. He didn't say where he was headed, nor why, nor has he come back this mornin'. If he ain't back soon, we need to go lookin' for him. Yet we don't dare leave the house unguarded or split up what manpower we got."

Amelia said. "There's no law says we have to stay here right now. When this trouble is over, we can take up where we leave off."

"Spell that out for me, Melia," Will said.

"It seems simple to me. We load up the wagons an' follow the herd awhile yet, until we can run off these killers."

Will's mouth fell open. Owen grinned. "Always said you married a smart gal," he said.

His brother frowned. "I don't like the idea of bein' run off my own place."

"I don't see it as runnin'," Owen said. "Sure would be easier to keep an eye on everyone with the women and kids nearer the herd."

"I can help with the cows, Daddy," Willy offered kindly. "An' I can fight too, if those men come."

Will reached to grip his little son's shoulder, and it was obvious that he did not take the boy's remarks lightly.

"Well, it makes sense, I reckon. We'll move the herd easy-like, stayin' within reach of the water holes. We'll still be easy to find, but we'll all be together."

"It's a good idea," Ginny said.

"No," Julia said sharply. "What would we do if they attacked? Those wagons would be no shelter at all. I think you're all crazy. We should stay right here, in the dugout."

"I'm mighty glad you've commenced to like our fine little home so much," Will said with the glimmer of a grin. "But we'd soon starve if we all tried to huddle here."

"I'd like to take the fight to the gang," Owen reflected quietly.

Will nodded sharply. "Might be we can arrange that too. Well, what's the first step?"

Owen stood. "Get the necessary supplies—nothing else—into two wagons. Move em' out to the herd and get it movin'."

"Galls me they'll think they've got us on the run," Will rumbled.

"Yeah, but it might make 'em overconfident," Owen suggested. "And we'll be ready for them when they try something."

Will grunted noncommittally. "Amelia, we'll fill the water kegs and load the bedrolls and such. Will you get together the food?"

She was already in motion. "Soon's we get the breakfast dishes cleared. Julia, you want to pack or wash dishes?"

Julia looked at her, a sharp line between her golden, arched brows. Her lips parted, but she apparently thought better of protesting.

"I'll ride out to the herd," Owen offered, "see if Georgie's come back. Jackson, you come with me. We'll start gatherin' the stock to be moved." He hefted the Winchester, which he kept at his side almost constantly these days. "One thing—what do we do with Crow?"

"Damn, hadn't thought of that," Will muttered. "I guess he'll just have to ride along with us. Even without weapons, he'll bear watching." He turned to Willy. "That will be your job, son. You see him do anything you think looks wrong, you tell your ma or Uncle Owen or me."

Willy gazed at his pa with round eyes. "Mr. Crow ain't so bad, Pa. He likes us kids, an' Virginia. He's always lookin' at her." The towheaded child giggled behind his hand as Ginny gave him an exasperated look.

Julia laughed aloud. "Well, then, let Virginia guard that verminous polecat. I reckon she can twist him 'round her little finger."

Amelia intervened. "Watch your tongue, Willy! Poor Mr. Crow's brains are addled since those terrible men hit him over the head."

Owen frowned. Poor Mr. Crow, indeed. It appeared that Amelia was fast forgetting that their uninvited guest had been one of those "terrible men" she mentioned. He made a mental note to keep an eye on Crow himself, at every opportunity. The captive had too damned many friends in camp.

Will must have had similar doubts. "Now you listen to me, Willy, an' you women as well. It don't do to trust a rattlesnake, just because he's shed his skin, temporary. He might still be inclined to help his old friends, even though he tangled with those varmints. Don't you give him a chance to try anything, you hear?"

Chastened, Willy nodded. Amelia and Virginia smiled at each other.

"If you're all through preachin', Will," Amelia said tartly, "we'll get to work."

It seemed odd, being on the move again, after thinking that they had come to the end of their journey. The kids, even little Melissa, seemed excited and pleased. Willy had his own horse now, a small, cow-wise pinto. Occasionally she bucked him off, or turned out from under him and then waited for him to scramble back on again. She was an education in horsemanship for the boy. Owen suspected the intelligent cowpony was fond of her little companion, and Willy thought she was the finest mount in the *remuda*.

True to his promise, Willy and his pony were usually not far from Crow, who seemed to accept the boy's presence cheerfully. What's more, the two of them began to take it upon themselves to ride drag with the herd. Willy had presented Crow with a decrepit old campaign hat of Will's, since Crow had lost his the night of the gang's attack upon the Terrel homestead. The man and the boy together just about added up to one pretty fair drover. Will did nothing to stop it, so Owen had to be content to continue to keep an eye, whenever possible, upon Crow. It occurred to him to wonder if Crow knew Willy had been set to watch him. If so, he seemed indifferent. And if he had questions about all of them suddenly leaving the homestead, he left them unspoken.

Ginny drove the second wagon part of the time. Whenever one of the men took over this chore, Owen had one of his favorite mounts saddled for her. The blood bay, Mexican-bred mare was stylish and spirited, and Virginia rode her gracefully. Owen often found his eyes searching for her and lingering longer than was wise. At such times he had to remind himself to keep alert for any sign of the Wardworth gang. He knew they were watching for their chance, and he found himself trying to think like the outlaws, assessing the weakest points of the Terrel defenses.

Likely, the wagons, always just ahead of the slowly moving herd, were as safe as any place. The men who scouted ahead several times daily probably were most at risk, at least during daylight hours.

The first day of scouting they found nothing but days-old tracks of Georgie's horse, moving westward. Since Will and Owen had already decided to push the herd toward the Caprock, the men were on the alert for further sign of the missing man. Owen and Jackson Dill rode ahead, following the trail Georgie's departure had left. They rode twenty miles before losing the trail where a handful of buffalo had trampled out every mark. Reluctantly, conscious of their responsibilities to the others, they turned back and could only report that Georgie had been alive and riding at a steady trot at that point.

Nor had there been any new sign of their enemies. The third afternoon after leaving the dugout, a hard afternoon shower refreshed the plains . . . and wiped out any old tracks. But they were out there, Wardworth and his men. Owen could not doubt the instinct, a kind of icy edge within his brain that often in the past had warned him of unseen danger.

That evening the Terrel brothers sat their horses near a spring that fed a shallow lake. The water kegs the wagons carried had already been refilled, and camp was being made a quarter-mile from the water. The men knew that wild things also used the water each night and left enough space open near the lake that these creatures would not be discouraged from drinking. This was not entirely from concern for the animals—the men hoped to find antelope or even a young buffalo to augment their beef.

As they rested their horses in the slow summer dusk, both men scanned the darkening plain that stretched away beyond their vision upon all sides. The evening was scented with the damp grass and earth, the air for once entirely free of dust.

"What do you think, Owen?" Will muttered. "Where are our little playmates? Be funny if they've given up an' here we are chasin' around the prairies, all for nothin'!"

Owen laughed. "I believe you'd be plumb disappointed."

Will grinned, but his voice was serious. "I'd like to meet the enemy an' have the issue decided one way or t'other. Makes me itch, waitin' around for the party to begin."

Owen touched his horse with his spur rowels, started him toward camp. "Reckon I feel the same way. An' I reckon those men out there know they've got us on edge."

"And they can take their time." Will's dun stumbled, caught himself. Will seemed not to notice. "Damn it all, Owen! They can keep us on edge from now on."

Owen shook his head. "No, sir, they can't. We keep movin' west, we'll reach the Caprock an' then the Pecos. Whatever it is they plan, they won't wait until we're that close to people again."

"You're right." Will nodded. "Well, let's go see what

Melia's cookin'." He lifted his horse into a gallop and Owen was not far behind.

The campfire was placed a little beyond the open end of a V formed by the parked wagons. Owen noticed that Crow and Willy were still mounted, and Crow rode a slow, wide circle about the campsite, his eyes seeming to search the distances. Was he watching for his old friends? For a long moment Owen studied the man, wondering about him. But he had to admit that it had been helpful to have him with the herd. Nor had he done anything to merit distrust since the day they found him injured and brought him in. Was he patiently awaiting his chance to betray them?

The other men had finished watering the cattle, chousing them away from the alkali-tainted portions of the shallow, white-rimmed lake. They had bedded the herd in good grass, a quarter-mile from the wagons.

Owen ate hurriedly and returned to the herd. He and Olaf were on first watch.

But nothing more alarming than a wandering skunk came near the camp or herds that night. Whiskey fell into disgrace, having investigated the white-striped intruder too closely. Worse, he jumped into the wagon where Amelia and the children and Julia slept. Julia became aware of Whiskey's pungent presence, and her shrieks brought the men at a run, ready to shoot. It required an hour to get everything settled down again.

At dawn Owen walked down to the lake and shot an antelope. Other antelope scattered swiftly as he came forward to gut his prize. Jackson Dill hurried from camp to help him. The big man stopped a few feet away with an exclamation. "Mr. Owen, look here!"

Terrel left the sleek antelope carcass to peer at the track Dill was bending over, the track of a shod horse, clearly marked in the mud.

"Well, what d'you know?" he muttered. "I recall that shoe—shaped it myself for the *grulla* mustang's left fore." The shoe was a lopsided U, painstakingly formed for the slightly misshapen hoof. "Georgie was ridin' that mount when he left."

"Yessir," Dill agreed. "He purely liked that horse.

Called him Pedro—never said it right, I remember." He straightened. "That there track's real fresh, Cap'n."

Owen nodded. "Last night, or yesterday afternoon late, Georgie's horse watered here. That don't necessarily mean Georgie was ridin' him."

"Somebody was, I s'pect. That track's deep."

"Maybe—but it's in mud. A free horse might have set it that deep," Owen mused. "But in that case, Pedro would have joined our *remuda*. I sure didn't see him just now when I turned my night horse in and saddled a fresh mount."

"No, sir, Pedro ain't there."

"Well, he might have got in with a herd of wild ones. No," Owen knocked down his own suggestion. "We'd have noticed other fresh horse tracks hereabouts." He moved around the area, studying the record of the night's visitors: antelope, rabbits, a coyote or two. These marks overlaid the tracks of the *remuda* and the cattle, watered early last evening. No other horse tracks were so fresh and clear as the ones they followed down to the water's edge. The *qrulla* cowpony had stepped to the spring, paused there to drink, then had moved away, directly east, too directly for a riderless horse.

"Wonder why Whiskey didn't bark? Well, he knows that horse, an' Georgie, though. Or maybe he was still out huntin' that goldurned skunk."

"Want me to trail him aways?" Dill asked.

Owen glanced back at the antelope, which had to be bled and gutted quickly before the morning heat shot up. "No, Jackson, I don't want anyone ridin' away from the group alone. This could be a fat, tasty nightcrawler on a hook, hopin' to draw somebody out, cut down our strength by one or two."

Jackson nodded. "Yessir, it do seem too easy. If 'twas Georgie, he'd have knowed we'd see them tracks first thing."

"Tell the others to keep their eyes open," Owen said. "Will wants to camp here a few days. Might be ol' Pedro—an' whoever's ridin' him these days—will come back."

The camp remained peaceful throughout the day. Amelia and Virginia took the opportunity of being near water to wash some of the family's laundry, spreading the wet garments upon mesquite bushes to dry in the white-hot sunlight. Julia helped when Amelia insisted, but she retreated to the shade of the wagons the moment Amelia's attention was turned to making the midday meal. As they ate, Will advised the women to rest during the afternoon. "Could be you'll need to sleep with one eye open tonight."

Thus commanded, the three women settled down in the shade under the wagons, with Whiskey curled near Ginny's feet, guarding his favorite against snakes and tarantulas. The dog had rolled in the mud at the edge of the lake. His looks were not improved by the patchy coating of dried mud, but perhaps it had served to diminish his skunk-flavored aroma enough to make his company bearable.

Owen rode quietly into camp in midafternoon and sat his horse, watching Virginia as she slept. As if she felt his presence, she sighed and opened her eyes.

He smiled lazily down at her. "No, don't get up," he said softly, not to awaken the other women and children.

Virginia promptly disobeyed him, rising and shaking out her crumpled skirts. "Would you like some coffee, Owen? I can get the fire goin' in a minute," she whispered.

"No, I just came to check on you."

"Why, we're fine!" She moved away from the sleepers and began to rekindle the fire. "It's broad daylight, Owen. What could happen to us here? Especially with Juan over there pretendin' to take a *siesta* when really you told him to watch out for us helpless women." She seemed both amused and indignant. Virginia was becoming more independent than Owen would ever have thought possible, remembering the gently raised girl fleeing from Miss Brown's Young Ladies' Seminary in Houston, with only the faintest idea of what lay beyond the school grounds.

Now he gazed at her thoughtfully, and the hot color rose in her cheeks. He realized that too much of what he was feeling, his desire to take her in his arms then and there, must be showing in his face. He tried to school his expression, but could not be sure how effective his efforts were.

"Ginny, I want you to keep your eyes open," he said. "Never forget—just because things seem peaceable—that there are men out there somewhere who mean to do harm to us all. Would you do somethin' for me?"

"Of course I will."

Owen wished he dared get off his horse and kiss her. Couldn't hurt, could it? The other women were asleep, and Juan . . . No, Juan wasn't asleep, even if his big sombrero was tilted down. Owen would bet a couple of good horses that the *vaquero* knew exactly what was going on in every corner of the camp.

Unconsciously he sighed and contented himself with smiling at the girl he loved. "Sleep with your boots on—an' most of your clothing as well—for a few nights," he instructed. "Keep your rifle at hand—fully loaded, you hear? And be ready!"

"Ready for what?" Her head tilted, and he found himself studying the soft planes and curves of her face, loving the wide dark gaze that held steady upon his, the gentle lines of her lips, set now in innocent gravity.

With an effort he brought his attention back to the matter at hand. "Just try to be ready for anything at all," he said. "If there's trouble, Amelia will have her hands full with the children. I'll have Will keep a span of mules harnessed. Could you hitch 'em to one of the wagons if there's no one else handy to do it?"

She thought for a moment. It was one of her endearing, rather childlike traits that she took time to consider a serious question. She never gave her word lightly, to be taken back later just as lightly.

Abruptly she nodded. "I believe I could hitch up Ratty and Babe. They're gentle, and I've harnessed them a time or two when everyone else was busy. They know me."

"I'll make sure it's the team you can handle." He was silent a moment, thinking. "Sleep in your clothes and boots tonight—tell the others to do the same, and keep your guns handy."

She looked doubtful. "That will get Julia all upset, Owen. You know how nervous she is. She's scared. Really scared."

"Yeah. Well, I'm sorry about that, but we all need to be prepared to move—or fight—at a moment's notice. Ginny. . . ."

He hesitated, wanting to say so much.

"Yes, Owen?"

He straightened, knowing he must get back to the herd and send Jackson to relieve Juan. "I'm proud of you. We all are. You've been brave, an' none of this is your fight."

She seemed honestly puzzled. "How can it not be my fight? You saved my life, when I had no one left. You and Will and Amelia . . ." She drew a deep, unsteady breath. "I'd do anything for Amelia. When you brought me to her, the Terrels became my family."

She met his eyes steadily and there was a pledge in their dark depths. Before he realized that he had yielded to the temptation, Owen stepped down from his horse and faced her, this slender, serious girl who had come into his life so strangely. Now it seemed to him that she had been a part of his life forever, and he knew he couldn't do without her.

She must have read his feelings in his eyes. She could have stepped away, given him a shy and coy look. But there was a deep, basic honesty in Virginia. She stood, awaiting his embrace, and settled into his arms as if her place had always been there. As perhaps it had.

"I love you, Ginny," Owen said.

He felt her soft breath against the bare skin at the open throat of his shirt. "Owen, are you sure?" she whispered.

He held her away, hands strong upon her upper arms. "Never been surer about anything."

"But . . ." Her eyes were troubled. "What about Julia?"

He shook his head firmly. "That's something from a long time ago. It don't mean nothin' now."

She seemed to be searching his face, measuring the truth of what he said. He bent and kissed her quickly, then grinned at her. "I'd better go, or Will will give me hell." Reluctantly he released her, swung into his saddle. With a last smile, he reined his horse away from the camp, and his heart was light and unworried. Someway they were all going to get through this, and then he and

Ginny would be together. Nothing had ever seemed more right, or more inevitable.

On first watch that evening Owen rode his circuit of the herd, reining in as he met Will, upon a bay gelding. The plains lay silent and empty—as far as their eyes could detect. Towering thunderheads sailed like great ships, backlighted by the last gleam of sunset. But Owen's horse was restive, head high, ears swiveling. A little gust of wind brought some scent that made him shrill a challenge.

"They're out there somewhere, Will, we'd best warn Jackson and Juan and Olaf."

Will nodded. "They won't try anything this early. Let's let the men sleep as long as they can."

Owen let out his breath harshly. "Will, I keep askin' myself what in damnation this is all about. Does that fool Wardworth think he can kill us all an' take Julia back to Houston, set up housekeepin' in the Talbot mansion like nothing's happened?"

"Don't make a great lot o' sense, does it?" Will turned his head, staring uselessly into the deepening dusk. "Owen, there has to be more than what Julia's told us."

"I hate to think she'd lie to us."

"Wasn't it the same as lying when she omitted to mention to you that Wardworth was callin' on her, even though she was betrothed to you?" Will said mildly. "She didn't even send word to you when she agreed to marry that scalawag—sprung it on you at her daddy's party. Ain't that a lie?"

It went against Owen's grain to have that bitter moment raked up again. But he knew his brother too well to think he would have mentioned it without good reason.

He was silent for a moment. "You're right, but what exactly do you think she could be hidin' from us?"

"I ain't rightly sure, but I can't help wondering what she's carrying in that valise she keeps nearby. She's got it with her in Amelia's wagon, did you know that?"

"Well, you know she sets a lot o' store by her trinkets."

"Owen . . ." Will hesitated, then plowed on doggedly. "I know you always thought the sun rose and set in Julia Talbot. That's your business, an' I ain't tryin' to tear her down in your mind. But we're in a fix here. Someway, Julia Talbot's at the heart of it.''

''I ain't arguing that,'' Owen said. ''Anyhow, the way I used to feel about Julia don't matter a hill o' beans anymore. But your children and Amelia, they matter, Will. They're in danger here. Them and—Ginny.''

Something in the way Owen said the girl's name must have alerted Will. ''Well, I'll be! Here I was wonderin' how to shake you loose of your daydreamin' about Julia, and you've been thinkin' about Ginny the whole time.''

But Owen was not quite ready to talk about Virginia, not even to Will. He spurred his horse into motion, hearing Will's soft chuckle behind him.

Owen woke suddenly, aware of several things at once: the low crackle of the fire fifteen feet away, a smell of rain in the air. Clouds now blotted out the stars. It was long after midnight, the herd was resting a scant half-mile away. Owen heard a bull bellow shrilly, an uneasy, sobbing sound. Probably that was what had wakened Owen. Olaf was standing guard just beyond the camp; if anything was wrong, he would have alerted them all.

Yet that icy edge was back in his skull, and his nerves were twanging with undefined alarm. He eased out of his blankets, reached for his hat. His hand closed upon his Winchester.

He stood listening, tuning in on the night. He heard nothing unusual.

Easing slowly back into the deeper shadow cast by the wagon top, Owen moved softly to Will's blankets, bent and touched his brother's shoulder.

He felt Will stir, knew he would make no sound as he rose. Battlefield experience taught a man to be sparing of noise in uncertain situations.

Abruptly lightning flared and the roll of thunder brought everyone in camp awake. Owen heard Julia give a whimper of alarm. Then Ginny appeared nearby, fully dressed, rifle in her hands.

Olaf hurried up to the wagons. ''I t'ink somet'ing happens,'' he said.

12

"What is it?" Virginia whispered. "What's wrong?"

"I don't know," Owen said. "Maybe nothin'. Get the others up and ready. Tell Amelia to keep Julia and the children in the wagon."

Ginny turned swiftly to do as he said.

Someone moved in the shadows. Crow, standing quiet, as if awaiting something. But Owen had no time to think about the outlaw now.

Will eased closer, just as the sky lit again. "Take the women and kids out of here, Owen. I'll get to the herd. Olaf, bring my horse."

"I left four horses saddled," Owen said. "Oh, hell, I forgot Crow. Rope out a mount for him."

Without waiting for a reply, he ran to get Beau and Strawberry, Will's thoroughbred mare, for Ginny. He had left them saddled and near his bedroll. Owen had the bridles on and the hobbles slipped in just moments, then brought both horses to the wagon where the children and Julia slept. Inside, he heard Willy's soft, sleepy mumbles and Amelia's quiet reassurance. To his surprise, Crow had already led the mules into place and was hitching them to the wagon. Ginny and Will were flinging things into the wagon—bedrolls, and the tin cups and the coffeepot, which Ginny emptied into the coals of the campfire.

"Ginny, leave that stuff. Get on this mare," Owen ordered. He tied Beau's reins to the wagon and ran to help Crow with the team.

"Hell of a storm comin'," the man said abruptly. Owen thought it was the first time Crow had ever spoken to him directly. "Them cows'll be restless. Want me to help with the herd? Or I could drive this here wagon if you want."

Owen was startled by the offer, and he wished that he

dared to trust the man. They were so damned short-handed, it would have been good if Crow could handle the wagon. But it might be a very good opportunity, under cover of night, for him to deliver Julia to the men who wanted her.

"Thanks, Crow. Let me think a minute."

Owen spoke to the mules. They seemed unusually nervous. Should he give the lines to Amelia, let her drive Julia and the children to a safer distance from the herd? Though God knew which direction might be safest! But frightened mules would be hard for Amelia to control, a recipe for disaster. Still, letting Crow drive was out. And the other men would have their hands full holding the herd. Owen would have to drive himself.

All this went through his head within the space of the next wildly flaring lightning flash. Olaf galloped up, leading Will's horse. "The other horses have broken the picket rope. They are gone," he said. "I could not catch one for Mr. Crow."

Will mounted swiftly. "Come with me, Olaf." The horses raced out of camp, headed for the cattle.

At that moment Owen heard shots from somewhere in the vicinity of the herd. There were shouts, and more gunfire.

"Dear God, what's that?" Amelia gasped, peering out of the wagon.

There was no time to reply. Owen knew what was coming next, even before the ground vibrated underfoot and the low, rumbling sound reached them, the sound of a thousand and some odd head of cattle leaping into a startled run. The sound was growing; the herd was headed toward the camp at breakneck speed.

Owen whirled to Crow. "Take my horse!" Likely Crow would see if he could escape for good on the fleet Beau, but Owen wasn't about leave a man afoot in front of a stampede.

"Ginny!" he shouted.

She appeared beside him, mounted on the dancing mare. "I'm here. Everyone's in."

Owen jumped to the wagon seat, gathered the lines, glancing over his shoulder into the lantern-lit wagon. Amelia held Melissa in her arms, and Willy was clinging fiercely to Whiskey. Julia was crouched near the rear of the wagon. "Put out that lamp. All of you hang on," Owen said, and let the frightened mules go. "Ginny, keep up," he yelled.

Jerking the whip from its socket, he lashed the already running mules, wheeling them in a tight turn. It was too late now to circle to the southwest as he had planned. The herd was sweeping down upon them, the thunder of the hooves of the huge, rushing mass of crazed longhorns growing louder and louder.

The wagon jolted. Julia shrieked, Amelia spoke sharply to her. Owen spared a glance at Ginny. She was bent low over the big mare's mane. Thank God Strawberry was fast and sensible. Ginny's dark hair whipped in the rain-threatening wind. Owen could not see Crow. Maybe the man had spurred Beau directly down to the lake and across its shallow expanse to save himself. The wagon could not take that route.

The trampling thunder of the herd was closer, a scant fifty yards behind them, and Owen felt the mules take the bits in their teeth, racing in total panic ahead of the herd.

"Hold on to the kids," he yelled over his shoulder.

"Willy," Amelia yelled at her son. "Willy, sit back down. Julia, take Melissa."

The wagon bounced hard over a slab of rock upthrusting from the prairie. There was a horrified shriek from behind Owen.

"Stop, Owen! Stop the wagon. Melissa fell out. Oh, dear God, stop, stop!"

Owen sawed at the reins, trying to stop his team, knowing with horror that it would not be the slightest bit of use, even if the panicky mules halted. They had gone many yards past the point where the little girl had bounced out onto the prairie. He could not hope to turn the team and go back in time to save the child. Stopping would only bring the herd down upon all of them in moments. Yet he had no choice, he must try.

But the mules were ignoring his pulls upon the rein; if anything, they were running faster, as the two women's shrieks goaded them onward. Cursing, Owen threw his full weight upon the reins—to no avail.

Through all this he had no idea where Ginny was. She had dropped back, out of sight. Then there was a burst of pounding hooves as Ginny's mare pulled alongside the wagon wheel. Ginny leaned to shout to him. "It's all right. Tell Amelia Melissa is safe—Crow has her."

Owen was to hear, later, what Ginny had witnessed. "Crow yanked his horse to a stop, Owen, with the cattle coming, so fast, so fast! And he—he leaned down! He grabbed Melissa by her little nightgown. He had her in his arms and the horse running again in just—just a breath of time."

But all Owen knew at the moment was that his stubborn mules kept running, even though he'd pulled their heads to the side, and Ginny was shouting that the baby was safe. As he relaxed the reins, he let out a yell of relief and elation.

After that, he concentrated on the team, fighting them gradually into a widely curving arc that took the wagon beyond range of the running cattle. The herd rushed by, perilously close behind them, with a sound that would be remembered in dreams for years to come. They were safe now, but it took long minutes to get the tiring mules to slow down. When the wagon halted at last, Amelia scrambled out, to receive her little daughter from Crow's hands, then fall to her knees in the prairie grass, rocking Melissa, tears running down her face.

"Thank you—thank you, Mr. Crow," she gasped. "How can I ever, ever repay you?"

Crow seemed embarrassed. He mumbled something and moved Beau away from the distraught mother, stopping alongside Owen, who had set the wagon's brake and climbed down, rifle in hand. Owen stood at the mules' heads, futilely scanning the darkness. Lightning flared across the sky and thunder rumbled ominously.

Owen's mind raced. It had been gunfire that started the herd. None of Will's men would have fired unless there was a threat from beyond the herd. Something like Wardworth's band of outlaws, taking advantage of the weather to spook the uneasy herd. Had they hoped to kill those in camp and then gather up the cattle at their leisure?

If so, the plan had come close to working.

But would Wardworth want Julia caught in that maelstrom of frightened, mindless cattle? It seemed impossible.

Owen turned to find Crow nearby, still mounted on Beau. The brown gelding was sidestepping anxiously, ready to run farther, though his sides heaved and he was soaked with sweat. Owen heard the first raindrops hit the wagon top and the parched ground as lightning showed him Crow's dark, bearded face.

"We owe you a big debt, Crow," Owen said, and held out his hand. "You saved somethin' mighty precious to all of us."

The man stared at him in surprise. "You maybe expected me to ride right over Miz Amelia's little girl? Terrel—I got a little girl of my own, back in Texas. Whatever's between the rest of us, this little child ain't no part of it."

Owen shook his head. "She's a part of it when her ma and pa and little brother are attacked by a bunch of men that wouldn't care if she an' the others got pounded to bloody rags. That was Caleb Wardworth and Comanche Jim and their gang out there tonight, and you know it. You want to tell me what reason they got to prey on this here family like a pack of damned wolves?"

Crow's shoulders seemed to slump. "I guess you got no reason to think any better of me than you think of them. But, well, I ain't one of that gang no more, Terrel. In case you don't remember, they tried to kill me, left me fer dead. Well, I ain't forgot! Nor I ain't quite forgot that you folks brung me in an' them good ladies doctored me and fed me, just like I was worth maybe as much as that pet dog Miss Virginia loves so much." He stopped abruptly and seemed to swallow before continuing. "Does that answer some of them questions I see in all your faces when you look at me?"

Owen snorted impatiently. "Crow, maybe what you say is true, an' you want no part of what those others are tryin' to do. But in our place, what would you think? You were with that gang the first time they tried to raid us."

Crow was silent for a long moment. "Reckon I cain't argue with that. And I would've put a bullet in the brain of the man that tried to harm me an' my family, even if I found him layin' half-dead." He dismounted, rubbed

Beau's neck absently. "To tell you the truth, I don't rightly understand it, Terrel. Why the hell did you help me?"

The rain was starting in earnest now as the little group waited on the empty prairie for whatever would happen next. Owen turned to look for Ginny. She had tied her mare and was urging Amelia and Melissa into the wagon.

"Well, Terrel," Crow said, "gimme a reason. Why didn't you shoot me while I lay helpless?"

Owen thought Crow seemed almost angry, as if he disliked being beholden to the Terrels. "Reckon we don't do things that way," he answered mildly. He moved to the rear of the wagon. Ginny stood there, ignoring the rain. He touched her shoulder. "Are you all right?"

"Yes, except my knees are still quivering," she said huskily.

"Climb inside, honey. No need to get wet. Hand me out your rifle, will you?"

She did so, and Owen walked back to hand the Henry to Crow.

"Help me keep watch?" he said.

The man stared down at the gun in his hand, then, through the wet darkness, at Owen. Owen thought he heard him let out his breath in a hard gust, as if something indefinable had taken place within him. "Yes sir, Mr. Terrel," he said. "Reckon I could do that. I'll walk out a ways to t'other side o' the wagon. See if you can keep the women and kids quiet. I got good ears—might could hear if a rider's comin'."

"Don't fire unless you know it ain't Will or one o' ours," Owen cautioned.

"I ain't a pure fool," Crow rasped, and handed Beau's reins to Owen.

Well, maybe I am, Owen thought as the man moved away, silent as a shadow. Have I armed the enemy?

But tonight Crow had earned the chance to prove he could be trusted. Owen tied Beau to the tailgate of the wagon. One of the women was crying. He climbed up, pushed the canvas aside. It was Julia, huddling near the front, who sobbed monotonously. For the moment Owen ignored her.

"Amelia, was Melissa hurt much?"

Her voice was unsteady. "I don't think so, best I can tell, in the dark. Can I light a lantern, Owen?"

It was the human craving they all felt, for light, for reassurance. But now was not the time.

"Not just yet. We can't afford to advertise our location. Best ever'one be quiet, wait until Will gets back."

"Oh, my God, Owen! What if Will—" Amelia's voice broke. "He could be hurt, or dead. He rode right out in the face of that herd. Please, couldn't you go find him, see if he's all right, him and the other men?"

It was precisely what Owen was aching to do, but he knew what his brother would say. "No, ma'am," he said gently. "Will expects me to guard all of you, not leave you out here alone and unprotected. Will can take care of himself. They had to let the cattle run until they could get 'em to circlin'. They'll be back by mornin', you'll see. Now, you try to sleep. We're standin' watch just out here."

He moved away and was grateful when Julia's muffled sobbing stopped and all within the wagon seemed to be sleeping. The rain pounded down fiercely and the only relief to the thick wet darkness was the sporadic lightning. Fortunately most of the strikes were not close by, though at times the thunder boomed like a huge gong suspended over their heads. The men stood in water, the ground about them was covered to the depth of an inch or so, the land so flat there were few places for the water to flow away. The water-sheeted mud reflected a mournful, dim light as the rain began to lessen and the clouds broke at last.

But morning was near, by the time the last drops fell, and the remaining clouds were stained blood-red in the east as the dawn announced itself.

Rain-soaked and tired, Owen looked about him. Nothing much to see. The prairie seemed totally empty and lifeless. There was no sign of Will or the other men as yet. There was a light, drifting ground mist that made vision uncertain.

Crow startled him as he moved near. "Want me to try an' start a cook fire, Captain Terrel?"

Owen blinked at the respect in the title, sounding strange to him so many years after the war. Only Jackson had continued to address him by his military title. "Good idea. Might be some kindlin' and some dry buffalo chips in that sack slung under the wagon. Hear anything in the night?"

Crow hesitated. "Thought I heard riders east o' here, maybe a hundred yards off, movin' purposeful. Half-hour before first light."

Owen felt a sudden lurch of alarm and an urge to ride out, seeking his brother. If those devils were still hunting the Terrels, they would catch the riders weary, maybe unprepared.

As if in response to his thought, there were several dull, distant reports, a heavy rifle. Might be Olaf Jones' old Sharps. He listened hard, thought he heard lighter gunfire, but it was too faint to be sure.

"They're at it," Crow observed. "Want I should ride over an' take a look? Might be I could help."

Owen hesitated, tempted to send Crow. But it wouldn't be a good idea. The man might be shot as one of the Wardworth bunch, and he was needed here.

"We got to keep Will's family and the others safe," he said at last, shaking his head. "I reckon Will would want us to wait."

"Well, I don't care what Will would want." Amelia climbed from the back of the wagon and ran to them. "Owen, there's shootin' out there. I want to help my husband if I can. If you won't go with me, I'll drive this wagon myself."

Her eyes were red from lack of sleep, and her face was set in determined lines.

Ginny moved up beside her and laid a protecting arm about her shoulder. "Owen, we wouldn't be in any worse danger moving toward the herd than we are out here," she said reasonably. "And maybe we can help. We've got guns."

Owen didn't tell them that by the time they could reach the herd, the shooting was apt to be all over. He bowed to Amelia's wishes, and soon they were all on their way across the wet, sweetly scented prairie, pushing the cranky mules as fast as they could. Crow took the lead, on Beau, the Henry rifle across his saddle.

Owen longed to be in the saddle, galloping to help

Will. It was agony to be tied to this slow wagon. As if she divined his thought, Ginny moved up beside him on the wagon seat and reached for the reins. "Take my horse and ride ahead, Owen. We'll be all right. If I hear shooting close, I'll stop and hide the kids in the brush."

He looked at her with all the love he felt. "Woman, you are one in a thousand," he said, and in moments he had untied and mounted the mare Ginny had ridden the night before. He spurred Strawberry into a gallop and caught up with Crow.

"Let's get on up there," he said to the other man. "Remember that our men won't be expectin' to see you armed. Let me go ahead, so they won't draw a bead on you."

The horses were ready to run. Soon Owen and Crow were far ahead of the wagon. Owen felt uneasy at leaving the women and children unguarded, but he could no longer resist the urge to join in that fight ahead. He could clearly hear the exchange of fire now. Their men must be holding their own—the gunshots from both sides were rapid, vicious.

Now they could see the herd, untended, some animals grazing, some resting after the frantic, exhausting run. The shouting came from somewhere beyond.

Owen couldn't be sure where Will and his men were. His best guess was that the nearer fire must be Wardworth's men. Accordingly he slowed his horse, Crow riding just behind, and moved behind that position. The sun was well up now and the mist had cleared away. Owen could see a knot of ground-tied horses off to the side, and they were not Terrel stock. His first impulse was to run those mounts off. But there was no cover, and he would lose the advantage of surprise if he went for the horses.

"Let's serve 'em up a little breakfast," Crow said. Owen spurred his mount and lifted his rifle. Neither man had qualms, under the circumstances, about attacking from the rear without warning. Their first shots brought an outlaw to his feet, whirling to see what menace approached. Crow had grazed the man's right arm. The outlaw held his forearm with his left hand, the fingers bloodstained, but was still able to steady a gun on the riders pounding toward them.

Owen let out a rebel yell, as much to alert Will to their arrival as anything, and he fired again, from the saddle. The mare flinched and broke stride. Owen spurred her onward. He saw a man fall, his rifle arcing away from him.

Then there was a long, undulating yell from the Terrel men, and Owen caught a glimpse of men mounting, heading their way. The Terrel men were on the offensive. It was enough to break the nerve of the outlaws. They ran for their horses, bent over and dodging, scrambling to mount. Owen raised his Winchester, took aim, shot. His mount, unaccustomed to gunfire, dodged, spoiled his aim. He levered another shell into the chamber. At that moment the mare, running full out, stuck a foreleg into a prairie-dog hole.

Owen heard her leg snap and felt a sick regret even as she went to her knees and the hindquarters rose to flip over the poor beast's head. Owen was propelled away, but his ankle was caught for a moment under the bulk of the crippled animal. He lost his Winchester and by instinct clawed his Colt from the holster even before he struggled to free his foot.

13

The mounted outlaws were scattering now, but one drew rein long enough to try for a shot at Owen, still prone upon the ground. The slug plowed into the mud inches from his face. Owen recognized Wardworth, came to his feet shooting. But the man had already put too much space between them for the Colt. Owen had the dubious satisfaction of seeing Wardworth clap a hand to his left upper arm, where the spent slug had grazed him.

A running horse slid to a stop near Owen. Will dismounted, his face creased with fatigue and worry. "My God, I thought he hit you, Owen. You came just in time. Those coyotes had us pinned down."

Crow trotted closer. "That mare has broke her leg, Captain."

"I know. Crow, ride back to the wagon. Take Jackson with you. Best not leave the women unguarded."

Crow nodded and reined his horse about.

"Here, wait," Will cried. "Owen, you lost your mind, givin' this man a gun?"

"Easy, Will. Crow saved little Melissa's life last night, an' stood watch with me, rode with me to help you men. I think we ought to trust him."

Will stared at them both, thunderstruck. "I want to hear more about this. For now, sir, I take my brother's word and ask your pardon." Will moved his horse nearer to Crow, extended his hand. Gladly Crow accepted the grip.

Will straightened. "Owen's right. Crow, Dill, find the family, bring them here."

When they were gone, Will turned back to Owen. He looked so exhausted that Owen was concerned. He turned and shouted for Juan. "First thing we need to do is make some coffee."

The jaunty little Mexican rode his weary horse near

Owen and dismounted. "*Señor,* you wish me to shoot the poor *yegua?*"

Owen sighed and shook his head. "That's my job. See can you build a fire. Soon as the wagon gets here, we'll get some breakfast together."

The others arrived within a half-hour. Juan had built a fire, upwind of the herd. Amelia moved swiftly to get coffee started for the tired men, and soon her big iron skillet was filled with bacon and Virginia had the biscuits in the Dutch oven.

"Will, you got to lie down and rest," his wife scolded worriedly. "I declare, one more night like that, an' you'll be down sick."

Will grinned and hugged her, then poured coffee for Juan, Jackson, and Olaf. He motioned for Crow to come forward, handed him a steaming cup.

"Amelia told me what you did for our little girl, Mr. Crow. I reckon I owe you just about anything you can name."

Crow shook his head. "No, sir, you don't owe me nothin'. You and Captain Terrel and the ladies—you saved me. My mangy hide ain't worth a whole lot," he grinned crookedly, "but it's the only one I got."

Will nodded. "Then we'll call it even. Owen, have some coffee."

"I'll take a cup, but I believe we ought to keep watch. Those men would still like to run off our herd. They might figure now, while we're tired, is the best time to strike again."

"We'll chance it," Will said. "They're just cattle, and we got more to lose than that herd."

Owen wondered if Will was thinking straight. He was mighty weary, that was plain to see. None of them had had a full night's sleep for weeks. Will was ten years older than Owen, and his age was showing this morning. For the first time Owen noticed that his brother's hair was graying and there was silver showing up in his beard. This morning the lines in his face were carved deep and his eyes were somber as he looked at his wife and the two children, the little ones heavy-eyed and subdued after the excitements of the night.

Will glanced at Owen, surprised at the look of worry on his face. "No, don't lay me to rest just yet, little brother. I ain't down and out, just mad as hell!"

"That makes two of us." Owen nodded. "I've about had enough of those buzzards." He hunkered down, poured another cup of the steaming black brew. The other men drew near, as if aware that momentous decisions were about to be made. "I been doing some thinking, Will. We need to go on the offensive, seems to me."

Will's mouth was thinned, his jaw clinched. He nodded. "My thought exactly."

It wasn't like Amelia to interfere in male planning, but she surprised her husband and brother-in-law this time. "You're not thinkin' to go after those murderers, surely!"

Will looked up. "Honey, we're still thinkin' out what to do. Don't fret, now."

Tears sprang to her blue eyes. "Will Terrel, I've been scared to death all night, afraid you'd been trampled to death by those awful cattle, or shot down in cold blood by those men. Now you're thinking of goin' out to fight again—" She buried her face in both hands, turning away from them.

Will rose and went to hold her. "Darlin', you got to look at it this way," he said quietly. "If we fear to go out after those killers, they're gonna keep comin' back, stalkin' us like starvin' wolves, waiting their chance. We got no choice. We have to put a stop to it someway, or we can never live in peace."

She wiped her face on her apron, looked at him pleadingly. "Can't we send someone for the law, Will?"

"Melia, we're hundreds o' miles from the nearest law, an' there's no saying if one of us could even get through. It's my belief that long before anyone could get to us, this fight would be over—one way or the other. We got to fight our own fight."

"That sounds just wonderful, Will Terrel," she cried. Owen had never seen his serene, sweet-tempered sister-in-law so upset. "But it never was our fight. That woman brought it down on us." She pointed to Julia, who was hovering near the wagon as if afraid to move away from its dubious shelter.

Ginny, giving the children their breakfast, looked up, startled at Amelia's outburst.

Owen stood. "Amelia, would you refuse to help a friend?" he asked in honest surprise.

Virginia came and wrapped both arms about Amelia. "She didn't mean that, Will, she's just worn out. She works too hard and she's worried sick for the children and all of us." She led Amelia to the wagon. "You climb inside and sleep an hour or so, Melia. We can manage all this. Julia will help—won't you, Julia?" Ginny turned hopefully toward the blond woman.

"You just leave me alone, you little hussy," Julia hissed, running shaking hands over her disheveled hair. "You all seem to think I'm some kind of servant, always ordering me around. If you tell me to do one more dirty chore, I'll—I'll slap your prissy little face."

"You try that, Miss High and Mighty, an' I'll undertake to knock you flat." Everyone stared at Crow, who stood with clenched fists, glaring at Julia.

Will looked confused. "Crow, you can't talk to Miss Talbot like that," he protested.

"Well, I ain't," Crow turned to them. "I ain't talking to no Miss Talbot. I'm talkin' to Miz Caleb Wardworth. Whyn't you ask her why she ain't told you it's her *husband* stalkin' all of you. An' while you're at it, ask her why he wants her dead, with no witnesses to say how it happened."

There was a moment of stunned silence, then Julia Talbot let out a screech like a wounded catamount, cornered and threatened. She dashed toward Crow, her hands lifted as if to claw his face. Without thinking, Owen grabbed her wrist, jerking her to a stop. She whirled angrily, then went suddenly limp and fetched up against his chest, one arm tight about his neck.

"Owen, if you ever loved me, you'll kill that filthy-mouthed scoundrel. He's insulted me. He doesn't deserve to live."

With difficulty, Owen freed himself. "Take it easy, Julia. Let's straighten this out."

Crow gave him a contemptuous glance. "You ain't gonna believe me, are you, Terrel? Well, I feel sorry for you. What I said was the gospel truth. Wardworth married her before he managed to rid Texas of her pa. Reckon he never thought she had the guts an' gumption to up an' slip away with the money ol' Osbourne Talbot had got from sellin' the cotton shipments he stole durin' the war.''

Owen narrowed his eyes. "What are you talkin' about? Julia's pa helped the plantation owners get their baled cotton past the blockade, sent it into Mexico.''

Crow's laugh was genuine amusement. "Hell, he was a slick ol' bastard. Sure he sent the cotton to Mexico—one caravan outta five or six. As for the others, he had Comanche Jim an' some of us standing by to take the carts and wagons off the drovers' hands, an' nobody ever knew who was behind it.

"We took an' sold that cotton," Crow said. "Most of the money went back to good ol' Talbot, shinin' light of Houston. I reckon he didn't dare have it known that he had all that cash—wouldn't look just right, you know. So he just tucked it all in a strongbox, hid it in his house. Wardworth sniffed around that mansion, all them times he was there courtin' Miss Julia. He knew where Talbot kept the money. He thought, as Julia's husband an' with Mr. Talbot outta the way, he could spend them thousands like he wanted. But it put Miss Julia's nose outta joint when Caleb laid her pa out. She commenced to pack that money in a valise an' run back to her old sweetheart. Ain't that right, Miz Wardworth?''

Julia's face was white. The glare in her blue eyes should have left Crow writhing on the ground. Owen glanced at Virginia, but she was staring at Julia with a grave expression.

"Crow, you told us you were a buffalo-hunter.''

He shrugged. "Sure I was, for a while. I had other occupations from time to time. Working for Talbot and Wilkins was one of 'em.''

"Julia, is there any truth to this?" Will demanded, and there was a hardness in his face that said he already knew the answer.

"No! No, Will, how can you believe anything this—this filthy varmint says?" She turned a melting gaze on Owen. "You don't believe him, do you?''

It was a bad moment. Owen could see, as he never

really had before, that Julia's lovely eyes were hiding lies.
He wondered how he could have been such a gullible
fool. His image of Julia Talbot had been no more real
than a mirage in the desert.

He looked at his brother. "Will, I think we'd best take
a look in Julia's valise."

"No," she cried, backing away from Owen. "Don't
you dare touch my—my personal things! You're no gentleman, Owen Terrel."

But Will had already turned to the wagon and was lifting out the leather valise. It was locked.

"Julia, you want to give us the key?" he asked mildly.

"No!" She whirled and tried to take the valise. Will
fended her off without trouble until Owen came to grasp
her arms as gently as he could, with Julia berating them
shrilly, trying to struggle free.

Amelia intervened. "Stop it, Julia. You'll wake Melissa."

Julia's shouting dissolved into angry sobs.

"Break the lock," Owen said.

Will used his hunting knife to pry open the valise. He
held it so everyone could see the tightly packed bank
notes and bags that looked as if they might hold gold
coins. Will lifted one, hefted it, nodding grimly. "Folks,
there appears to be a tidy little fortune here. Julia, why
are you carryin' all that money?"

Julia jerked herself free from Owen's hands and moved
to shut the valise. Will let her take it, and she stood with
the heavy bag clutched protectively in both arms. Her
face was splotched with weeping and temper.

"You had no right to open it. It's mine. Will Terrel, I
never would have believed you would take advantage of
a woman's helplessness to pry into her little secrets—"

"This ain't no little secret," Will said. "There's an
almighty lot o' money in that bag, Julia. I reckon there's
nothin' wrong in that, unless your pa got it by dishonest
means, working against the Confederacy while he was
claimin' to be a patriot."

She tossed her head defiantly. "Well, an' what if he
did, Will Terrel? He didn't see it as wrong. He knew the
South couldn't win. All he did was take a little advantage
of the situation. Who's to say you wouldn't do the same,

if you got the chance?'' Her defiant glance moved to Owen, who regarded her with naked disgust.

"Anyway.'' She shrugged. "It had nothin' to do with me. I just knew Papa had some money hid in the house. Caleb tried to get me to say where it was so often that I got suspicious, but I'd already said I'd marry him, because Papa insisted Caleb was goin' far in politics.

"Then—'' Her voice faltered and for a moment she hung her head. When she lifted her face again, there was real grief in her eyes. "He murdered Papa and gave out the story that Papa challenged him to a duel. But I wasn't fooled. I knew Caleb shot him because he wanted Papa's money, and I made up my mind he'd never get it. So''— her expression became crafty—"I pretended to be prostrated by grief, an' when he went out to drink with his low friends, I just had my maid pack a few things and I got the money an' got on the steamboat headed for Galveston. I left a note sayin' I'd gone to New Orleans, hoping he'd never find me—''

She fell silent. No one said anything for a few moments. Melissa cried out, in the wagon, and Amelia climbed back inside the canvas walls to see to her daughter. Virginia bent to the forgotten breakfast, poking the fire.

"You'd better eat,'' she told the men, and they began to fill their tin plates.

Julia stepped back until she was against the wagon wheel, watching all of them with angry eyes. None of the men seemed inclined to look at her. It was as if she had ceased to exist.

Virginia filled a plate for her. "Here, Julia. Set your valise down and eat something. It may be a hard day.''

But Julia turned her back on the other girl and moved around the end of the wagon. When she did not reappear, Ginny shrugged and handed the plate to Crow.

"Thank you, Miss Ginny.''

Amelia brought Melissa out. The little girl had a scrape on one cheek from her fall last night, and her arm was badly bruised. But she sat upon her daddy's knee and ate hungrily. Amelia seemed calm now, though Will watched her worriedly.

"All right, men," he said. "I want to hear any ideas you got."

Juan smiled. "Let us go to Mexico, *Señor!* We can cross the Rio Grande, and I can find *muchos hombres, muchos bandidos* to help us fight our enemies."

Owen found himself grinning, imagining the border bandits coming to their rescue . . . and then taking the herd in payment.

Jackson Dill hunkered down with a fresh cup of coffee. He seemed to be moodily studying the scuffed and worn toe of his right boot. "All we got to do is wait. They'll be back, tryin' us out again."

"Reckon we can depend on that." Will nodded. "But I'm for goin' after that bunch, track 'em down like the cowardly coyotes they are. What's your thought, Owen?"

Owen held his peace for a few moments, watching Ginny and Amelia as they cleaned up the breakfast pans. Julia had climbed into the wagon to sulk.

"Before we go after 'em, we'll have to get the family to safety. We can't leave the women and kids out here, even with a couple of men. They'll surely try to hit us where we're weakest."

Will sighed. "You're right. And I won't have the women and children in the line of fire again if I can help it. But we can't go on the way we have, trying to guard the herd, gettin' next to no sleep, wonderin' where they'll strike next. What we need is a way to divide their forces."

Crow looked up, eyes sparkling with amusement. "Now there's a good thought. Captain Terrel, can we figure a way to manage that?"

"Maybe you can tell me, Crow. How many men has Wardworth got?"

"Wardworth, or Wilkins?"

"Yeah. That's exactly what I mean," Owen murmured.

Will's eyes sharpened with interest. "I think I see what Owen's gettin' at. Whose men are they, Wardworth's or Wilkin's?"

Owen nodded. "We keep thinking of these owlhoots as one gang. But they have two bosses. Could be they have two different objectives."

Crow came nearer and set his cup down. "That ain't a bad guess, Terrel. Maybe I can give you a hint or two. Comanche Jim has his eye on that herd. His men has worked many a stolen bunch of stock over the river into Mexico. A cow sells for three or four dollars a head over there, an' all it costs them is a little work."

Owen nodded. "Go on. We're listenin'."

Encouraged, Crow continued. "Now, then, Wardworth wants the Talbot money."

Will rubbed his beard thoughtfully. "Well, sir, what about Julia? Reckon he hopes he can tame her enough to take her back to Houston an' get her to play the part of the lovin' Miz Wardworth while he runs for office?"

Crow shrugged. "I get the feelin' he's figgerin' on goin' back a grievin' widower."

"Wonder how he'll explain why she left home in the first place?" Owen put in.

"Easy enough, I reckon," Crow said. "He could say she's been away visiting relatives, gettin' over the loss of her pa, then had some accident or other. Who's to know different?"

"Does Comanche Jim know about the money?"

Crow shrugged. "Not unless he and Wardworth have got chummier than they was when I was ridin' with 'em. Wilkins thinks that Wardworth's out here to get his wife—and a share of the herd. I only found out about Talbot's money by makin' a point of listenin' in on a couple of little secret confabs among Wardworth an' his three men. He keeps them in line with promises to share Papa Talbot's money—long as they can keep their mouths shut around Wilkins' crew."

"An' you never bothered to mention all this to Comanche Jim? Why was that, exactly?"

Crow grinned. "My ol' daddy used to smack my mouth for speakin' out of turn."

Owen nodded. "Then that gives me an idea or two. Let me think about it a while, Will. I'll keep watch while the rest of you sleep. Forget the herd for now. Those cows ain't goin' nowhere until they've rested some. Relieve me this afternoon." He stood and went to get his horse.

14

There was no alarm during that day. Perhaps the Terrel enemies needed rest and food as badly as their prey. Owen rode slowly, patrolling in a wide loop about the camp and the herd. The dog had joined him, trotting tirelessly at the horse's heels. Owen had more confidence in the senses of Whiskey and Beau than he had in his own. His mind felt leaden with weariness, but he forced himself to think, going over and over their situation and all that had led up to it.

He wasted little time blaming Julia Talbot. It was hard to believe that she was—had always been—so very different from his cherished mental picture of her. But he was not a fool boy to weep over spilt milk. He was angry at her attempt to hide her marriage to Wardworth and at her refusal to tell the Terrels the true story when she took shelter with them, thus endangering them all. No use worrying about all that now. Owen didn't give a spit in the Rio Grande if the Wardworth bunch took over every stick and stone of the property that Osbourne Talbot had gotten by betraying his fellow Texans. Let those sneaking coyotes tear one another to bits over the money Julia hoarded in her precious valise.

Julia's life was in danger, too. Owen had neither love nor respect for her now, yet he could not refuse to protect her life. But the welfare of the children and the other women would damn sure come first.

That was hardly a consideration, when all was said and done. They were all in equal danger. Even if Wardworth had both Julia and the money, he could not leave the Terrels alive. Law might be a rare commodity out here, but Wardworth was smart enough to know that the Terrel brothers and their men would never rest until the score was evened, if it took a lifetime.

So . . . this had to be a fight to the death.

The sun was hot and high, thunderheads building again west and south of the herd. But Owen felt a chill to his bones. The plans they made now might well determine whether any of them survived the mess Julia Talbot had brought down on them.

Could they afford to merely wait and defend themselves each time the outlaws struck? The gang had the advantage, for they had no such vulnerable baggage as the women and children, let alone the livestock. They alone knew when and where they would strike, and the advantage of surprise seemingly must remain with them. Last night Wardworth had used the Terrel herd against the camp. What would it be next? Owen and Will had as much stamina and gumption as most men, but it didn't take much to see that they had too much to guard and too few men. Already many of the horses were missing, because of the stampede.

Will's remark this morning about the cattle had set Owen to thinking. If they tried to hold on to the herd and defend the family as well, they stood to lose both. If they were willing to, say, use the herd as bait . . .

Owen stopped his horse for a moment, eyes automatically scanning the plains. Nothing moved except a buzzard circling in the near distance, over the carcass of the dead mare. As his horse moved restlessly sidewise, tugging at the bit, a rattler buzzed loudly from under a shinnery bush a few feet away. Owen drew his Colt and shot twice. The snake's thick coils flopped and slid in its death struggles.

Owen heard a shout from the camp and turned to see Will mounting, spurring toward him. He rode to meet his brother.

"Only a sidewinder," Owen said. "Everything's quiet."

"Damn!" Will grinned widely. "I was rarin' to take on those scallywags again."

"Sounds to me like you've been at the snakebite remedy," Owen said, glad to see his brother in better spirits. "Never knew it made you so happy to be shot at."

"Now you mention it, I can think of a couple things I like better. Seen anything movin' around?"

"No."

"I was hopin' some of the *remuda* would follow the saddle stock. Dang it, I purely hate to lose them horses." He pounded his saddle horn with one big fist.

"They won't stray too far from the water. We'll find 'em when we have time."

"If someone else don't find 'em first. Well, we ain't got a lot of choice right now."

"No," Owen said quietly, "but I figure we got a few moves we can make. Might mean riskin' the cattle, though."

"As I see it, we can worry about the cattle once we get the women an' kids safe."

"I agree." Owen tried to shrug the tired ache out of his shoulders. "Has it struck you that Wilkins and his men might see the herd as somethin' too good to pass up, even if Wardworth loses interest in it?"

Will's heavy brows were drawn in puzzlement, but he nodded slowly. "I'm with you that far."

Owen continued, "On the other hand, Caleb Wardworth is not likely to pass up the chance to get Papa Talbot's little valise, in favor of the herd or anything else. So . . ."

Will straightened, beginning to smile. "So, if we split the money and the herd, we may split the enemy."

"Seems so to me."

Will was quiet for a long moment. At last he nodded. "I agree with your thinkin' on this, except for one thing: if we abandon the herd, make a run for the Pecos, maybe, what's to keep the whole gang from coming after us, then takin' the herd at their leisure?"

"That's the fly in the ointment," Owen admitted. "I think I can take care of that."

"How?" Will was watching him narrowly, as if he sensed that this part of Owen's plan would not meet with his approval.

"Lordy, I'm too beat to talk about it now." Owen did not have to fake his long sigh of weariness. "I think I'll go and grab a little sleep before night. They're likely to be onto us again, come dark, and we need to be ready."

"Yeah. I told the other men to sleep all they can. I'll keep my eyes open out here."

Owen loped back to the camp, released his horse, and

saddled a fresh one, in case of need. He found a shady mesquite, flung down a blanket, and stretched out, asleep almost at once.

He woke to the coolness of dusk, conscious that the quiet hours had been healing to his overtired body. His stomach rumbled hopefully at the scent of coffee boiling. He sat up. Was that steak frying? He lost no time in making his way to the cook fire. Ginny was turning generous slabs of meat in two big skillets.

"That smells better'n roses and honeysuckle," he said, helping himself to coffee.

She turned to him with a smile. "Will says we're leavin' the herd behind, so we might as well eat one of those nice tender calves before the outlaws get 'em. He butchered one while you and the other men rested."

Little Willy pounded past the fire, whooping like an Apache, Whiskey racing behind him. Amelia, walking into the firelight with Melissa in her arms, reprimanded her son. "Come and sit down, Willy, it's time to eat." She set the little girl down. Melissa promptly toddled toward the fire. Owen snatched her away from danger, handed her to Ginny.

Will and the other men were gathering near the fire now, with only Olaf, who was standing guard, missing.

Ginny handed Owen two full plates. "Would you take some food to Julia? She hasn't eaten anything all day."

Owen did not move. "I'd rather not, Ginny."

She sighed, but did not take the plate back. "I know you must be angry at her, Owen, but it won't do any of us any good if she makes herself sick. She won't speak to Amelia or me. Maybe you can get her to eat, at least."

Owen saw that Ginny looked tired and strained, and he couldn't argue with her. It was the last thing he wanted to do, but he supposed he could stand to spend ten minutes with the girl he had once loved. "Where is she?"

"In the wagon. She won't come out. Thank you, Owen."

He took the food and moved to the back of the wagon. It was dark inside. "Julia, it's Owen. I brought you some supper."

She said nothing, but he heard a muffled sob. More irritated than sympathetic, he climbed into the wagon,

found a place to sit upon a wooden chest, and set the
plate of steak, biscuits, and beans near Julia, who was
lying on one of the bedrolls.

"Come on now," Owen said briskly. "Sit up and dig
in. Might be a while before we get any more hot food."
When she did not move, he reached down, caught her
wrist, and pulled her upright.

"Here, try this." He cut a bit of meat and held it out
to her. She must have been painfully hungry. After a
moment she took the meat.

Silently Owen ate, enjoying the good food. He was
relieved to see Julia reach for her own plate and continue
to eat. He had the feeling that if it had not been dark,
she would have stuck to her pride and refused the food.
He wondered how many times in the past this same sulky
tactic must have gotten her her way with her doting father.

As he cleaned his tin plate, Owen started to leave the
wagon. She reached suddenly and caught his arm.

"Owen, wait," she begged. "I need to talk to you."

"Julia, anything you need to say to me you should've
said long ago. Seems you and your pa kept way too many
secrets. I don't know why you couldn't be straight with
me, but I guess you had your reasons. None of it matters
now."

He heard her plate clatter as she flung it aside. "You
don't understand," she cried, apparently not caring that
the others would hear. "I loved Papa. Maybe what he
did was wrong, I don't know. For that matter, I didn't
know exactly what his business was. I only knew I
mustn't talk about it, or he'd be in trouble. What would
you expect me to do? If—" Her voice broke pitifully. "If
you and I had married, I would've told you . . . someday."

"No," he replied evenly, "I don't believe you would,
knowin' how I would feel about your pa's dealin's." He
kept his voice low, but there was no mistaking the cold
finality of it. "As for us bein' married, maybe you've
forgot that you chose Caleb Wardworth."

Without waiting for her response, he moved to the tailgate of the wagon, sprang lightly down. After finishing a

second cup of coffee, listening quietly to the conversation about him, he stood.

"What's the plan for tonight, Will?" he asked. Everyone fell silent. There was a feeling of great portent to the moment. Even the children seemed to sense it, and they were very quiet.

"Most of this idea is yours, Owen. I want you to take charge. All of us will take your orders from this minute." Will glanced at the other men, received their nods.

Owen was taken aback. In his mind, he had always considered his older brother should have final word in important decisions. "Will, that ain't necessary—"

Will interrupted, "Owen, arguin' wastes time. Let's hear what you want us to do."

"Right, Will." Owen paused a moment, gathering in his thoughts all the things he had run through his mind every waking moment the past forty-eight hours.

"Folks, we're pretty well agreed that we're losin' ground by wearing ourselves out trying to guard the camp and the herd both. So we need to leave the herd for now. That means we risk losin' the cattle. But it also means that Wardworth's buddy, Wilkins, may see that as an opportunity for him and his men to run our stock over the border. That would leave Wardworth and his men still sniffin' after Julia's money. Be a hell of a lot easier to fight off three or four than the whole passel."

"Owen, if we lose the herd—that's our livin'," Amelia protested.

Owen smiled slightly. "I don't figger to lose that herd for long," Owen said.

"Don't worry, Amelia," Will put in. "It's a long way to the border, an' cows travel slow."

"Then what do we do?" Ginny asked.

"We head west, for the Pecos, Roswell, maybe. The main thing now is to get the children to safety."

"We're lettin' them bushwhackers get away with what they done?" Jackson Dill exclaimed. "Now, that just don't sound like you, Cap'n."

"I don't believe I said that," Owen drawled. "I think we can set a little trap an' see what varmints we catch."

Quickly he outlined his plan. "Will's takin' the women and children out, horseback, with one man to help."

"I will go, *señor!*" Juan offered.

"*Muchas gracias, mi amigo,*" Owen said. "But first I want to set up a little bait for Wardworth, try to decoy him so Will's group can slip out. Wardworth would expect the women—and Julia's valise—to be in the wagon. Crow, Jackson, and Olaf will start out as soon as possible with the wagon.

"There's risk," he warned them, "but I believe this is better than waiting for Wardworth to decide where we fight."

There was some discussion, and again Will brought up the problem of how to lure half the gang to try again for the herd.

"I think I have that figured," Owen said, "but give me a little more time on it, will you? Right now, we ought to be gettin' ready."

"Captain Terrel's right," Crow said. "One more night raid might leave us in worse shape. If we're gonna do it, let's do it now."

It was odd that Crow, once their enemy and captive, cast the deciding vote. In moments Amelia had almost forcibly evicted Julia from the wagon, while she rummaged in the food stores, handing things to Ginny to be packed in saddlebags the men brought. Juan was saddling horses, the freshest of the ones they had left. But all were careful not to let their activities be visible to anyone who might be—who almost surely was—watching from the distance. The fire had been put out almost completely, so that the movement of people and horses would not be outlined against the flames.

Owen saddled Beau and led him to where Will was supervising the distribution of food and water. "I'm gonna scout around a little," Owen muttered to his brother. "Send the wagon out as soon as the men are ready, an' I'll catch up. You and Juan ride out just as we planned, with the women and kids. Move north for a few miles, then ease around toward the west and don't look back until you get to the Pecos."

Will turned on his brother sternly. "Owen, you foolin' around out there alone ain't part of the plan."

"You said I was in charge, remember?" Owen grinned.

"Now you got to live with that. Don't worry, I'll be fine."

Owen left Will, moved to the wagon. Ginny seemed to know it was he even though she couldn't have made out his face in the nearly pitch dark. "Owen," she whispered, "I want to stay with you. Don't send me with the others."

He led her a few feet into the darkness and took her in his arms. Her kiss was tender, pleading. Owen held her close for a few silent heartbeats. "I wish you could stay with me," he said softly. "Reckon you know now I want you with me for the rest of my life."

She pulled away and he knew she was trying to see his expression in the darkness. "Owen, do you mean that?"

"I don't say a lot I don't mean. I never said anything in my whole life I meant more." His voice was low, its very quietness compelling.

She nestled back in his arms. "I'm afraid," she whispered. "I'm afraid I won't ever see you again if I leave you tonight."

He hesitated, then spoke the truth. "I know. I'm afraid of that too, but it's somethin' we have to do. We got to get those children out of danger."

Her long sigh said as plainly as words that she knew he spoke an unarguable truth. "Promise me," she said fiercely. "Promise me you'll come and find me."

He held her so tight that it must have been painful. "I'd search until my dyin' day for you, Virginia. I love you, more than I knew a man could love a woman."

"I love you too, Owen," she whispered, and kissed him once more.

"Now go back and help Amelia," he instructed. "Ask Crow to give you back the Henry rifle. He can use the extra Winchester we found with that dead rustler this morning. Keep your rifle loaded and ready as you ride."

He touched her cheek, felt tears upon his calloused fingers. Then she was gone and he went back to take up Beau's reins. He swung into the saddle just as Jackson Dill stepped to the horse's head.

"Owen, they's somethin' I meant to tell you earlier. I believe Georgie's ridin' with Wardworth."

Owen leaned down. "What makes you think so?"

"Durin' the gunfight, after we got them cattle stopped, I heard that boy yell out somethin'. Too dark to see who 'twas, but I knowed that was him, all right. You know how he always talks through his nose, whiny-like?''

"Damn,'' Owen swore softly. "You reckon he just rode out of our camp an' went to find that bunch an' joined up?''

"Yes, sir, I do. He was real mad about the work he was made to do. He's too shif'less to dig wells an' the like.''

"Yeah, Jackson, I know, but I'd never have thought he'd put in with those killers against people he's worked for all his life.''

"Don't forget, Georgie's brother Simon was hung before the war for horse-stealin. That family is trash, Cap'n.''

"Well, if he's helping Wardworth, that means one more against us.''

"Yes, sir, an' Georgie may be shif'less as a blue-tick hound, an' a coward as well. But he's a dead shot with a gun.''

Taking this latest bit of unpleasant news with him, Owen reined his horse around and headed away from camp.

He headed north, letting Beau move at an easy trot, trusting to the horse's night vision to avoid obstacles. The night was very dark, but that suited his purposes.

He had not realized how tightly wound-up his nerves were until a soft sound behind him had him whirling his horse and drawing his gun almost simultaneously.

A dimly seen patch of white, low to the ground, made him relax. It was only the dog, taking a notion to follow Owen. The rider wondered if he ought to try to send Whiskey back. Likely it would be useless, and certainly it would be noisy. Better to let the dog accompany him, hope he didn't get in the way of Owen's plans.

15

A short distance from the camp, Owen drew his horse to a halt and looked back. Little was to be seen except a glow from the banked fire, and the only noises were the bawl of a cow and the voice of a rider singing to the herd. It was Will, he thought. Good touch, that. It might give the impression that all was as usual at the Terrel encampment.

They would all be leaving soon, the wagon pulling quietly out, moving slowly on newly greased wheels to avoid creaking, heading due west. The others would wait an hour or so, trying to rest in their bedrolls.

Owen turned, rode on, trying to scan the darkness on three sides. Finally, he caught the glimmer of a fire, a mile north. They were getting bolder then, figuring the Terrels would not dare to come looking for them. Unless that campfire was a lure to pull the defenders away from the camp—and thus from the herd and Julia, with her hoard of ill-gotten wealth.

But it was all Owen had to go on. He spurred his horse to a trot and rode toward the little beacon of light.

He had hoped to stumble onto one of the watchers who doubtless had been set to keep an eye on the Terrel camp, perhaps eliminate a man who could report Will's departure with his group. But he saw and heard no one.

Owen reined in some fifty yards from the campfire. He could make out horses hobbled and grazing here and there. That was smart, to hobble them and leave them scattered. It pretty well prevented a quick sweep of the gang's mounts, leaving them afoot.

The dog whined softly.

"Quiet, boy," Owen muttered. He dismounted, tied one rein to a mesquite to be sure Beau would be waiting until he returned. If he returned. He checked the load of his Peacemaker, leaving the Winchester on the saddle.

Then he moved swiftly and silently toward the camp. The dog paced silently at his heels.

He could make out sleeping forms, prudently back from the tiny fire. Owen stopped, stood rock-still, listening, watching, patient as death now. He must try to spot the man who would be keeping watch over the camp, and that before the watcher spotted him. The chances of it were slim, but Owen had no choice now save to see it through.

It turned out to be laughably easy. Whoever was in charge in the outlaw camp was overconfident, or had placed his confidence in the wrong man. The guard was half-concealed, leaning against a stout shinnery bush—sound asleep. Owen was on him, one hand covering the man's mouth, the cold lips of his Colt against the man's ear, before the outlaw jerked awake.

"One more move and you're a dead man," Owen murmured gently.

His captive froze. Owen tied the man's hands with a strip of rawhide he'd brought, then made him stand and walk ahead of him. Holding the outlaw's collar in a choking grasp, Owen moved a few steps toward the sleeping outlaws. "Wake up, men!" he shouted. "I have a little announcement."

It was almost comical, the resulting scramble as the outlaws rolled out of their blankets, reaching for guns.

Calmly, Owen put a shot through the calf of one of the nearest. "Leave the hardware where it is," he said. "Raise your hands, or some of you won't see the sun come up."

It was a tense few seconds before Owen could be sure that someone wouldn't simply grab a rifle, plug his hostage, and get him with the next shot. Confusion and perhaps uncertainty as to whether he had arrived alone held the outlaws still. But that would last about as long as a squirrel in a bobcat den. Owen lost no time in getting his message across.

"Just dropped in to let you know we sent our man Juan across the Mexican border for an uncle of his. You might have heard of him. Feller name of Juan Cortina."

The effect was fairly satisfying. Cortina's brutal rustler gangs were known and talked about all along the border, and he was said to be fanatically loyal to kin. If these vermin believed Owen's story, it might cause a bit of nervousness in the ranks.

Not that it was likely to alter their basic objectives, or send them back to Texas in defeat. The border was days away, and there was ample time, if the outlaws moved fast, to make the Terrel herd—and the Terrels—vanish among the buffalo bones on the vastness of the Llano Estacado. But it might inspire them to move on the herd more quickly, and that was the result Owen hoped for.

"Now, then," Owen continued amiably, "we figure to take our women and children out of this fight. If you want to try us again, you'll find us ready and waitin'. But I advise you to go back to the filthy holes you crawled out of. And as for you, Georgie," he called suddenly to the skinny fellow who seemed to be trying to hide himself behind a barrel chested outlaw, "Georgie, you'd best hightail it outta here. If you let Will draw a bead on you, after you helped try to run the herd over his wife and kids—God help you."

With a sudden movement, Owen hooked a leg around his captive sentry's ankle, shoved him hard. The man fell almost upon the campfire. With his screams and a few random shots to hold them for the needed few moments, Owen was gone, sprinting in the darkness for his horse.

He reloaded as he ran—something Will had drilled into him when he was a boy after their pa died and the two of them were the protectors of their family. Whiskey raced happily alongside Owen. The dog seemed to think their adventure a marvelous game.

The dog's sense of direction was a help. He led Owen directly to Beau. Owen could hear yells and hoofbeats behind him as he snatched loose the rein and flung himself into his saddle. Beau was running even as Owen's boot toe found the stirrup. Owen jerked his rifle free, levered a shell into the chamber.

He rode the thoroughbred in a wide half-circle past the camp, racing close enough to make sure the outlaws knew which way he went. In a matter of moments he was leading hastily mounted pursuers eastward. He hoped the entire group had been goaded into trying to hunt him down, so he could draw them away from the route his friends and family would be taking. A flurry of gunshots seemed to promise a determined pursuit.

As he rode, bent low in case one of the recklessly fired rifle slugs came nearer than he expected, he passed through his mind the things he had learned. Georgie was indeed one of Wardworth's men now. Altogether, Owen had counted seven men in the camp. Caleb Wardworth was not present. Probably he was watching the Terrel camp—not an encouraging thought. Owen calculated there could be at least one more, possibly as many as three, that he had not seen tonight.

Wilkins had been in the camp. There was no mistaking his bulk. He was known to be half again as broad as most men. Grimly Owen wondered if he'd have been smarter to simply shoot Comanche Jim Wilkins, hoping the gang would fall apart. Certainly none of those vultures would balk at outright murder to achieve their ends. But some personal sense of honor held Owen back from such an act.

It was an hour or so past midnight when he judged that he had put enough distance between himself and his pursuers. He pulled the brown gelding down to a trot and turned him at a right angle, moving south now. He hoped that the gang would spur on east, thinking he was still ahead, thus gaining a few hours' time for them all. At least, he must have provided enough confusion to give the two Terrel parties, moving west in the darkness, a better chance.

And then? It was anybody's guess. Would Wilkins and his men argue for sweeping down on the unguarded herd, pushing the cattle southwest before Juan's mythical kin arrived? There was a good chance they would smell a bluff, simply find the Terrel trail and attempt to finish them, planning to go back for the herd in their own good time. If so, the Terrel chances were sharply reduced.

But not down to zero, Owen reminded himself. If only Will and Juan could get the women and kids to safety, Owen and his men would cheerfully take on all of Wardworth's and Wilkins' ruthless bushwhackers. And if the outlaws won, there would be precious few of them left to enjoy their victory.

He drew Beau to a halt, listened. The sounds of pursuit

had faded. His pursuers had not yet realized that he had doubled back.

He breathed deeply, relieved, and touched Beau with the spurs. At a gallop, the dog following swiftly, Owen headed back toward the point where he would meet Jackson, Olaf Jones, and Crow with the wagon.

He rode rapidly for an hour, guiding upon the stars, thankful that the earlier clouds had not developed. It would be dead easy to get lost on these trackless plains where there were virtually no landmarks within hundreds of square miles.

Abruptly, Beau's gait altered. The horse began to limp, favoring his left foreleg.

Quickly Owen got down, lifted the brown's hoof, feeling for the trouble. There was no stone lodged in the hoof, and the shoe was still secure. Running experienced fingers above the ankle, he felt along the cannon bone and the tendons below the knee. The swelling was not hard to find. Somewhere in the long miles Beau had put a foot wrong, strained the tendon.

Cursing softly, as much for the faithful horse's pain as for his own predicament, Owen unsaddled Beau and pulled the bridle off. He shoved his gear under a mesquite, hoped he would be able to find it later. He untied his canteen, dismayed to find it very light. In his hurry he'd forgotten to fill it. Owen sighed. Better hurry and intercept the wagon. If he missed it in the darkness, by midday he would be in serious trouble, on foot and without water.

Owen picked up his Winchester. He hoped Beau would find his way to water, that his leg would mend, with rest. Maybe Owen would even find the good horse again one day, grazing with wild mustangs and running free.

The brown nosed his shoulder. Owen's throat tightened as he rubbed the sleek, sweat-damp neck. "You take it easy, boy," he said. "You've done your part."

With Whiskey panting alongside, he moved out across the silent desert at a trot, setting himself to cover a considerable distance before dawn. Strange how vulnerable he felt, now that he must leave the horse behind. A man came to take for granted the mounts he used, some willing and smart, like Beau, others stubborn or lazy or dull-

witted. Now that Owen's boot soles were pounding the
desert sands, and he was no longer elevated above scorpion, mesquite thorn, sidewinder, and bruising stones,
he would have given a year of his life for one of the worst
of the horses and mules he'd known.

He was glad of the dog's presence. A man alone could
find his nerve crumbling, faced with the incalculable expanse of barren wasteland. The sky arched immensely,
deep and black and spattered with stars that seemed to
watch him, indifferent to his fate. The miles between
Owen and the place where he might hope to spot the
wagon, at dawn, had seemed negligible when he was carried swiftly by Beau. Now they stretched out before him
in a different way. Would he be able to make it in time,
or would the others, unaware of Owen's predicament,
simply move on, farther and farther away, as his strength
ebbed?

Owen pulled his thoughts up sharply. He had no energy
to spare for fear. This was not the first crisis he had
faced, and if he faced his problems coolly, it would not
be his last.

He controlled his mind, narrowing it in to the moment
at hand and the needs of that moment. He must cross ten
or twelve miles of harsh terrain within two hours, at most.
And he'd better be ahead of the wagon, or if not, he'd
better pray that he did not unwittingly pass over the wagon
tracks in the predawn dark.

So he set himself to run, not at full speed, which he
could not hope to keep up for long, but at a ground-
eating trot. He and Will had trotted thus for many miles
when they hunted deer in the Big Thicket. But Owen had
been younger then, a thin, wiry youth with boundless
energy.

Well, he was still able to do what was needed! Pushing
aside thoughts of weariness or worry, Owen concentrated
upon keeping his feet moving, checking the stars often
to be sure his direction was right. When he could bear
his thirst no longer, he and the dog shared the last few
swallows of water left in the canteen.

And then they moved on at a steady pace. Owen ignored his growing fatigue. Time stretched out, and Ow-
en's consciousness boiled down to the drawing of breath,

the lifting and putting forward of one foot after another. He allowed himself a short breather. The dog immediately lay down by his feet. Owen rubbed Whiskey's head, grateful for the animal's loyalty. With a deep breath, Owen forced reluctant muscles into motion once more.

His passage disturbed a bull bat resting under a cholla. It sliced upward on delicately curved wings, with a whistle of alarm. Owen was conscious once or twice of the movement of some small creature scrambling softly out of his path. His feet, unaccustomed to continued hard contact with the ground, ached within his boots. Owen ignored the discomfort. He had his second wind now. He had a fair chance of making it to the area west of the last Terrel campsight where he calculated the wagon would pass.

Daylight was coming, just the dimmest glow at first, then a rosy illumination that made the desert a weirdly beautiful landscape. Owen began to scan ahead of him for wagon tracks.

But there was nothing. As the light grew and he could see around him, he hoped to catch sight of the wagon and team. Nothing was in sight. Nothing but desert growths and grass and sand and rock and the huge, luminously blue sky.

Owen stumbled to a halt, needing rest badly. He bent double, dragging in air, conscious of the ache and tremble of his legs. Whiskey whined and lay down, panting hard. Owen pitied the tired, thirsty dog. Too bad the animal must suffer too.

Owen tried to assess his situation. Had he run far enough—or perhaps too far? Straightening, he gazed around him again, turning slowly.

Then he wished he had not turned. He experienced an unsettling sense of disorientation. The stars were gone now. There was nothing to guide upon. How would he know if he strayed from his direction? He should continue moving south . . .

Owen's throat was suddenly very dry and he fought the feeling of helplessness, the conviction that he was the only human left alive within hundreds of miles. He was utterly sure that he was lost, with nothing at all to guide upon. Yet he could not stay here. He must find his companions, or he would almost surely die in this arid, god-forsaken place.

In those bad moments Owen Terrel fought back from the edges of panic that could have unmanned him. The sun was rising, already hot. High overhead, a hawk called thinly, and a fitful breeze kicked up.

Abruptly Owen felt foolish. The wind most commonly came from southwest. And the rising sun should be marker enough for anyone. Keep the sun at his left shoulder until midday, and he would not become confused and move eastward. That still left ample room to miss his objective, but it was enough to steady him. He faced about, felt the breeze against the right side of his face, and started to walk. The dog paced faithfully at his heel.

Immediately Owen felt more confident. Simply being in motion served to ease the sensation of helplessness. He made himself breath deeply, forced his eyes to scan for the wagon, for tracks, even as he chose his path, weaving among the shinnery and cactus and stone slabs upthrust from under the surface of the soil. He was conscious that the daylight brought new hazards. By noon the sun would have the power to drive a man to his knees. Thirst that was bearable now would soon become intolerable. And Owen was very conscious that he could be seen from the distance of a mile or more, in this flat expanse. If one of Wardworth's friends spotted him, he would be ridden down very quickly.

Again he reminded himself that an armed man, particularly one taught wilderness tactics by Will Terrel, was far from helpless. He knew how to go to ground, blending into this monotonously featured landscape, and appear under the very hooves of a man's horse, as if out of the sand itself.

Nevertheless, he spared a glance over his shoulder from time to time as he continued to strain his senses for a sight of the wagon.

At that moment, he found the sign he'd prayed for, but it was not hopeful. Twin wheel tracks crossed his path, winding to his right. He was too late. The wagon had passed ahead of him before dawn.

Owen wasted no time on regrets or worry. He had two choices. He could follow the wagon, not knowing how far ahead it might be, perhaps running to his death from thirst without the slightest chance of ever gaining the least sight of it.

Or he could backtrack along the marks of the wheels. Olaf and Crow and Jackson Dill would have detoured to fill the water kegs before starting out. Those tracks would lead surely to one of the water holes. No guarantee how far Owen would have to walk before he reached the life-giving water. And he would lose any chance of being with the men when they engaged the enemy.

Without the slightest hesitation, Owen turned and trotted west, following the wagon, steeling himself to the coming hours, perhaps his last, and most painful, hours on earth.

16

Later Owen would find it hard to recall that devilishly unending day. Maybe his mind refused to recount the burning, choking thirst, the weakness that grew with the rising temperature, eyes that blurred as he peered ahead, longing to make out the dingy wagon canvas bobbing in the heat-shimmering distance.

At times, even if it had been there, Terrel might not have realized it. His head pounded and his throat ached with thirst. Sweat poured into his eyes. He was walking more slowly now, at times only staggering. Twice he became aware that he was walking at a tangent, away from the twin tracks, and knew he was losing his alertness. He feared that he would simply wander away unknowingly from the trail and fall, never to be found. Yet he could not stop and rest, could not let the wagon pull even farther ahead. His stubborn mind would not allow him to stop. Through it all, the dog kept close, looking up at him now and then with a whine.

Owen was aware that the sun was ahead of him now, and then lowering until it was slanting into his eyes, the day almost gone. He thought, vaguely, that he must reach the wagon before dark, or he was lost indeed. He could not continue at this pace much longer.

A merciful dullness invaded his mind. He walked in a mental fog, not even knowing he was falling, until the sandy ground slammed jarringly into his face.

It was the sweetest relief Owen could have imagined, simply to be lying still. The struggle was over. He need not push and punish exhausted muscles any further. He could sleep now. It was really quite comfortable, his aching body stretched out in the sand. The heat was going now, but the sand would stay warm most of the night, the long, restful night . . .

Something touched the open palm of his hand, moved

damply. Then there was a tugging at his sleeve, a whimper. Someone crying? Ginny's face drifted into his numb mind, dark eyes pleading, silky hair escaping along the temples.

Terrel rolled over. He was awake now, and aware of his danger. The dog whined eagerly and licked at his face. Darkness had fallen, cool and refreshing.

Forcing himself to his knees, Owen looked for his rifle. Thank God he had not lost it in his exhausted stupor. Instinct had made him cling to it, and it lay nearby. Grimly, knowing it was perhaps his last chance, Owen lifted the gun, fired three times into the air. He waited a moment, then fired three shots again. After that, reloading at intervals, he sent the signals four times into the dark sky. If his men were near enough to hear, perhaps one of them would ride back.

It was also possible that the Wardworth gang might be drawn to him. Fiercely, making himself walk slowly along the tracks, Terrel hoped that they would. He made sure both his weapons were fully loaded, and listened for the approach of horsemen.

When he began to hear the quick, galloping hoofbeats, at first he thought it was another hallucination. Yet he stopped and sent three shots booming over the plain.

There was a faint halloo. Owen tried to answer, only then aware that his dried throat would emit no more than a croak. He allowed himself to stop walking and waited, wondering if the approaching rider was friend or enemy.

"Where at are you?" came a shout.

Whiskey barked joyfully and Owen let out a low, hoarse sound. The rider's horse plunged to a stop. Jackson Dill was at that moment the most beautiful sight in the world to Owen, who was managing to keep from falling to his knees only by the greatest effort.

"Lord A'mighty, that you, Cap'n?" Dill was off his horse and untying his canteen. He gave the water to Terrel, who had to restrain himself from gulping it. His hands shook as he lifted it to his mouth. Nothing had ever tasted so good. It was the taste of life itself. Staggering, he bent and poured water into the palm of his cupped hand for the dog, who lapped weakly.

Dill took the canteen back, tightened the lid, and replaced it on his saddle.

"Cap'n I ain't askin' you what happened till you got a chance to rest. Let's git back to the wagon."

It took the last ounce of Owen's strength to climb on behind Dill, and he was grateful when Jackson caught his arm and hauled him up

"The—dog—" Owen gasped.

"Don't you fret, if he cain't make it, I'll walk an' carry 'im. That there's a damn good dog, ain't he?"

Jackson let his horse move forward at a slow trot. Owen felt himself reviving slowly, as much from the relief of being found as from the water Jackson had given him.

"Reach in that saddlebag, Cap'n. They's jerky an' a biscuit or two. You must be mighty hungry."

Owen obeyed, and the food quickly strengthened him. He dropped one biscuit down to Whiskey, trotting by the mustang's rear hoof.

"Any sign of Wardworth's boys?" he asked huskily.

"No, sir. Nary hide nor hair."

"Might be a bad sign."

Jackson Dill nodded. "Well, sir, wagon's 'bout a mile on ahead. Rest if you can, Cap'n."

Jones had halted the wagon, letting the mules rest, giving each animal a hatful of water from the kegs. He and Crow greeted Owen with sincere pleasure. It was the first time Owen realized that he had formed a liking for Crow, who had been their enemy and now was accepted as a comrade.

Olaf Jones's broad, honest face was concerned. "Mr. Terrel, where is your fine horse?"

"Went lame. Just let me crawl in the wagon and you can get movin'. Oh, man, I thought Jackson was wearin' wings when he handed me that canteen."

They laughed, and Olaf slapped Terrel's back, nearly bowling him over.

"You sleep gude, Mr. Terrel. We will call you if there is trouble." The Swede also lifted Whiskey into the wagon, and the tired dog curled up with an almost human sigh.

Owen had no difficulty taking Olaf's advice. His exhaustion put him under in minutes, and he did not wake until dawn.

The wagon was stopped. He crawled out, found the men getting a pot of coffee boiling.

Crow glanced around at him with a grin. "You look most nearly alive this mornin'," he remarked.

"Some of that coffee will set me right again."

He poured himself a cup, then helped Jones grain the mules and water them sparingly.

Within minutes they were on the move again, breakfasting on cold corn bread Amelia had left in the wagon for them. As they had planned, two men remained out of sight in the wagon. Owen drove this morning, his Winchester ready at hand. Crow, who had had a bit of rest in the night, rode Dill's horse, while the others slept.

"They should have caught up to us by now," Owen said quietly, and Crow nodded.

"Yes, sir. I been thinkin' the same. Somethin's gone wrong."

Owen's jaw tightened, thinking back over the plan. Will and Juan were to take the women and children to safety, while he and the others decoyed Wardworth and his men into attacking the wagon. Hopefully, the unguarded herd would lure Wilkins and his followers away from the Terrels—if Wilkins had bought Owen's tale about Juan's friends among the border bandits. Comanche Jim would figure that the herd could be taken, but only in the next few days, before Juan Cortina's men took over.

But somewhere, the plan had failed. Otherwise the Wardworth faction would surely have found and hit the wagon by now.

Tension gnawing at his gut, Owen kept the wagon moving west. He was alert, ready for anything. It was the first time he could remember actually wanting trouble to erupt. And he was pretty sure the other men felt the same, for if the wagon went unmolested, it must mean that Wardworth and his men had gotten onto the trail of Will and the family.

They moved through the hot morning. Noon came and went. They paused long enough at the small water hole to fill the kegs and canteens and rest the team, then moved on.

As often happened during the afternoon this time of year, clouds were building. This time they looked as though they meant business. The towering thunderheads built, miles high, rushing to fill the western sky, losing their pearly sheen, turning a bruised purplish color.

"Gonna get some weather," Crow commented.

Just then Jackson Dill poked his head out of the wagon. "Mr. Crow, I'll ride, you rest now. Bring that horse 'roun' to the back." Owen stopped the wagon to allow them to make the exchange.

Jones had awakened too, and he was rummaging for cold food for them all. But he did not leave the wagon. If someone watched from a distance, likely he would not spot the fact that there were more men, and no women, inside the vehicle.

The wagon rolled on. Owen worried over the fact that they would have to rest the team tonight and allow the mules to graze. He felt driven to get to Will and Ginny and the others. If their one saddle horse had been rested enough to take the strain, he would have been tempted to ride ahead at full speed. He was nearly certain now that his plan had not only failed, but had perhaps put the others in greater danger. A sick dread lay at the pit of his stomach.

He scanned once again the area ahead of them and to either side. His warning cry alerted Dill and the men in the wagon.

"Riders comin'! Get ready." He peered ahead, counting six riders.

"Captain, two of 'em are women," Crow shouted.

But Terrel already realized that Ginny and Julia were on the lead horses, their mounts being flogged ahead by the men who rode behind. Those men wanted those at the wagon to know at once that Ginny and Julia Talbot were captives. And if the gang had taken these two women alive, had they left the others dead? Fears for Will and Amelia, for the children, made an intolerable ache in his throat.

Owen spoke urgently over his shoulder. "Crow, you and Olaf drop out the back, go to ground by the trail. I'm gonna bring 'em back to you. Don't let yourself be seen."

Dill was riding alongside, his face worried and questioning. "Cap'n we dassn't shoot—might hit Miss Ginny or Miss Julia. Or else them bushwhackers will kill 'em. My God, you reckon you done gunned down Mr. Will and Miz Melia an' them babies?"

Owen interrupted. "No time for that, Dill! Listen to me. Cut outta here, like you're tryin' to get away."

Dill's black skin looked grayish, and his mouth went grim. "Cap'n, what kinda man you think I am!"

"Jackson!" Owen's voice carried the ring of command. "Pretend you're makin' a run for it. It might draw a man or two your way. Then circle back and see if you can get the women out of the line of fire."

Comprehension dawned in Dill's honest face. "Yes, sir," he snapped, and gigged his horse into a run even as he made the sturdy mustang whirl to the south. He bent low over his saddle, knowing there would be a hail of rifle fire following him and his game, agile cowpony. Owen was glad to see one of the outlaws leave the bunch and whip his horse to try to cut off Dill. If he caught up to Jackson, who was nearly as good a shot with a running target as Will, he would be wishing he hadn't made the effort. And that lessened the threat to the women by one man.

A moment later, Owen caught the boom of Dill's rifle, repeated once, and the gunfire from that direction ceased. He grinned. Good for you, Jackson, he mentally saluted his old friend.

Owen was whipping his mules into a run, straight toward the approaching outlaws and their hostages. At the last moment he pulled the team around in a perilously tight circle and raced back the way he'd come. Bullets sang viciously past. Owen looked back through the open canvas flaps, his heart twisting as he saw that Ginny and Julia were still being driven ahead of the outlaws. Julia was bouncing painfully in her saddle, clinging desperately to the saddle horn, the reins flying free. She had never been a good rider. They must have tied her feet to the stirrups, or she would have fallen off long ago.

He caught a glimpse of Ginny. She was in control of her horse, even though someone was lashing the roan savagely from behind, forcing him to a reckless run. Owen was amazed to see her reach out and snatch Julia's rein. Ginny risked her life as she reined hard aside, dragging Julia's mount with hers. In that one daring move she removed herself and Julia as hostages and shields for the oncoming outlaws.

But not without cost. One of the gang leveled a pistol and fired directly at the women. Ginny's horse went down. Owen heard her cry out, then roiling dust concealed the scene.

Owen's mules dragged the swaying, jolting wagon almost precisely along the tracks he'd left minutes before. Olaf and Crow had burrowed down behind shinnery and slabs of stone so well that even Owen could not spot them. But he knew when the wagon wheels spun past their position, for there was suddenly a new batch of rifle fire behind him. He jerked the mules to a halt, leapt from the wagon, rifle in hand. He targeted a running horseman and hesitated infinitesimally as he recognized Georgie, handgun pouring lead at Olaf and Crow. Then Owen's finger tightened and Georgie fell. His horse dashed aside, almost ramming another rider. Owen saw that it was Caleb Wardworth. He snapped a shot, missed.

The next shot burned the rump of Wardworth's horse as Wardworth whirled the black gelding and spurred away, bent low over his saddle.

But there were two other men pounding up. No, only one. Olaf Jones had reached out with a huge hand and jerked one of the riders out of his saddle, shot him point-blank with his handgun. The other man tried to follow Wardworth. Crow nailed him even as he attempted to turn his excited horse. The gunman was flung out of the saddle, but his foot hung in the stirrup. The terrified mustang raced away, dragging and kicking at his burden.

Owen spared him no more than a glance. He was already running, limping on feet that were still swollen and sore from his long walk across the desert, willing himself to get quickly to the spot seventy-five yards away where Virginia's horse had gone down.

Julia was still mounted, bent over to snatch futilely for the dragging rein. Fortunately her horse was too weary to run, for the blond girl was screaming, a monotonous, repeated squeal that seemed to be as much from anger as fear. Owen ignored her as he ran past, looking for Ginny. Her horse was up, standing with head drooping low. Jackson Dill was galloping back, and he slid his horse to a stop just as Owen reached the scene.

"See can you shut her up." Owen jerked a thumb toward Julia.

His own attention was only for Virginia, who lay crumpled in the dirt, face hidden in a swirl of dark, silky hair. Owen's heart pounded painfully as he saw the red, spreading stain upon the side and back of her dress bodice.

"Oh, damn it," he whispered, touching her gently, trying to see how badly she was hurt. The bullet wound was in her right side. There was a lot of blood. Carefully he ran his fingers over her neck and spine. He'd seen broken necks, shattered backs when mounts wounded in battle went down upon their riders. If Ginny's horse had rolled upon her . . . He heard the wagon wheels, the hoofbeats of the mule team.

Crow leapt down and came running with a canteen and a blanket. "My God, Terrel! How bad hurt is she?" There was genuine grief in his words. For the first time Owen saw what should have been obvious to him for many days. Crow was in love with the girl who had shown him kindness.

"I'm tryin' to see," Owen said. "No bones broken that I can tell. Help me ease her over. Careful now."

Dill had managed to quiet Julia. Releasing her roped feet from the stirrups, he helped her down, led her away, and let her sit down. No one was surprised that she did not offer to help with Ginny.

When Ginny was lying upon her back, head propped upon Owen's rolled-up leather vest, they attempted to assess the severity of the bullet wound.

"I wish Amelia was here," Owen groaned. "I've got to get this damned dress off that wound."

Crow drew a razor-sharp bowie knife from a neck sheath. Astonished, Owen took it. "How did you manage to keep this?" He began to cut the cloth away from Ginny's side. "We thought we'd pulled all your teeth."

Crow shrugged. "Man feels lonesome 'thout a weapon. I made shift to hide this in my boot afore you fellers caught me first time. Now don't you cut no more of her dress than you have to," he instructed Owen severely. "She wouldn't like us men undressin' her."

Owen obeyed, wishing his damned hands wouldn't shake. "Find me somethin' to stop this bleeding."

Crow moved immediately to rummage in the wagon, was back by the time Owen had the calico cloth sliced away from Ginny's wounded side, together with the fabric of her chemise. He flung aside the blood-soaked rags, took the whiskey Crow handed him and poured it generously over the place where the pistol slug had exited, and pressed pads of soft, absorbent flannel onto the wound.

"You ain't bad at that," Crow said.

Owen sighed. "Did plenty of it during the war. The bullet went through. If it didn't hit something vital, we may get lucky. When we find Amelia, maybe she can tell better." *If* we find Amelia, his mind agonized.

Jones came quietly near. "How may I help you, Mr. Terrel?"

"Could you an' Crow lift Ginny up while I wrap these bandages around her waist?"

Olaf's huge hands slid very gently under Ginny's back and legs, lifting her carefully. From the other side Crow assisted Owen to bind the makeshift bandage. Then Owen made a place for Virginia in the wagon, and they lifted her inside. Owen tilted her head and touched her parched, colorless lips with water, let a very little seep into her mouth. Still she did not waken.

"Poor little miss," Olaf worried as he and Crow watched from the tailgate. "Maybe she has hit her head?"

With a new sense of dread, and ashamed that he had not yet thought to check, Owen moved his fingers tenderly upon the back of Ginny's head, feeling for a wound under the luxuriant, rich fall of hair. But he found only the slightest bump above her ear.

"Nothin' here that seems bad." He bent and placed his ear upon her chest. "Heart seems steady and she's breathin' okay. God, I wish she'd wake up."

"Terrel, you might try a drop o' whiskey," Crow suggested. "Be careful you don't choke her, though," he warned fiercely.

Owen poured a teaspoon of whiskey into a cup and lifted her shoulders and head once more. As he let the liquor go drop by drop across her tongue, he felt her shudder. She coughed—Crow let out a new cry of anxiety and warning.

Owen set the cup aside. "Ginny, can you hear me? Wake up now!"

Her lips parted and she let out a small, sighing breath.

17

Her eyelids moved, struggled to lift. Her eyes looked unfocused. After a few moments, she drew a sharp breath and cried out weakly, "Run, Julia!"

"It's all right, honey. Julia's fine."

She blinked dazedly and turned her head. "Owen? What—"

"You were hurt," Owen said shakily. "You'll be all right. Lie still now, and drink a little of this water." He held the canteen to her lips. She sipped and swallowed weakly.

"Owen, they—they made us ride—"

"Honey, we know."

"They took her money." Virginia sighed, the sound of a tired child.

"It don't matter," Owen said.

"Captain, we oughtta get out of here purty soon," Crow said. "Wardworth got away. He might bring the rest of the gang down on us in a few hours."

Owen nodded. "Right. See if you can catch any of the horses those men were riding. Olaf, would you drive? Best put Julia in here, I reckon. But if she disturbs Ginny—"

"Then I will make the lady walk." Jones grinned sunnily, his broad, sunburned face creasing from cheek to chin.

Owen leaned Virginia back on the blankets, but before he left the wagon, there was something he must ask.

"Ginny, where's the family?"

He saw her delicate jaw tighten and his heart sank. Her dark eyes filled. "I—I think Amelia and the children are safe. Those men came out of nowhere. They shot Juan right away. A-After Juan went down, Will yelled at Amelia to keep going. He and I stopped and got down to try to stop those devils, but it was no use. They hit

159

Will before he could shoot more than once." Her voice broke, tears slid down her dust-grimed face.

"Is he dead?" Owen's words came out short and brusque, because he dreaded her reply.

She nodded, sobbing tiredly. "He was . . . There was blood all over his head . . . Oh, Owen!" She gasped, and her face was blue-white. He knew she must be in pain.

"Ginny, steady now!" He caught her shoulders in both hands.

She gulped, swallowed. He could see the effort she made to control her sorrow and fear. After a moment she continued her story. "Julia couldn't keep up with Amelia. After they grabbed me, they caught her. Amelia . . ." She had to pause a moment, swallowing. "She was far ahead, holding Melissa, and Willy was running his pony alongside. The men left off chasing them after a few minutes. They had Julia, and the money—"

"Okay," Owen soothed. "Okay, sweetheart. You rest now. We're goin' to find Amelia and the kids. And"— he controlled his voice with an effort—"and Will."

Her eyelids closed, the tears sliding down her cheeks. Owen watched her for a moment, wishing only to stay with her, listen anxiously for every new breath she took. Had she lost too much blood? Was she strong enough to withstand her wound and the stress her body had absorbed in the past weeks?

But he could not stay. There was too much to do.

As he climbed from the wagon, Olaf Jones approached, assisting Julia, who leaned weakly against him. She was talking to the big, blond man eagerly, her hands fluttering. But when she caught sight of Owen, she straightened and moved away from Jones, to Terrel.

"I'm glad you killed them," she burst out, clutching at his hand with both hers. "I wish you had tortured those brutes to death. Owen, they took my money. We have to find it. Caleb had it on his saddle. We have to find his horse—"

Owen pulled his hand free. "Wardworth got away. Get in the wagon, Julia. We're goin' to find Will and Amelia and the kids."

"Wait!" She grabbed at Owen's shirt frantically.

"What are you going to do about my money, Owen? We have to find it. Oh, what will I do? Won't anyone listen to me?"

Her voice was rising hysterically. Terrel saw that she could not be allowed to ride with Virginia, in this state. She would inflict her uncontrolled emotions upon the wounded girl without a thought of anything but her own loss.

"Olaf, best put her on a horse," he said. "Ask Crow to keep an eye on her."

Jackson galloped up, leading a buckskin horse that had been ridden by one of the dead outlaws. "You gonna ride ahead, Cap'n?"

"I have to see if I can find my brother. Ginny saw him shot down."

"Oh, not Mr. Will," Dill burst out. "Let me go with you."

"Thanks, Jackson. You and the others guard Miss Ginny and follow as fast as you can."

Jackson nodded emphatically. "Yes, sir. Don't you worry, we'll watch after her, Cap'n."

Owen reined the buckskin over to the wagon, took a short-handled spade, which he quickly tied behind the saddle. He spared one moment to bend and look inside at Ginny. She had fallen asleep. Owen wheeled the horse and galloped to the west, along the tracks left by the outlaws.

It made his stomach clench painfully to leave Ginny behind. But he owed Will and Amelia too much to hesitate. If all he could do for his brother was to see him decently buried, then he would do that last favor.

He pushed his horse hard, hoping to find Will before nightfall. At least the tracks were plain. He should have no difficulty locating the spot where Will had fallen.

The miles moved past too slowly. The clouds were thick overhead now and the breeze picking up sharply. Owen glanced at the threatening sky, hoping the storm would pass south of them. When he reached the next water hole, he paused to water the horse and allow him a few minutes' rest. It was beginning to rain. Owen mounted again and moved at a gallop along the trail. A rush of oddly cool wind, carrying dust and sand mixed in with the fat drops of rain, swirled about him and his mount. Abruptly the sprinkle became a downpour. Owen cursed under his breath. This would soon wash out the tracks. He pushed ahead as hard as he dared.

He estimated that the Terrel party must have reached an area roughly ten miles farther before the gang had attacked them. Water was standing in every low spot now. The trail was lost. Owen could only pray that he was not veering from the direction Will and the others had taken. The heavy clouds smothered the sunset, and darkness fell early, complicating his search. He rode more slowly, clinging stubbornly to hope of finding Will, knowing it was nearly impossible now.

Owen's horse broke stride suddenly, with a shrill nicker. Owen heard another horse answer, and spurred forward. Now he could dimly make out their outlines, standing head up, watching his approach. The buckskin he rode shied suddenly away from a dim shape in the mud. Owen recognized the wide *sombrero* at one side. It was Juan's body, facedown.

"Vaya con Dios, amigo," Owen murmured, remembering the loyal, hardworking man who had done so much for the Terrel family since leaving the Santa Gertrudis Ranch in Texas.

"Stop, whoever you are," someone shouted shrilly, and a shot whined over Owen's head.

"Amelia?" he yelled.

"Owen? Is that you? Oh, dear God, Owen!"

He hurried to reach her, dismounting quickly.

Amelia dropped Will's rifle and ran to him. She was soaking wet, shivering, her dripping hair tangled about her face. "Oh, thank God you've come! Will's hurt bad."

Owen grabbed her shoulders. "He's alive?" Beyond her, he saw a blanket-covered form. Releasing her, he ran to his brother.

"Will, it's me!" He sank to one knee, touching the colorless, still face. Amelia had managed to rig a partial shelter with a blanket draped over a shinnery bush to shield her husband's face from the worst of the rain. A bloody bandage circled Will's head. He was breathing shallowly.

"He hasn't wakened," Amelia said, her voice reedy with fear.

"Amelia," Owen asked quietly. "Where are the children?"

She blinked, seemed confused. Owen realized that she was near collapse. "They . . . I put them there, near the horses."

Owen turned, saw the two little forms, huddling together in a blanket. He frowned with concern. "We got to make a fire, get some food together for the children."

"It's so—wet—"

Owen left his brother and reached back under a thickly leafed shinnery for leaves and twigs dry enough to ignite. "Amelia, you got any paper?"

She thought, then went to her saddlebag and with shaking hands brought out her Bible, offering it to Owen.

"No," he said gently. "We won't use that. I think I might . . ." He rummaged in his wallet, found the bill of sale Richard King had given them. In a few minutes he had a good fire going. "Willy, bring your sister over here," he said. "Make some coffee, Amelia, and find some food for us."

Owen's brisk instruction seemed to steady his sister-in-law. She hurried to do as Owen had directed, finding the things she needed in her saddlebags. Owen uncovered Will and checked to see if there were other injuries. Mercifully, there were no other bullet wounds, no broken bones.

When Amelia had the coffeepot on the fire, she sliced bacon into a pan, then she came to bend yearningly over her husband.

"How bad is his head?" Owen asked, voice tense. If Will had a bullet in his brain, it would only be a matter of time until they lost him.

"There's a gash in his skull. It bled real bad, Owen. And he doesn't wake up. Owen, I'm so scared!"

He gripped her work-roughened hand for a moment. "You think the bullet only creased him?"

"Yes." She was positive about this. "I felt along it, real careful. But he laid here for an hour or more before we could get back. He'd told us to run—get the children safe—'' She was overcome for a moment and had to bury her face in her hands.

''But you came back,'' Owen said, and he felt a deep affection for this strong, loyal woman.

''I couldn't leave him. I couldn't just . . . I waited until I was sure they weren't followin' us, then I turned back.'' Her tearful eyes clung to his. ''They took Ginny, and Julia, too. And they killed poor Juan.''

''I know, Amelia. Now, stop frettin'. Julia's safe. Ginny was hurt. I think she'll be all right.''

''You got the girls away from those vicious men? Thank God for that. But they may come back, Owen.''

''Most of them won't be going anywhere, ever again,'' he assured her. ''You have any whiskey in your saddlebags?''

Her fingers knit together, whitening. ''No, I left it in the wagon. Oh, why didn't I think to—''

''Never mind. Likely it's best to just let Will rest, anyway. I'll moisten his mouth with water.'' To his surprise, Will's mouth opened at the touch of the canteen, and he swallowed the cautiously administered drops of water.

Amelia let out a cry of hope. ''Owen, that's a good sign!''

''I believe you're right.'' He examined the bandage, eased Will's head down. ''The bleeding's stopped too. Let's get those children fed. Damn this rain. Wish we had the wagon here.''

They gave each of the children a thick slice of bacon and a slab of corn bread. Owen poured coffee for Amelia, made her sit and drink it and eat. She seemed steadier and less white when she had finished. He was grateful himself for the hot, black brew and the strengthening food. They were in for a rough night. Fortunately, the rain was stopping.

As Amelia tended her tired children, Owen was thinking, hard. For safety's sake, they should put out the fire. But they badly needed the warmth. And he was virtually sure Crow and Olaf would keep the wagon moving into the night, trying to reach them. They would need a beacon.

After the children were fed and put to sleep in damp

bedding near the fire, Owen insisted that Amelia rest. "I'll keep watch, and wake you to take over later."

But he did not wake her until the creaking of wagon wheels and the eager greeting of the frisking dog, running ahead, gave him the glad news that their group was about to be reunited.

Amelia drowsily built up the fire and started fresh coffee as Owen went to help the tired men with the mules.

"How's Ginny?" he asked quickly.

"She's sleepin'," Crow said. "I think she's doin' fine."

Owen breathed a deep sigh of relief. "I want to see her."

"I'll git a lantern. Julia's in the wagon too. She finally got tired enough to shut up."

Owen had completely forgotten Julia, but her presence would not deter him from spending a moment with the girl he loved. He took the lantern, climbed onto the wagon seat, and leaned into the wagon, letting the light fall upon Ginny's face. He touched her cheek. She was warm, but not fevered, as far as he could tell, and her breathing was quiet, natural. Relieved, Owen withdrew. He climbed down, went to check Will. Amelia was with him.

"He spoke to me," she said tearfully.

"Amelia, he's gonna live," Owen said.

The rest of the night passed quietly. Dill took the watch and Owen slept exhaustedly, waking to the blissful comfort of hot sunlight making the ground steam, taking the damp chill from the air. Coffee was boiling on the fire and Amelia was stirring flapjack batter. Julia was sullenly dishing cornmeal mush for the children, who seemed little the worse for the soaking they'd had yesterday.

Owen went at once to look at Virginia. It was a joy to find her awake. Her quick smile was enough to tighten Owen's throat painfully.

"Good morning," she murmured.

"How do you feel?"

"I've been better," she said honestly. "But I've been up and around, with Amelia's help, this morning. And I'd have stayed up if she'd let me."

"No, you've got to rest, build back your strength. We'll be movin' again soon as you and Will can travel."

Her eyes brightened. "Owen, it's wonderful about Will! I'm so thankful that Amelia found him alive. Do you think he'll . . ." She hesitated.

"I think he's tough an' stubborn an' he'll be up orderin' all of us around before we know it," Owen said, and he prayed that he was right.

Ginny's wide dark eyes were warm on his face, as tender as a caress. "That's just what I'm hoping for. I love your family, every one of them. Amelia's been like a sister to me."

He grinned. "I'm mighty relieved you're so fond of my family. Do you think you could find some little leftover corner in your heart for me?"

Her lips turned up and her eyes were glowing. She touched his bearded cheek gently. "The best part of my heart will always belong to you, Owen Terrel."

He bent to kiss her, but they were interrupted by Amelia as she twitched aside the wagon flap. "Owen, you get out here an' eat before ever'thing gets cold," she scolded.

Ginny laughed weakly as Owen scrambled to obey.

But first he went to Will's bedroll. The sick man's eyes were closed. Owen peered at him worriedly.

Amelia came with a dampened cloth and began to bathe her husband's face. "Will, open your eyes before your little brother starts blubberin'," she commanded briskly.

Will blinked, focused on Owen. "Why, if that ain't the dirtiest face I ever—laid eyes—on," he murmured.

"Will, how you doin'?" Owen asked.

"You just—spit over that—line an' we'll—rastle." Will grinned crookedly.

"God, you like to scared me to death." Owen clasped Will's hand, hard.

"Thought you seen a ghost, huh? Amelia said you was totin' a shovel when you rode up."

Owen had to restrain a shudder. "I was told you'd had your head blown off, big brother. Figured to save your worthless carcass from the coyotes."

Will nodded soberly. "Cain't quarrel with that."

Owen grasped his brother's shoulder. "You try to rest

some more. Soon as you feel strong enough, we'll give you a nice easy wagon ride down to the Pecos.''

Will smiled, closed his eyes. Owen moved to the fire and accepted the plate and tin cup Julia handed him.

"Owen"—she bent near to whisper—"when will you go after Caleb Wardworth? I must have my money back.''

Owen was suddenly sick of her preoccupation with her lost money. "Julia, look around you and see what you and your precious money have caused. My brother and Virginia bad hurt, several men dead, little children bein' menaced. You're lucky Caleb Wardworth hasn't shot you down or dragged you away to God knows what fate. I advise you to forget the damned money, or else find some other fool to go after it. I ain't about to risk one more life for it, not my own, not anybody's!''

He turned sharply away from her and moved out to where Olaf was tending the mules and horses. He ate as he walked. There was much to do and he knew he had hard decisions to make.

Crow rode up at a trot. Owen paused to wait for him.

"I looked for new sign. Ain't nobody been near us. Only tracks nearby are ours. I guess Wardworth's figurin' to help Wilkins with the herd, get his cut from that, though I'd have thought he'd take the money an' go enjoy it.''

Owen shook his head. "Whatever else he does, he'll be back for Julia sooner or later. He can't afford to let her live to go back to Texas an' spread the word about him. There's still enough honest men there to hunt him down like the coyote he is.''

Crow's grin flickered. "Reckon they'll hunt me down too, if I go back.''

Owen gave him a straight look. "It don't have to be that way, Crow. You've earned the gratitude of this family, an' we stick with our friends. We'll give you a start of cows. The land is here for the takin'. A man can get a fresh start, if he wants to work for it. You could send for your family.''

Crow seemed overcome. He dropped his head, seemed to study the saddle horn. After a minute he took a deep breath, met Owen's gaze again. "You don't know me,

Mr. Terrel. I done things—well, that I ain't too proud of. An' I don't rightly know if I can change.''

Owen shrugged. ''Seems to me you already have.''

Crow's shoulders straightened. ''Yes, sir. I'd be a fool not to accept your offer. I—I'm much obliged.''

Owen grinned. ''Good. But first we got to get the herd back. You can bet your last dollar that those cows are gettin' used to new owners about now. That's why I'm goin' back, as soon as I'm sure Ginny and Will are all right. I'm goin' to save our herd.''

Abruptly Crow leaned and thrust out his hand. ''I'm goin' with you, Terrel. You can count on me. I know my word ain't worth a buffalo chip, an' I cain't remember when any man trusted me, until you an' your brother did. But I swear I won't let you down.''

Owen shook the man's hand. ''Let's see what Jones has to say. Where's Jackson?''

''He took the last watch, rolled into his blankets at daybreak. I reckon that's the first decent sleep he's had in days.''

''Let him sleep. We'll bring him in on it later.''

Owen hailed Olaf, who left the mules and joined them. The three of them discussed the situation at length, then Owen gave instructions to the other two and moved back to the camp.

Amelia was just leaving the wagon as Owen approached. She put a finger to her lips. ''She's asleep. Best let her rest.''

He nodded and followed her back to the fire. ''Amelia, we can't stay here,'' he said bluntly.

She sighed, glanced at him as she cleaned pots and pans. As usual, Julia had vanished as soon as the camp work began. Owen bent to help Amelia, scraping the last of the cornmeal mush and a couple of leftover flapjacks out for Whiskey.

''I know,'' Amelia said. ''Those men could come back anytime.''

''I doubt it, but we can't be sure. What really concerns me—Will and Ginny ought to see a doctor as quick as possible.''

She nodded. ''How far are we from help?''

''I calculate about two–three days to reach the Caprock, travelin' slow, not to jolt your patients too much. It ain't too far from there to South Springs Ranch. Mr. Chisum will send for a doctor. I want you to get everything packed and ready to go."

Her intelligent eyes lifted to his, startled. "You aren't comin' with us, are you?"

He laid a big hand on hers. "Now, don't worry. Olaf and Jackson will be with you."

"And where are you and Crow going?"

Owen smiled. "Will always said you had a mind that went right to the point. Says it keeps him hoppin' to stay ahead of you."

She smiled, and it lightened her tired, worried face. "Who says he stays ahead of me? Now you quit joshin' me, Owen Terrel, an' give me the bad news. What fool thing are you up to now?"

"Gettin' our cows back."

"Owen, no! If anything happened to you . . . Oh believe me, Will wouldn't want you to try it. Let the cattle go! We'll manage somehow."

"Now, Amelia, you heard Will say I was in charge, didn't you? This is my decision, an' I won't be askin' Will's permission."

She threw up her hands. "Oh, you Terrels are all alike! I declare, I might as well save my breath. All right, Owen. You do what you think you have to. I promise you I'll take good care of your girl and see her safe if I can."

"I know you will."

"When do we leave?"

"Do you think Will and Ginny are well enough to move on tonight?"

Reluctantly she nodded.

"Good. Soon as it's dark, Crow and I will go bury Juan, then ride out. We might give those rustlers a little surprise. One thing, though. I don't want Will to know we're makin' this try. Don't tell him until you have to. He'll just fret and stew, an' it ain't good for him."

Amelia nodded, but the eyes she lifted to his were wet. "All right. But you promise to come back to us, Owen Terrel. You hear?"

Owen grinned. "Yes, ma'am, I hear you fine."

18

Virginia slept most of the day. At dusk, Owen carried her from the wagon to a little area Amelia had arranged for privacy. He left her there with Amelia. When the two women returned, Ginny was walking slowly, leaning upon Amelia's arm. Her face had been washed, her hair freshly brushed. She sat down upon a bedroll near the fire, breathing hard but obviously proud of her feat.

Owen brought her a plate of food. Little Melissa cuddled up to her gladly, and the dog lay at her feet, staring up with adoring eyes.

She laughed weakly. "I never had so much attention before."

"I got somethin' for you, Miss Virginia," Crow spoke up. He had been whittling most of the afternoon on a bit of mesquite wood, and now he presented Ginny with a little figure of a bird. She looked up at Crow, her smile so delighted that Owen had to squash a foolish twinge of jealousy.

"Why, Mr. Crow," she said, "that's so thoughtful of you! It's a mockingbird, isn't it? How did you color it?"

"I used a little twig an' some soot and grease." Crow beamed as Ginny cradled the figure in her hands.

"Well, it's just pretty as can be," she said. "Look, Owen, it's exactly like a mockingbird, isn't it?"

"Real nice," Owen was forced to admit, surprised at the outlaw's skill. "Say, you think you could carve a longhorn steer for me, Crow?"

"Why, I'd be glad to try, Captain."

"Thank you, Mr. Crow," Ginny said, and with natural friendliness extended her hand to him. She pressed his rough fingers. "I'll treasure this. We're all glad to have you with us, Mr. Crow, and grateful for your help."

"You can count on me, Miss Virginia," Crow said.

He looked around at the rest of them. "You can all count on me. I'm givin' my word."

Amelia brought Crow his plate. "Ginny's right," she said firmly. "We're grateful to you, more'n we can say."

He seemed overcome at these kind words. Quickly, mumbling thanks, he took his plate into the shadows and sat down to eat. Owen received his plate from Amelia and hunkered down near Ginny, watchful of her, in case she tired.

She ate sparingly, but seemed much stronger. When she had finished, he helped her back to her bed in the wagon. He bent to kiss her. Her hand rested upon the back of his neck. As he drew away, he caught her fingers.

"Got something to tell you. I know you'll take it right."

"You're leaving us, aren't you?" she said quietly.

"Now how did you guess that? Did Melia tell you?"

She shook her head. "I've been thinking. You wouldn't let those killers have your cattle, even"—she paused, then went on with obvious difficulty—"even if you have to risk your life."

He struggled to put his conviction into words. "I'd never feel like much of a man if I ran away from that bunch of no-goods."

"I don't think it would be running."

He was silent for a long moment, holding her fingers against his cheek. "Do you understand that I have to decide that?"

She sighed. "Yes. But I don't know what I would do if—"

He interrupted her, firmly. "You don't need to think about that, Ginny. Before you know it, Crow and I will have the herd safe, and then I'll come for you. Jackson and Olaf Jones are takin' all of you back to the Pecos Valley. They'll find a doctor for you. When I get back there, will you be my wife?"

She drew her breath in and her voice was hiding tears. "Yes, Owen Terrel. I'll be counting the days, and my prayers will go with you."

Owen kissed her once more and left her to rest.

Amelia was helping Will eat. His appetite was better tonight, but his head pained him a good deal. When he had finished, Owen and Jones helped him to the wagon, where a place had been prepared for him to lie down.

"We're gonna get you and Ginny back to the Pecos Valley," Owen told him, omitting to say that he would not be going along.

Will seemed to accept this as sensible. He slid into sleep almost before Owen left him.

As soon as it was dark, Jones put the mules to the wagon while Owen and Jackson saddled all the horses. Amelia lifted the children onto the wagon seat to a silent, sulking Julia and then climbed up herself.

She gathered up the lines and turned to her brother-in-law. "You know, Owen, when we started this journey, I was scared the Comanches might get us. Funny, only Indians we saw were hangin' around the forts, an' it's white men we've had to fear."

"Reckon there's bad men in all races. Good ones too."

"I won't ever forget that again." She clucked to the mules and the wagon moved out, creaking softly in the darkness. On horseback, Jackson Dill took the lead and Olaf Jones rode watchfully behind. Owen had tied the dog inside the wagon, feeling he'd be a comfort to Ginny on the long, uncomfortable trip.

Terrel and Crow turned their horses the opposite direction, letting them move out fast in the clear, warm night.

They found Juan's body without difficulty and buried him with silent respect. When the grave was filled, Owen removed his hat and spoke solemnly.

"This man was a friend and a loyal and brave comrade. May he rest in peace, with God."

The two men mounted in silence and left the lonely grave.

They rode without talk, keeping the horses at a steady trot, pausing every few hours to rest them. The horses were not in the best shape. Owen was hoping to remedy that situation by dawn, but he could not afford to take chances. He'd had enough of being on foot in the plains.

By sunup they were about a half-mile from the alkali lake where they had camped the night of the stampede. Owen signaled a halt, got down to loosen his cinch and let his mount grab a few mouthfuls of grass. "We're in luck. That's most of our *remuda* grazin' by the lake."

"Look at 'em." Crow grinned. "Fat, slick, an' fresh! I was scared they'd done taken up with a wild bunch by now. I'll go for the black on this side. Which one you want?"

"Give me a little time to circle around to the other side. We'll use the lake as a barrier. They won't cross it unless they're forced. I'll try to rope the big dun. When I wave, you come arunnin'."

Crow nodded. Owen urged his tired sorrel to a trot, circling to the far side of the lake. If the horses grazing there had been wild mustangs, they would have taken alarm and lit out already. These ranch horses would not take fright at sight or scent of a rider, though they would not be easy to catch once they began to run. Owen hoped to get close before they spooked. His weary mount would not be able to run fast or far.

He glanced around to see Crow moving his horse quietly into position. When Owen judged they were as close as possible without disturbing the *remuda*, he waved to Crow. The two of them spurred their horses into a run, straight toward the lake.

There were nine stock horses grazing in a loose group. Among them, Owen was glad to see, was Will's good stallion. Later on, if all went well, he'd be back to get him and the mares they'd brought from the Santa Gertrudis. But for now, it was a tough, canny cowpony he needed. He readied his loop and charged directly at a black-maned zebra-dun.

The dun flung up his head. His tail streamed out like a silky black banner as he burst into a run away from Owen's mount and toward the lake edge. But the dun was clever and he was already dodging away from the lake, racing along the edge of the acrid water.

Owen had made an educated guess as to the dun's probable move: would he wheel left or right? The stallion and his mares were running east. The dun would likely try to join them. It was a good guess. Owen's mount had already cut down half the distance by veering right. He spurred his horse to a minute of killing speed, then let the loop fly. It settled securely about the dun's neck.

With a whoop of pleasure, Owen reined in gradually, not to injure either of the horses as the dun hit the end of the lariat. As they stopped, the dun whirled to face Owen and stood, ears irritably laid back, but accepting the rope's authority.

In minutes Owen had the excited, snorting dun saddled and had turned loose his long-suffering sorrel. The tired horse rolled in the grass to ease the sweaty itch of his hide, then stood and trotted to the spring at the head of the lake.

Owen turned to see if Crow had succeeded in catching his mount. He had apparently missed the black he'd wanted, but was saddling a roan, one of the King mares, bred in Mexico. She had size and plenty of reach. Owen nodded in unconscious approval. The roan mare would do.

When the two men were mounted, they wasted no time moving southeast, hoping to cut sign of the Terrel herd. They rode watchfully, rifles ready. But all they saw for hours were a herd of fleeing antelope and, in the distance, a half-dozen buffalo, a somewhat rare sight.

Owen felt a twinge of regret, seeing those remnants of the huge herds that once had roamed these plains. Slaughtered for their hides, they were fewer and fewer in number as the years passed. The decimation of the buffalo herds had been a major factor in the struggle to control the Indians on this frontier. No settler could regret that result; tales of Comanche and Apache savagery abounded in west Texas and in New Mexico Territory, where the red men had tried by the only means they knew to hold back the tide of settlement from their hunting grounds.

Nevertheless, a man had to be sorry that the buffalo would soon be mostly a memory.

By midafternoon Terrel and Crow found the unmistakable trail of the Terrel cattle, being pushed south and west, by riders on shod horses, just as Owen had figured. The men paused to allow their horses and themselves a mouthful of water from their canteens. The day was bright and hot, but the usual summer banks of thunderheads had once again formed. The mountains far to the west would doubtless have rain this day. Whether the storms would reach the Llano was a question.

"They'll be plannin' to water these cows at the Pecos

'bout nightfall tomorrow,'' Crow guessed. ''Hell, if we had cut south from where we left Will and the others, we'd had 'em by now. They'll push on across the border about here—'' He bent to draw upon the dry soil, pushing aside a flat rock and disturbing a six-inch centipede. He paused to crush the ugly insect under his boot heel.

''They'll be pushing hard,'' Owen agreed. ''Maybe they believed my little story about Juan Cortina.''

''What story?'' Crow looked around, startled. Owen explained about his visit to the Wardworth-Wilkins camp. To his surprise, Crow let out a hoarse bark of laughter.

''What's so funny?''

Crow shook his head. ''Well, sir, if you'd bothered to ask, I could have told you Comanche Jim is well acquainted with Cortina. Still, he couldn't know you were spinnin' him a tall tale, an' he wouldn't much like to cross that ol' bandit. I believe he is steerin' this here herd away from Cortina's favorite river crossin'.''

''At least it split the gang. If Wilkins' men had been with Wardworth's boys when they attacked Will and the family, they wouldn't have left anyone alive. But damn it, why didn't they hit us and the wagon, instead?''

''I would guess that that young rascal Georgie figured you wouldn't put the women and children in that wagon. He likely guessed you'd try to decoy Wardworth. And it wouldn't be hard to figger that you'd send 'em west, to the Pecos. Closer to help, thataway.''

Owen gave him a glance of surprised respect. ''Crow, I should have thought of that.''

Crow screwed up his leathery, bearded face thoughtfully. ''Now, then, Wilkins' main plan will be to get this beef over the Rio Grande as fast as he can. We'll be lucky to catch 'em this side of the border. They got a jump on us, for sure.''

''I expect you're right,'' Owen agreed. ''Far as it goes, anyhow. But they won't be expectin' us. We'll grab a couple hours' sleep and push on through the night. Those cows will be tired by tomorrow night, and hungry, slowing down, tryin' to graze after they drink.''

''And we got fresher horses than they have,'' Crow said.

Owen grinned. ''One more thing. We got the benefit

of your experience at runnin' herds across the Rio Grande. Why, Mr. Crow, you get more valuable ever' day!''

Crow laughed. "Remember that when it's time to cut me out some prime mother cows an' help me set up as a rancher. I'm expectin' you to help me get a well dug and make a soddy before winter. I hear you are mighty fine at diggin', Captain.''

"Lordy, what have I got myself into? All right. You help me get that herd back an' put Comanche Jim's polecats to flight, I'll help you get your homestead goin'. I'll even throw in a couple of good cowponies.''

Crow grinned widely. "You know, I believe I like bein' a honest man. What you reckon my cattle is worth, right now?''

"Not a plugged nickel, until we get 'em back. But we ain't gonna do it by killin' these horses. Let's make camp.''

Both men were glad of a rest, though they might have enjoyed a heartier meal than the jerky they chewed, washed down with a minimum amount of water. Owen eyed the scudding clouds. No rain tonight, he guessed.

They took the chance of doing without a watch and slept hard for two hours. Then, in the darkness, they saddled their horses and moved out once more, resting briefly at dawn.

By midafternoon of the following day thunder was muttering low in the distance and the heat was intensified by the muggy feel of the day. The men had reached the Caprock. They made their way down a steep and treacherous game trail to the bottom of the rugged, broken bluffs.

Owen located a spring bubbling from the foot of the upthrusting cliff. Once more they stopped to let their horses graze and rest, and Crow cooked a rabbit he'd shot earlier. Even without salt, the fresh meat was good. Both men longed for coffee, and Crow was out of tobacco, a matter of great dissatisfaction to him.

When they were finished with their scant meal and the horses had enjoyed an hour's grazing, Terrel and Crow climbed into their saddles once more, heading across the sand dunes below the escarpment. As the hot afternoon wore into evening, the heat sultry and heavy, the men had cause to feel gratitude for their horses, moving tirelessly and willingly. Since they had found the wide, unmistakable path of the herd, even the horses seemed to sense the urgency of their trek. Owen was careful to save their mounts as much as possible. Upon these horses rested the success of their mission, for the men could literally do nothing without them.

Nor did either man need to be told that his own life might depend upon their ability to cross these dry miles and find water. Thus they did not begrudge the time required to rest the horses. Owen had brought the last of the oats Will had packed in the wagon. At dusk the men unsaddled and let their horses roll, easing the sweaty itch of their backs. They gave them each a double handful of oats and again allowed them to graze for a brief time upon the nutritious prairie grasses. They would be suffering soon for water, but by Crow's calculations, they were only a few miles from the Pecos.

"We'd best eat a bite now, rest a few minutes," Crow said. "We won't get no chance later." He nodded toward the sky. "Unless I miss my guess, we are gonna get wet. That there's a mighty bad-lookin' cloud, Captain."

They chewed the last bits of jerky and cold flapjacks that Amelia had put up for them, allowed themselves a swallow of water, then saddled up and moved on. Lightning flared and swept across the face of the hovering clouds.

"This weather will make the herd hard to hold," Owen said. "What do you say we take a little advantage of that?"

"What you got in mind?"

"How many men you figure Wilkins has?"

Crow shrugged, deftly controlled his horse as lightning and a quick-following crash of thunder shook the earth. "Man, that was too close," he exclaimed. "Well, there's five men—six if Wardworth has joined up again. 'Course, he ain't worth much. Scare him a little an' he'll cut out, like he did when they hit the wagon. He's better at backshootin' than a open fight—but his bullets will kill you just as dead."

They were in rough terrain now, erosion-cut gullies

making it hard for the horses to move very fast. The men allowed the surefooted beasts to make their own way. The horses smelled water now and would find the quickest way to the muddy Pecos without the direction of the riders.

"The odds bother you, Crow?" Owen asked the question with real curiosity. He was learning that Crow had surprising depths. If he hadn't taken the wrong path, somewhere back down the years, he'd have been the kind of man Terrel would have been proud to have with him in battle. Hell, he was glad to have him alongside now. Owen had discarded his last doubts about Crow. If he could not be trusted, it was far too late to worry about it.

"Well, sure." Crow's leathery face creased with a humorless grin. "Ain't you a trifle bothered, Terrel?"

Owen glanced at him. "My pa used to say, 'Us Terrels get bored in an even fight.' But to tell you the truth, I wouldn't grieve if one or two of Wilkins' owlhoots would bog down in quicksand or get struck by lightnin'." As if illustrating his words, the early darkness exploded with light all around them once again. His dun plunged convulsively forward, ready to buck. Owen held the horse's head up, spurred him into a faster gait, to distract him.

Crow's horse galloped to catch up. "Lordy, I'm beginning to think you made a mistake, wishin' for a storm." He laughed unsteadily. "It's just as likely we'll be the ones fried by lightnin' as Wilkins' men. You reckon the good Lord ain't noticed yet how I've changed my ways?"

Owen smiled. "Maybe you should say a little prayer an' remind Him."

"Best do any prayin' real fast. We're getting close to the river."

Crow was right. The horses struck a game trail that wound through the *bosque,* the belt of cedars and cottonwoods along river. In moments they were at the river's edge, gratefully drinking. The men climbed down, drank upstream of the horses, and filled their canteens. They moved carefully, testing the muddy ground. Neither man wished to learn how it felt to encounter quicksand.

As soon as the horses had slaked their thirst, they led them away from the water, moved south along the *bosque.* It was darker under the trees, and the clouds were heavier now, the thunder muttering at intervals.

"They been here," Owen said, a half-mile along the river. "Didn't try to cross, far as I can tell. Reckon they had their hands full, thirsty as those cows were bound to be. They likely lost some along here."

"Yeah. Wilkins wouldn't take time to comb the bushes for the last few. He's in a hurry now. This here's John Chisum's stampin' ground. Chisum's hands would know some of this gang on sight, and say hello with a rifle slug."

"All right. Let's move on. Best be a little careful now. These tracks are fresher than I would have expected." Owen swung up onto the dun, checked this rifle, and loosened the Peacemaker in its holster. Then he led the way at a fast trot.

The wind was gusting hard and had the smell of rain in it. Lighting hit a tall cottonwood across the river. The flash gave the illusion of daylight for an instant. Both men had their hands full with their mounts. Owen's dun was near to panic. Crow cursed eloquently as he got his mare under control and brought her back alongside Owen's horse.

"Damn it, Terrel, I plumb hate lightnin'," he confessed. "If we get through this night, I swear I'll never set foot out of doors in a storm again."

"I'm not rightly fond of it myself," Owen said softly. "Reckon it did us a favor that time, though. I saw two riders up ahead, bringin' up the rear of our herd. Wasn't for that lightnin' flash, we might've rode right up to 'em."

"Damn, we're closer than we thought," muttered Crow. "What's your plan, Terrel?"

"I been thinkin'. It's too dark and stormy an' there's too many trees to get an accurate notion of where all Wilkins' men are. We can guess they won't have anyone next the river. There's the two I saw, prob'bly two others on their left a few yards, an' the rest along the east side of the herd. They're pushing the cattle on south fast as they can. What say we help 'em out?"

Crow gave a quiet laugh. "Wouldn't take much to scat-

ter these cattle to hell an' gone. Take some work to gather
'em up afterward.''

"Reckon we can do that at our leisure—after we finish
with those mangy coyotes.''

"Jumpy as those cows're bound to be, they might do
a little bit of the job for us,'' Crow said. ''Just like Wilkins and Wardworth figured when they started the stampede through our camp up on the Llano.''

"He liked the idea then,'' Owen said. ''Let's see how
well he likes it now. One thing, though, let's try to stay
together long as we can. We don't want to mistake each
other for the enemy.''

"I hear you, Captain Terrel. When do we open the
ball?''

The world went glaringly yellow as lightning ripped
the clouds. Both men caught a glimpse of riders and cattle not more than thirty yards ahead. They were close
enough now to hear the click of horns bumping together,
the jingle of bit chains and spurs.

"Reckon now's as good a time as any,'' Owen said,
and touched spurs to the dun's sides. He raised his rifle,
let off a shot skyward. It would serve as a warning to the
cow thieves, but it would also act as a trigger to release
the pent-up energy within the herd.

Crow's rebel yell and shots fired at the two nearest
rustlers completed the job. With an impulse that ran
throughout the big herd instantaneously, the cattle were
running.

19

No one could accuse Wilkins' men of cowardice. With Terrel's and Crow's first shots, both the men Owen had spotted earlier whirled their mounts toward the attackers, guns blazing. Bent low over their saddles, Owen and Crow swept toward them. Crow took the one on their right while Terrel's Winchester lifted the other rustler from his saddle.

After that, it was all confusion, punctuated by gunfire and yells as the rustlers made their choice; to fight, or to try to hold the herd. Wilkins himself raced back toward Terrel and Crow, his rifle cracking again and again, and incidentally saved his own life for a few minutes more, as the herd thundered over the very ground he had vacated, carrying at least one outlaw to his death within the unstoppable maelstrom of big, racing bodies.

Meanwhile, Wilkins, yelling his hatred and perhaps his joy of the conflict he rode to meet, charged full into Terrel's horse.

Owen felt the dun going down. There was no time to kick free of the stirrups and leave his saddle. The outlaw's horse jumped over the tangle of Terrel and his mount. A hoof grazed Owen's temple, stunning him momentarily. He experienced the brush of death as his horse came within an inch of rolling completely over Owen. His fate hung in the balance for the space of an indrawn breath, with the ground vibrating under him from the pounding retreat of the stampeding herd.

In a dazed way he knew when the weight of his mount broke his leg, felt that crushing weight lift as the horse managed to regain its feet. The shaken dun stood, head down and heaving, a few feet from Owen's position.

Owen became aware of several things at once as his head cleared. There was rain on his face, big, warm, pelting drops, the first offering of the storm. And his leg

was afire with pain. Lightning lit the scene. He saw a
horseman approaching at a run, and for a moment that
was almost fatal, he believed it was Crow. Then he realized that it was Wilkins, returning. The outlaw held a
pistol, steadying it for the shot that would finish Owen.

Owen rolled, grabbing for his Colt. He had one second
to aim and fire. Time seemed to stall and move with
uneven slowness. Oddly, a memory flashed through Terrel's mind; of a long-ago summer day when a lanky,
overall-clad boy of ten had gone hunting with his older
brother. He heard Will's voice quite plainly, ''You gotta
hold it real steady, little brother. Don't jerk the trigger,
now, just squeeze . . .''

The gun recoiled. Wilkins let out a shriek, as if furious
at the accuracy of Terrel's aim. His body hit the ground
only a few feet away. But Owen was not sure the outlaw
was finished until a new wavering sheet of lightning
showed him Wilkins, on his back, arms outflung. The
dead blue eyes reflected the momentary light. He seemed
to stare dully at Owen, unblinking as the rain began to
pound savagely into the trampled earth.

Thunder seemed to make the earth shudder and shift
about Terrel. Slowly he realized that the danger was over,
for the moment at least. There was no sound but the beat
of the rain. The running herd was too distant to hear.
The cattle would run themselves out by morning, scattered for miles along the Pecos. No way of knowing if
enough of Wilkins' gang had survived to round up the
cattle and drive them away for good, but there wasn't a
hell of a lot that Terrel could do about that now.

He shifted, groaned as the bones in his leg grated together. Rainwater poured heavily over him. He'd lost his
hat in the fall—and his rifle as well. Cautiously he groped
about him in the streaming darkness, hoping to find the
gun. After the events of the past few days, he felt very
lonely without the Winchester.

But all his hands encountered was mud, rocks, roots.
Owen set his jaw and waited for lightning to illuminate
his surroundings. The dun horse was still nearby, and the
rifle lay where the horse had fallen. Owen dragged himself to the gun, gritting his teeth against the pain of
his broken leg. Now, if he could manage to mount his

horse . . . But where would he ride? He must wait for daylight, hope Crow would return. Apparently the former outlaw had continued after the herd and the surviving outlaws, not knowing that Owen had gone down.

His leg hurt devilishly now, but he struggled to get nearer to the horse. The gelding snorted and backed nervously. Owen caught a dragging rein, tied it firmly to a cedar limb. It made him feel a good deal better to have the horse secured.

The rain had settled down to a moderate, steady downfall. Owen hitched himself close to a bush, leaned tiredly back. It promised to be a very long, wet, and painful night.

Sunlight and pain roused Owen from a fragmented, haunted, shivering sleep. He found himself seated upon muddy ground, soaked to the skin. His rifle lay across his lap.

The day was moving toward noon, the sun nearly directly overhead. Birdcalls sounded about him. Owen could hear the river, somewhere off to the right. It made him aware of his thirst. He swallowed dryly, his throat burning. There was a canteen upon his saddle.

But when he turned stiffly to look for his horse, he found the dun gone. He must have pulled free in the night: he might be anywhere along the river, miles away by now. Instinctively Owen looked for tracks. What he saw made him frown. His horse's tracks moved away toward the Pecos, alongside the marks of another shod horse—and the tracks of a man's boots. Damn, had someone stolen his horse, practically out from under his nose?

Then a cheerful whistle announced someone's approach. The tune was "Turkey in the Straw," one Owen had heard often enough in the past days. It seemed Crow knew no other tune.

The other man stepped into sight, carrying saddlebags and canteens. Owen grinned at him, never more glad to greet a friend.

"Well, look at you," Crow said. "Wide awake an' ready to take on the world again."

"Hand me that canteen," Owen croaked.

Quickly Crow came and gave him the water. "I'll have

a fire made in a jiffy. Soon as the coffee's started, I'll see to that there leg.''

''Man, I'm beginnin' to be glad we hauled you in to camp.'' Owen studied his unlikely partner. ''I see you dragged Wilkins' carcass away.''

''If you miss him, I'll bring him back. The thing is, he ain't any purtier now than he was when he was alive, an' he don't smell a lot better.''

''I can do without his company,'' Owen said. ''Tell me how things went last night. I had to leave the party early. Did they get away with the herd?''

Crow gave him an odd look. ''No, sir, reckon not. Best I can tell, only one man got away, an' he lit out for the border. One got pounded into the mud. We did for the other three. The cows are tuckered out, scattered to hell an' gone along the river. I think they'll stay put until I can get some help to gather 'em.''

Owen sighed with weariness and relief. ''Man, you keep this up, you're liable to get us Terrels obligated for life. Be a terrible burden to you. Will tends to take these things serious. He gets plumb sentimental.''

Crow set the coffeepot onto the fire. He grinned at Owen. ''Never fear, I'll cure him of that in a hurry—just run off a couple hunnerd head of Terrel beef. Now, then, let me look at that leg. Broke, is it? Damn, I hope it ain't gonna go gangrenous. I purely hate to take off a feller's leg.''

''You ain't takin' this one off, friend,'' Terrel assured him. ''I believe it's a simple break. You splint it, heave me onto my horse, an' get me to South Springs Ranch.''

''Whatever you say.''

Crow set to work, ripping Owen's pants leg, setting the leg and binding it between straight cedar limbs. It was a painful process. When Crow was finished, Owen felt weak and dizzy. A cup of black and bitter coffee helped. There was nothing to eat, but Owen's stomach wouldn't have tolerated food at that moment, in any case.

''Too hot to travel,'' Crow pronounced, spreading blankets in a shady place. ''You rest until late afternoon, an' we'll move out.''

Ashamed to admit his weakness, Owen lay back and fell into a restless, pain-disturbed sleep. He was roused by a tantalizing odor and opened his eyes to find his companion frying catfish from the Pecos. He came over to bring the food to Owen. "Look what I got, Captain."

"Oh man, how'd you manage this?"

"Made me a little ol' fish trap while you were snoozin'. Ain't no salt to go on it, though."

"It'll go down so quick I'll never miss salt."

They ate, drank their coffee, then Crow readied the horses and brought Owen's nearby.

"If you can prop me upright, maybe I can get myself on," Terrel said.

In the end he required a little help, but the results were two mounted men, headed north along the river.

Riding jolted Owen's splinted leg. He rode in silence, enduring the pain. He was determined to get back to his family and Ginny. They had traveled some twelve or fifteen miles when they were spotted by one of Chisum's riders. The man, mounted on a good bay cowpony, galloped nearer.

"One of you fellers Owen Terrel?" he asked.

"I'm Terrel." Owen made himself sit straighter. He felt feverish and dizzy, and clenched his teeth, determined to stay on his horse until they reached their destination.

"Looks like you need some doctorin'. We got your brother an' a passel of ladies an' kids at South Springs. Mr. Chisum told some of us to keep an eye out for you folks, give you a hand if we can. He sent some riders out lookin' for the men that stole your herd. Reckon we know one or two of them skunks."

"We pried 'em loose from the cows," Crow said, "but we had to leave the herd."

The puncher nodded. "I'll get some men an' see to the cattle. They's a line camp 'bout two miles on. Make yourselves to home. I'll send somebody for the doc." He spurred away.

Crow gave Owen a concerned look. "Can you make it, Terrel? You ain't lookin' too pert."

Owen managed a grin. "I'll make it. Let's move on."

By sheer will he managed to stick on his horse until the line camp was reached. The ground seemed to heave like ocean waves as he maneuvered his broken leg over the horse's rump. Crow caught Terrel as he touched the ground. Good thing, too, or he would have passed out on the spot. Crow supported him until he was steadier, then helped him to a place under a tree. He spread blankets, got Owen settled, apparently knowing that Owen would prefer this to bunking under the cabin's low roof.

Owen slipped into a doze, dreaming that he was still on horseback, crossing wasteland that burned under a hellish sun. He did not know when Chisum riders arrived, bringing food and a doctor from Roswell.

But he woke to the doctor's examination and gratefully accepted a tin cup of whiskey, pressed upon him by one of the Chisum men. The fiery liquor hit his empty stomach and sent him spiraling into a semidaze. Later someone brought him coffee, tender steak and biscuits. He could eat only a little.

Afterward, Owen sank into a heavy sleep. Tangled, meaningless dreams plagued him, seemed to go on forever. Once he roused a bit to voices nearby, but could not seem to make himself want to reply to them. He felt intolerably hot, even though the sun had set.

"He's fevered, but that should break soon," the words buzzed around like lazy horseflies in his skull. "Let him rest, try to get him to eat, make him drink all he will."

Life became a series of broken fragments of awareness, moments when someone woke him, gave him water or sips of cooled coffee, a few spoonsful of soup. He heard bits of conversation. Mostly he slept, but nightmares were tossed about in his unconscious mind like colorful shards, landing in meaningless patterns. He saw Ginny moving toward him, smiling . . . and then it was not Ginny but Julia who touched his face, her smile deceitful, hiding shameful secrets. Will was being attacked, Owen tried to move, to help his brother, but his limbs would not respond. Agonized by his helplessness, he struggled, until something cool touched his face and the dream vanished. He sank into sleep again almost at once.

At last Owen knew a gradual return of awareness of the world about him. People were talking nearby. Owen listened drowsily, feeling weak but free of pain and illness. He recognized Jackson Dill's rich, deep voice, and that was Crow's wry laugh.

"Mr. Will, he's frettin'," Jackson said. "Cain't keep him down. Miz Amelia, she makes him rest an' won't let him git on a horse yet, or he'd be here with Mr. Owen. She's rented a little house in Roswell, an' she's makin' Miz Julia help with the work while Miss Ginny gets well. Miz Julia goes around lookin' like she's swallered vinegar."

"Heck, I figgered that was her natural expression." Crow said. "For such a purty woman she sure can be a fright."

"My ma use to say, 'purty is as purty does,' " Dill chuckled.

"You fellers gonna be movin' Terrel down to Roswell?" Owen did not recognize this voice.

"Soon as he's able. If we don't, his brother'll be on the way here, an' the doc says Mr. Will, he got to rest for a month. That head wound was real bad."

Owen opened his eyes, concern for Will giving him the strength to shake off the daze of fevered weakness. It was about midmorning, he judged, a hot, fly-humming day. The men he'd been listening to were hunkered around a dying fire. Crow was stirring something in a fire-blackened pot.

Cautiously Terrel shifted, found that he had little pain in his leg. Mostly he was conscious of thirst and hunger.

He drew a deep breath. "Hey," he called, voice ridiculously weak. "How can a man get a slab of steak around here?"

Dill and Crow rushed to bend over him, grinning. "Well, what do you know?" Crow said. "It's alive!"

"Not for long, unless I get somethin' to eat," Owen said. "What's that you're cookin', Mr. Crow?"

"That there's son-of-a-gun stew. I'll bring you a plate."

"Dill, help me sit up, will you?"

Jackson gently propped him up against a saddle. Owen waited until his head quit swimming, then took the tin plate in shaking hands. It was hard to get the spoon to his mouth. Damn, he was like a year-old child. Wisely, his friends let him solve the problem for himself. "Don't I get some coffee?" Owen pleaded.

"Man, he no more'n opens his eyes and he's yellin'

orders,'' Crow complained, but there was a smiling look in his dark eyes when he brought the cup and held it until Terrel could steady his grip on it.

"How long you fellers been playin' nursemaid for me?'' Owen asked.

"You been takin' your ease for a week, Captain,'' Crow replied. "Jackson rode in this mornin'. Seems your folks is gettin' right tired of waitin' for you. Sent this here man to haul you home.''

"I believe I'm ready to go—after somebody dunks me in the river a few times. I've seen cleaner corpses.''

Crow grinned widely. "Shoot, it didn't seem worth it to wash your face—leastways, not till we could be sure you wasn't gonna die. That much less dirt to shovel.''

Owen found himself laughing and clutched his plate, afraid his shaking hands would lose it. The food was energy he had to have. As soon as he could manage it, he dipped another spoonful. His hunger had gone; maybe his stomach had shrunk. Nevertheless, he forced himself to eat most of the portion Crow had brought him, and gratefully drank the coffee. He felt stronger already.

"When do we leave?'' he asked.

"Not today,'' Dill said. "You rest some more, Cap'n. We'll borrow one of Mr. Chisum's wagons in the mornin'.''

"I want to go see Mr. Chisum, thank him.''

The Chisum cowboy, who had been leaning against a tree, whittling a stick, turned his head. "Oh, you already thanked him. He was here two days ago, on the way to where the boys are brandin' calves thirty miles west of here. You shook his hand an' thanked him over'n over. Might' near embarrassed him.''

Owen shook his head. "Now, I don't remember that at all.''

"You was burnin' up with fever, out o' your head,'' Crow explained. "But he took you as sincere. An' after he saw all them poor cow thieves laid out ever' which-away, he remarked that the Double T brand must stand for Double Trouble.''

Owen took Jackson's advice, rested most of the day. He asked Dill to build him a crutch. When it was done, they helped him up. He fought his weakness and practiced moving about. Afterward he felt abominably tired, but a half-hour's rest was sufficient to make him feel more like himself. He made himself hobble about the camp on his crutch just before lying down for the night, and he was sure his strength was returning.

At dawn he woke to the smells of smoke and coffee boiling. Gritting his teeth, Owen managed to pull on his left boot, lever himself upright onto his crutch, and make his way to a crude bench against the cabin wall.

Joe, the Chisum puncher, was cooking indoors on the cast-iron stove this morning, and he had biscuits baking in the oven. Mr. Chisum would be missing a calf, it appeared, for the tin plate Crow brought Owen was half-covered with tender steak.

"Oh, man!" Owen grinned. "Crow's stew wasn't bad, but this is what I'm cravin'."

He ate with real appetite, then asked Joe for water to wash a bit. Ignoring the smiles of the others, he washed his filthy shirt, wrung it out the best he could, and put it on. The sun would soon dry it.

"Man must be thinkin' to see his girl," Crow remarked to Dill.

"Well, he's still ugly, but he smells a mite better," Jackson remarked.

It went against the grain to lie down on a bedroll in the wagon for the trip. Terrel would have given years off his life to ride in horseback, like a man, but the doctor had given orders that he mustn't ride for a few more days, or the healing leg could be ruined. Dill and Crow refused to be persuaded otherwise.

Dill chucked to the team borrowed from the Chisum ranch, and the wagon creaked slowly into motion.

20

Two days later the wagon rolled across the Pecos at the Horsehead Crossing. Owen relaxed on the wagon seat, having complained about lying in the wagon bed until his men gave up and let him sit up and watch the slowly passing scenery. He was happy in the knowledge that soon he would see his family . . . and Ginny.

"Crow," he said thoughtfully, "what say we stop by the barbershop before we go to the house."

Jackson, riding alongside the wagon, gave him a shrewd look. "You takin' a almighty int'rest in sprucin' up lately, Cap'n."

Terrel tapped the rump of Dill's horse with the tip of his crutch, making the hammerhead gray crow-hop. "You could benefit from my example, Dill. Reckon all of us look like a passel of buff-hunters, beggin' your pardon, Crow."

Crow flapped the lines, urged the horses forward. "Yes, sir, Dill, we're goin' to town. There's ladies in town, remember. We gotta keep up appearances."

Jackson hooted at this, but when they reached the barbershop, he too took advantage of the wooden tubs of hot water in the back room, and though he drew the line at getting a haircut, he was willing to take Owen's twenty-dollar gold piece over to Van Smith and Wilburn's store to buy clothes for all of them. By the time the barber had finished, he was back. When the trio left the barbershop, they could scarcely have been recognized as the three travel-worn men who had entered earlier. Only their boots and hats were the same, with the dirt brushed off. That wouldn't last, as far as the boots were concerned. Apparently, there had been a hard early-morning rain, and the streets of the little town were deep in mud. One step off the plank walk placed a pedestrian in clinging muck.

Owen's healing leg twinged as he climbed awkwardly into the wagon and placed his crutch against the seat.

Then, something abruptly registered itself in his consciousness as a warning, like a spider scuttling over a web, setting the fragile strands trembling. It was something his eyes had passed over a moment before that belatedly rang alarm bells in his mind.

He frowned as Crow released the brake and drove the tired team out into the muddy street. What exactly had he seen? He had the uneasy notion that he had failed to pay attention to something important. Something . . . no, someone. It had been a man, just a glimpse of his trim back as he strode jauntily around a corner. Owen looked back, but there was no one there now. He faced forward again, shaking his head. What was it about that barely noticed figure? The man was dressed fancier than others on the street, in a dark suit and top hat, a cane in his hand. Owen had not seen the stranger's face, not even in profile. Likely he was a salesman bringing samples of his wares to the frontier town. But there was something about his stance, or the set of his shoulders . . .

Then he knew what was nagging at his mind. The briefly glimpsed dandy had reminded him of Caleb Wardworth, the way he'd been dressed the first night he'd seen him at Julia's home in Houston.

He smiled, relieved that he'd tracked the uneasy prickling of his mind to its source. Would he always be suspicious of a man dressed like a carpetbagger? He supposed he would.

"Thinkin' about Miss Virginia?" Crow asked.

Terrel glanced at him, saw the naked envy in Crow's eyes. He regretted that this man who had become his trusted comrade should be made unhappy by the love between Owen and Virginia Morgan. Crow had given her his devotion. Owen could not dislike the man for that.

"Reckon she's never out of my mind," he said quietly.

Crow's jaw set and he was quiet for a moment as he worked the team and wagon past a bogged-down freight rig and around a corner. "She's a fine little lady," he said at last. "I know . . ." he paused, and Owen saw Crow's prominent Adam's apple bob as he swallowed. "I know you'll take good care of her. Would—could you promise me one little thing, Terrel?"

"Let me hear it."

"If she an' you ever need help, send for me, wherever I'm at?"

Owen was taken aback. It was the last thing he would have expected to hear.

Abruptly he turned on the wagon seat, extended his right hand. "You got my promise, but you don't need it. I'd have called on you in any case."

Terrel was never to forget that odd little moment, in a lurching wagon, passing curious townspeople and modest little homes, on his way to meet the people he loved best in the world. Crow's bearded, weathered face glowed with pleasure. Owen glanced from him to Jackson Dill's broad back and knew himself to be a most fortunate man, possessed of friends like these.

"Yonder's the house, Cap'n," Dill said. "End of the street, past them fields." He spurred his horse and raced ahead. They could hear him shouting and see figures hurrying from the house to the road. Crow urged his team to a trot for the last hundred yards. As he pulled them to a halt, there were glad greetings from those who waited: Julia in the gate, smiling brightly, Will and Amelia moving forward, Willy and Melissa racing about their feet. Will still wore a neat bandage about his head, and he leaned on a cane. Owen saw that he seemed unsteady when he walked, as if he still suffered from dizziness.

Virginia stood a few steps behind the others, her eyes fixed upon Owen's face.

"Jackson, yank my little brother off that there wagon," Will said. "I believe I'll give him a thrashin' for worryin' us half to death."

"Owen, you look starved to a shadow," Amelia scolded. "I've got dinner on the stove. Mr. Crow, we're so glad to see you. You must come in and eat with us, too."

"Thank you, Miz Amelia," Crow said, and set the brake. "I got to tend these horses first. They been a long way."

"There's prairie hay and oats in the shed out back," Will said.

Owen managed to get down without too much awkwardness, putting his crutch down first and letting his weight down upon his good leg. He waved Dill away a bit fiercely. He wasn't about to let Ginny see him lifted down like one of the kids.

"How's the leg, Owen?" Amelia asked anxiously. "And they said you had fever—"

"It was nothin'." He looked past her to Ginny, longing for a moment alone with her. "I broke my leg, but it'll mend. I just need some of your good cookin'."

Amelia glanced at the target of his eyes, and her smile was sympathetic. "Maybe you'd like to sit there on the porch until dinner's ready. Ginny," her voice lifted. "Come and help this man up onto the porch. I'll get the food on the table. Julia, Melissa, come and help."

Julia lips thinned, but she went with Amelia. Will climbed up onto the wagon seat to accompany Crow and Dill to the shed to tend the team and the dun gelding tied on behind. Jackson remounted and trotted his horse ahead of the wagon.

So Owen found himself almost alone with his girl. Only little Willy remained, staring curiously at Owen and Virginia. But Amelia reappeared in moments and shooed her son into the house. They could hear her admonishing him, "No, you can talk to your Uncle Owen later. You leave him be now. Don't put your fingers in the cake icing, Melissa. That's for dinner."

Owen was extremely conscious of Virginia's light touch upon his arm as he climbed the porch steps.

"Sit there, Owen," she said softly, indicating a bench against the wall. He obeyed and leaned back to take in her slightly rosy face.

"Girl, you look prettier than a nestful of baby swallows," he said, catching her hand. "Sit here beside me."

Almost shyly she settled onto the bench.

"You're feelin' all right now?" he asked. "Your wound all healed up?"

She nodded. "I'm good as new, but Amelia won't believe it. She won't let me do anything but the lightest chores."

He grinned. "Good for Amelia. Will looks good too."

She nodded happily. "The doctor says he'll be fine, but he must be careful for a while. Amelia says he must hire new men to tend the herd until you and Will are completely well." Her wide dark eyes fastened anxiously upon his. "Owen, you—you will be completely well, won't you? I've been so worried."

He pulled her into his arms. "Don't worry anymore,

sweetheart," he said. "I'm gettin' better every day. I had that blasted fever—reckon it was from bein' rained on all night. That's all gone now and my leg will be fine soon. You wait and see, we'll be on our way home in a few weeks. Got to be. I've got a house to build."

"You and Will already built a house."

"That's Will's house. The next one's ours."

She lifted her head sharply and leaned back, studying his face. Her lips parted, but she seemed unable to form words. Owen smiled, ran a calloused fingertip along her cheekbone.

"Don't you remember that you promised to be my wife?"

"I remember," she whispered, and her eyes seemed to glow with an inner light.

He kissed her brow. "You know it won't be easy. It's a hard life for a woman, so far from other folks, with nothin' fine about to take pride in."

"I'll take pride in you," she said, and her voice was unsteady. "Yes, Owen Terrel, I'll be your wife. And you'll never, never be sorry you asked me."

He hugged her again, laughing. "I'm relieved you said that. It was a heavy burden on my mind."

Now she was laughing too, and for a few moments the two of them were oblivious of the rest of the world. For Owen, it was a time stolen from the hardships and dangers they had all faced. Somehow it made everything worthwhile.

Someone cleared his throat. Will was coming onto the porch. Owen released Ginny. Cheeks flushed, she hurried indoors.

Will had to pause, as if steadying himself, then he moved to a rocking chair and sat down.

Owen watched him, worried. He drew a bag of tobacco from his shirt pocket, leaned forward, and tossed it to his brother. "We picked that up for you in town. Does the doc let you smoke?"

Will smiled with gratitude. "He says one pipe a day cain't hurt." Drawing out his pipe, he packed the fragrant tobacco into the bowl. Then he leaned back and crossed his long legs. Owen recognized the signs: Will was ready for serious talk.

"Tell me about the herd, Owen."

"The news is good, Will. We may lose a few head, but the Terrels are still in the cattle business. Crow an' I got lucky when we waded into them thieves. We think only one got away. Chisum's men are keepin' an eye on the herd. Soon as we get sorted out, we'll hire a man or two, take 'em home."

Will sighed. "I can't wait. Too damned many people around here."

"Yes, sir, this is a real city." Owen laughed. "I believe I counted three stores. I know how you feel, though. Something about the Llano Estacado makes anywhere else seem small and crowded."

They were interrupted as a Mexican boy of seven or eight darted up on the porch.

"Hello, son. What can I do for you?" Will asked.

"Una nota para la señora." The lad pulled a crumpled fold of paper from his pocket.

"Amelia," Will called into the house. And when his wife hurried out, wiping her hands upon her apron, he gave her a look of mock reproof. "Who are you receivin' love notes from, woman?"

She tilted her head, puzzled.

"Boy here says he has a letter for you."

But the lad had backed up, holding the paper protectively behind his back. *"No, no, la otra señora*—other lady. *Es para la señora rubia."*

Owen began to understand. "He means the note's for Julia."

But Julia was already shoving past Amelia to snatch the crumpled note from the boy's hand. She turned away to read the contents as Will gave the child a coin and received his delighted thanks.

"What is that, Julia?" Amelia asked. "You don't know anyone in town."

Julia was smiling as she turned. "I asked the man at the general store to let me know if he got any new bonnets in. I think I'll run right down and look at them." She was untying her apron as she spoke.

"Why, we're nearly ready to eat, Julia. Surely it can wait."

Julia's smile vanished. "If I wait, the women here in

town will have picked them over. I want to go now.'' Her eyes narrowed, catlike, and her expression dared Amelia to protest further.

''But you shouldn't go alone. Wait until I can—''

''Amelia, you aren't my mother,'' Julia snapped. She stalked back into the house and was out again in minutes, tying a dark, rather dowdy bonnet over her fair hair, draping a totally unneeded black shawl over her bright dress.

Owen supposed that his game leg rather excused him from offering to escort her. He grinned inwardly. Sure would be disappointing to miss the good meal he could smell cooking. First time he'd ever thought of a broken leg as lucky.

Looking at no one, Julia strode off along the edge of the muddy street, for once careless of her shoes and skirt hem.

Amelia stared after her worriedly. ''I don't know what to make of that girl. Now, why did she take my shawl and bonnet, instead of her own things?'' She gave a shrug of complete puzzlement and went back to her cooking.

Will turned back to Owen. ''Was there any sign of Caleb Wardworth with Wilkins' gang?''

Owen tilted his head back against the warm adobe wall. ''No, I don't believe he ever rejoined Wilkins' bunch. I'm thinkin' he wouldn't have wanted to risk one of his old buddies seein' what was in the valise he'd turned up with. My guess is he put as much distance as he could between himself and the gang.''

Will nodded slowly, then fixed his brother with eyes that were much like Owen's own. ''Any chance that skunk has lit out for Mexico, or back to Texas?''

Owen sighed. ''Now, that's the other question. He had a pretty good plan under way back in Houston. He was gettin' ready to make a splash in the political pond, as Talbot's son-in-law. Besides that, there's a mess of property that belonged to Talbot.''

''And now belongs to Julia. But if Julia has an accident and never comes home, her husband would surely inherit.''

Characteristically, the brothers were onto the line of

reasoning like two skilled coon hounds, closing swiftly and surely upon the logic of the situation.

"Then he has to be sure Julia don't step off the steamboat someday and move back into the Talbot mansion," Will muttered. "Not now. Not ever."

The two men sat in silence for a few minutes. Owen was conscious of feeling tired and wishing the damned business would get over with, once and for all. "Well, maybe he don't know where she is."

Will gave a short laugh. "If he don't, he soon will. He can't risk her kitin' back to Texas ahead of him, tellin' her story. There's still a few men back there that would ride him on a rail down to the bayou and see he's never found. It'll only take a few questions to track her down. She don't exactly blend into the landscape, not Julia."

Amelia called the men in to eat. Cheerfully the family gathered about the kitchen table and were served Amelia's succulent roast hen, sweet potatoes, and corn bread. Owen sat across from Virginia. He had only to lift his eyes to enjoy looking at her. Perhaps he overdid it, for Ginny grew quite rosy, conscious of his gaze. Likely everyone else at the table was aware of his concentrated study of the girl.

At last Ginny gave a flustered glance at the smiling faces about her and bent forward. "Owen Terrel, you keep your eyes on your plate, or I'll take my dinner out into the back yard."

"Fine idea, let's go!" He stood, took up his plate, grasped his crutch, and strode out the back door, to the general merriment of the family. She could have refused to follow him, but in moments she came quietly out, carrying her plate. Owen sat upon a chair under an apple tree. She sat upon the grass. The skirt of her pink muslin dress spread out about her. Her hair was drawn smoothly over her ears and coiled softly at the back of her head. Owen's fingers itched to remove the tortoiseshell pins and let the gleaming chestnut mass flow over her shoulders. She looked very young and vulnerable. It was something in her wide dark eyes, the delicate bones beneath the lightly tanned skin of her slender face. If Owen hadn't known, he never would have guessed that this girl had survived so many harrowing experiences, had come so close to death.

Nor, if he had not witnessed it again and again, would he have suspected the courage beneath her quiet, unassuming exterior. She might have been any innocent, well-bred, sheltered young girl on the threshhold of her life as a woman.

"You're doing it again." She gave an exasperated laugh. "Owen, I really can't eat if you keep watching me like a hawk hovering over a pullet."

He threw back his head an laughed. "Sounds like a mighty dangerous situation for the pullet. Are you scared of me, Ginny?"

She bent her head and he could see the clean line of her parted hair. "Well, maybe a little," she murmured. Then she looked up, smiling, and he saw that she was joking.

Owen lost interest in his dinner. He set his plate on the ground and took hers away as well. Then he pulled her into the chair with him, onto his lap. They kissed, and he found himself wondering how he was going to wait for her until he could stand up in church without a crutch. Well, damn it, he wouldn't wait. If she was willing, he'd find a minister this very day.

Ginny drew away a little and gazed up at him soberly. She laid a slim hand against his cheek. He caught it, kissed her palm.

"Damn, Ginny. I'm so crazy about you I can't see straight."

"I know," she murmured. "It's the same for me. I felt like dying when they brought word you'd been hurt, and were sick, and they wouldn't let me go to you."

"You were scarcely well yourself."

"That didn't matter. I begged the men to take me to that line camp, and you."

He kissed her lingeringly, then drew back to enjoy her lovely blush. "I love you, Ginny."

"I never want to be apart from you again, Owen." Her eyes were solemn, as clear and honest as a small child's.

"If it's in my power, you never will be," he promised, and drew her close again.

A burst of laughter from within the house, as Will finished some tall tale or other, reminded the lovers that they were not quite alone. Ginny pulled away.

"You eat now, Owen Terrel. Your food's getting cold."

He gave a mock sigh. "Already soundin' like a wife! How does a man get himself into this trap?"

"By dogged persistence," she asserted.

When they had finished eating, Ginny returned their plates to the kitchen. Will came out into the yard, frowning.

"Too much chicken and dressing?" Owen grinned. "Or are you thinkin' the Terrel brothers make a fine pair, hobbling around on canes and crutches?"

"Nah, that only evens the odds 'twixt us an' them," Will said. "I was thinking about what we were talkin' about earlier. Reckon we should have let Julia go out alone?"

Owen looked at him sharply. "Wasn't much 'letting' to it, was there? Anyhow, surely Wardworth ain't—"

The memory crashed into the forefront of his mind like a rifle shot, that glimpse of a well-dressed gent, top hat jauntily tilted . . .

"What is it, Owen? You look like you found a tadpole in your soup."

Owen grabbed his crutch and got up, already moving toward the corner of the house. "I think I've been a damned fool, Will. Get someone to saddle me a horse. Where's Crow?"

Will kept up with him. "Owen, what the devil's got into you?"

But as Owen emerged at the front of the house, he came to a relieved stop. A hired buggy was just pulling up at the yard gate. Julia was driving, and she was alone. She was smiling, and she hopped lightly to the ground as they stared at her. Rather awkwardly she tied the buggy horse, then turned back to get something out of the buggy. It was so familiar that for a moment it didn't hit Owen what the blond woman was holding—a scuffed leather valise, weightily packed.

21

As she hurried up the path toward the porch, Owen moved as swiftly as he could to block her path. "Julia! Where'd you get that?"

She backed away from him a step, her face defiant. "Stand aside, Owen. I'm goin' in to pack my things."

Will moved up beside Owen. "You didn't answer his question, Miss Julia." Owen had never heard his voice so cold.

She held the valise against her as if daring the men to touch it. "It's mine. You know it's mine."

"Where'd you get it?"

She stared at Owen, a hint of fright in her pale eyes. "If I tell you, will you leave me be? I declare, I never saw so much fuss over nothin'."

Owen pointed a rigid finger at the valise. "What's in there may be nothing to you, but it has cost the lives of some good men. Our men. It has brought danger and hurt onto our family an' come close to makin' you pay a mighty steep price for it. I want to know where you got it, Julia—and I want to know now!"

He made no effort to dilute the threat in his voice. He wondered how he could ever have imagined that he loved this cold, scheming female. She was beautiful, but that beauty covered unspeakable selfishness.

She seemed about to defy him, then her face softened and she gazed at Owen appealingly. "All right. I'll tell you. But I want to talk to you alone." She gave a meaningful glance at Will.

Will snorted and moved away, going back into the small house. Julia nodded toward the buggy.

"Come where we can't be heard. You know how curious Amelia and Virginia are."

She retreated to the gate, leaned against the post. She

set the valise down near her foot, as if afraid he would snatch it and run.

He did not respond to her wheedling smile. "All right. Where did you find the bag?" An icy snake of foreboding was coiling in his stomach.

She bit her lip, obviously considering how much she would be forced to reveal to him. One slender shoulder moved in a shrug. She removed the unbecoming bonnet and shawl she had borrowed, without leave, from Amelia. She tossed them over the yard fence. "You've already guessed it. Caleb Wardworth is here in town."

"How long have you known that?"

She fluttered her eyelashes prettily. "Owen, don't be so mean to me. I've known for two days. One of the first things I did when we arrived here was to ask some people to watch for a man of his description. He was only just hours behind us."

"Why didn't you tell Will?" Owen's voice was steely.

Her face arranged itself in concerned lines. "Owen, surely you wouldn't have wished for me to disturb your dear brother when he's been ailin'."

"What if Wardworth had decided to murder all of you in your beds? You owed Will some warning."

"Owen, you—you're frightenin' me! Please don't shout." Tears appeared magically in the pretty eyes, slid down her soft, rounded cheeks. "If I did wrong, I'm sorry. I just—I only thought I ought to start handling things for myself. It isn't right for all of you to be dragged into my little ol' problems," she murmured virtuously. He stared at her in amazement. Was it possible she believed her own excuses?

"Tell me the rest of it, Julia," he ordered. "What happened after you heard he was in town?"

"Well, I found out where Wardworth was staying. An' I paid the desk clerk at the hotel to watch where he went. Didn't that work fine? He found out that Caleb goes to the saloon to play poker most every day at this time. I told him to give me the word when Caleb left his room today, and he sent that note—"

"You went to Wardworth's room?"

She nodded. "I had told the room clerk I'm his wife. Well, it's true, for heaven's sake! That smirkin' idiot let me have the key. So, here I am!'' She smiled brightly. ''Caleb was stupid. He left the money in his room. He hadn't used much of it yet.''

Owen stared at her, picturing her lingering in that room to count her precious money.

''And you just walked in and took it? Don't you know the clerk will tell Wardworth you were there? He won't have a lot of trouble describin' you, either. Caleb will find you, Julia. And that brings him down on my family again. I won't have it.''

She gave him a pert, somehow vicious smile.

''Well, then, do something about it!''

Terrel stared at her narrowly, putting it together. ''You rented a rig—and you were going in to pack. I thought you were smarter than that, Julia. Do you think you can run fast enough and far enough to keep ahead of Wardworth?''

Again that careless shrug. ''I might—if you come with me. And if he does catch up . . .'' Her eyes glittered. ''Well, I know you're miffed with me, but I don't think you'll stand by and let him harm me, or take what belongs to me.''

He shook his head, stunned. ''You expect me to come with you? Julia, you've gone plumb out of your mind.''

She lifted her hand and would have touched his face if he had not moved back. Impatiently she stamped a small foot. ''Oh, Owen, don't be so pesky! I know you're mad I married Caleb, but that was Papa's doin'. You know it always was you I loved.''

''You had a mighty strange way of showin' it.''

''But I came to you, didn't I? I ran away from Caleb and came to find you. Don't that prove that I love you, Owen darlin'?''

His jaw tightened. ''You knew the Terrels would protect you. I reckon that's all it proves. You lied to us, no matter if it put Will's family in danger. And now you've done it again.''

She tossed her head, eyes icy. ''I didn't ask you Terrels to go get this from Caleb's hotel room.'' She indicated the valise. ''I did it all by myself.''

He gave a short laugh. ''Sure. You wouldn't trust us to bring it back to you, would you, Julia? You figure everybody's just like you, do anything for a wad of money.''

Her eyes flickered and he knew he'd hit the truth. But her protest was very prettily done. ''No, Owen, that's not true. Of course I trust you, dearest. Or I wouldn't ask you to go with me now.''

He regarded her with a kind of inner wonder. She was so beautiful—even more beautiful than she'd been as a young girl, the girl he'd dreamed about through all the years he'd waited for her. But the dream was gone now. He could look past the flawless skin, the gleaming hair, the tempting lips. There were currents in those pale eyes that, had they been the eyes of a man, would have made Owen wary at once.

''Well, I fear I'll have to disappoint you, Mrs. Wardworth,'' he said deliberately. ''You get your things and go. I believe this family can do without you.''

Her nostrils flared and suddenly she was not so beautiful. ''You don't mean that, Owen. You wouldn't send me out unprotected, carrying this.'' She picked up her valise as if she could no longer bear to leave it lying at her feet.

Owen shrugged. ''It was your choice to burden yourself with the money your daddy stole from hardworkin' honest folk. You can always take it back to your husband.''

She dropped the case and sprang for him, fingers arched like claws. He caught her shoulder hard with his free hand. She gasped with pain, and became subdued. ''You're wasting time, ain't you, lady?''

She froze for a moment, staring at him. Then, incredibly, she grinned. There was nothing feminine or soft about her now. He let her go, and she stepped back, rubbing her shoulder.

''You think you can drive me away, just like that, Owen Terrel?''

''Yes, ma'am, I think I can,'' he said easily.

She bent, lifted the case, put it back in the buggy. Then she turned, and Owen wondered why she had become so calm.

''And I think you'll go with me,'' she said. ''Because if you don't, I'll simply tell Will I need help. He don't

hate me like you do, Owen. An' maybe I should mention
Caleb won't come after me alone. That never was his
way. He'll hire a little help, an' he won't be lookin' for
men who give a hoot about little children.''

Owen had never felt like striking a woman before. Now
he had to clench his fist at his side, struggling for control.
The devil of it was, she had the upper hand. Will would
let her stay, let her turn his home into a besieged fort. It
wasn't in him to refuse to shelter and protect a woman,
no matter how unworthy.

She tilted her head, eyes sparkling. ''Well, Owen?
Who's wastin' time now?''

He let out his breath slowly. ''Looks like you win this
one. I'll get my horse and rifle.''

He turned away, but she stopped him with an urgent
hand upon his elbow. ''And don't stand about sayin'
good-bye to that little hussy Virginia. You won't be
comin' back. It wouldn't be fair to lead her on, now,
would it?''

Without comment, Owen jerked his arm free and hurried as quickly as his crutch would allow, around the
house to the sheds at back. He grasped a saddle blanket
left-handedly, flung it and then his saddle upon the dun
gelding's back, cinching it up with one hand. It was
harder to bridle the horse. He had to lean the crutch aside,
balancing on one foot.

Fortunately Owen's rifle was still with his saddle. He
wouldn't have to go back to the house. It wouldn't do to
have to explain to the family where he was going. Will
and the others would try to stop him, might even follow
him and leave the women and children unprotected. Owen
intended to make it very clear to Wardworth that Julia
and the money were nowhere close to this place. But
Wardworth was smart enough to realize that Will just
might take a notion to track him to the ends of the earth,
make him pay for the grief he'd caused the Terrel family
and crew. Could be ol' Caleb would send a couple of
fellers here too.

Dill and Crow and Jones would take care of that. And
with that in mind, Owen mounted, awkwardly sliding his
bad leg over the cantle, unable to use the stirrup on that
side. He bent to open the gate, maneuvering the horse

out, replacing the gate without dismounting. He trotted his horse to the side yard, where Olaf Jones and Crow were loafing under a big elm.

Owen whistled softly, conscious that Virginia was watching curiously from the kitchen window, where she and Amelia were washing up after the meal. God, it was hard to leave Ginny without a word!

Crow sprang up, came over to Owen with a curious look.

"You shouldn't be ridin', Owen."

"Never mind that for now," he said urgently. "There may be some trouble. I want you to keep alert. Pass the word to the others. Watch the family real close, will you? And take care of Ginny for me. I'll be back as soon as I can."

Crow studied him frowningly, then nodded once, briskly. No amount of talk would have been more expressive of his loyalty. "Reckon you could tell me where you're headed?"

Owen considered for a moment. "My brother mustn't know," he said at last. "Leastways, not for a few hours, or until you hear from me. Wardworth's in town, got him some new little helpers, most likely. Julia's gone and got back her damned money. Her lovin' husband will surely be after it with ever'thing he can muster. I'll get her away from here."

Crow studied him for a long minute and there was a hint of suspicion in his black eyes. "Has that blond filly got to you, Captain?"

Owen met his stare with a harsh laugh. "Oh, yeah. Same way a rattler underfoot gets to me. She's brewed up a new batch of trouble, and she's fixin' to spread it around my family again. Might be I can head it off."

"I hear you. I'll poke Jones awake an' get Dill. We'll keep a eye out."

"I'm obliged." Owen touched the gelding with his heel.

Julia was ready to go. She gave the buggy horse a smart sting with her whip, sent it stepping smartly along the street, catching up with Owen. "Aren't you goin' the wrong way?" she asked. "I want to go to Santa Fe."

He said nothing at all, continuing toward the tiny busi-

ness district of the town. His eyes were busy, checking
for riders headed their way. But there was nothing that
looked out of the ordinary. A bony cow grazed in a field
with several goats. A string of brilliant red chilies hung
upon the outer wall of a tiny, sun-warmed adobe-house,
and dark-haired children played with a litter of spotted
pups in the sand near the open door.

"Owen, hold up," Julia called. "Where are you going? Owen, stop!"

He glanced at her, saw the dawning alarm on her face
as she realized that he intended leading her into the cen-
ter of the town. She started to rein her buggy horse about.
He reached and caught the line on his side, snapped it
out of her hand. He spurred his horse to a lope, leading
the horse and buggy along at a pace too fast for Julia to
risk leaping out of the vehicle.

For a few moments Julia screeched protests and pleas.
Then she raised the whip and slashed at Owen. The tip
stung his shoulder. Owen refused even to look back at
her. She struck him again, then seemed to give up her
efforts to stop him, as if realizing that she would draw
dangerous attention to herself if she continued.

There were few people about on the streets. It was
siesta time. Owen saw what he was looking for in front
of the town's only hotel. Three men were gathered at the
hitch rail, urgently conferring. Even as he watched, they
broke apart and mounted.

"Owen," Julia cried, fright making her voice hoarse.
"Look out, there they are. Let me go, Owen, please!"

With contempt he flung the line back to her. "Good-
bye Julia, hope you like Santa Fe." She turned the horse
and whipped it into a run. The buggy wheels hit a puddle, the muddy water splashing. Owen kept going, directly toward the hotel, and Wardworth.

But Wardworth had spotted Julia. He shouted at one of
his men, gestured wildly. Wardworth's man drew his
handgun and kicked his horse into a run, prepared to
dash past Owen, to pursue the buggy. Calmly Owen lifted
his Winchester, sent a slug through the rider's left shoulder. As he fell, his gun was flung far out of reach.

Owen urged his horse into a full run. Ahead of him
Wardworth and his other hired gun dismounted, diving

into shelter behind a horse trough, from which they opened fire.

Terrel bent low, racing toward the trough that hid the two men. His charge must have been unnerving. The shots went wild, though a couple whined menacingly close.

Terrel drove the horse directly at the wide water trough. The dun soared up and over as the second of Wardworth's hired gunmen let out a yell and scrambled away on all fours. The dun's leap had carried Owen past Wardworth, who cringed back against the thick, water-dark planks of the water trough. Owen caught a glimpse of his pasty face, eyes popping with fright and rage.

Owen spun his excited horse about as a slug ripped past his body, nicking the cantle of his saddle. Now he was facing Wardworth, who desperately leveled his pistol again. Owen's rifle barrel lifted. He knew that death could be no more than a heartbeat away. It seemed unimportant. There was time enough for what must be done. His finger drew steadily upon the trigger.

The Winchester roared, shattering the afternoon. Wardworth's gun echoed and reechoed the shot. Something seared Owen's neck. He was bleeding, he could feel the sticky warmth under his shirt collar.

But Wardworth was bending forward, the front of his black suit and snowy-white shirtfront splashed red. He went down like a jointed wooden doll, his top hat rolling aside in the mud.

Terrel looked for the last remaining gunman, but he had apparently decided the fight was not rightly his; he was running, far along the street.

So, it was over. Terrel sat his horse for a long moment, staring at the dead man, facedown before him. He felt nothing much except a deep fatigue and a sharp ache in his bad leg.

He reined his horse out into the street again, letting him walk. He passed the wounded gunman, who lay carefully still, hands in plain sight and empty. He stared up at Owen fearfully. "Mister, could—could you get me some help?" he asked hoarsely.

Owen nodded, rode on. He looked about for Julia's

buggy, but there was no sign of it. Likely Julia wouldn't slow down this side of the Sacramento Mountains.

Terrel breathed deeply, lifted his shoulders. He must find whoever passed for law here in this little town, report what had taken place. Then maybe he could go home . . .

Funny that he was thinking of the little rented cottage, where he had never so much as spent a night, as home. Not too hard to figure why. Everything that mattered to him waited there.

As he stopped his horse and prepared to dismount at the small, rock-walled jail, a rider came racing along the street. Owen looked around, startled to see Virginia, dark hair blowing loose, skirts flying. She slid her horse to a stop, quickly climbed down.

"Owen, we heard the shooting. And I saw you leaving with Julia. Oh, dear God, you're hurt."

"No, no, it's only a scratch. I'm okay."

Awkwardly Owen got down, balanced on his good leg until he could lean against the hitch rail. Virginia rushed into his arms. He could feel her trembling, and he held her for a long, healing moment. Another rider galloped up to them. It was Crow, looking sheepish. He carried Owen's crutch in one hand and handed it down to Terrel.

"Sorry, Captain. Miss Virginia got away from me."

"No matter, Crow. It's all over with. I wish you'd find a doctor for that man layin' in the street yonder. The undertaker will do for the other one."

Ginny leaned back in his arms, her face still pale with worry. "It was that man Wardworth, wasn't it?"

Owen pressed her face close to his shoulder again. "He won't be botherin' anyone anymore. Now, you go back with Crow. Tell the family I'm okay an' all's well. I'll be home directly."

She stepped back, gazed at him for a moment with eyes that said things a man would give a lifetime to hear. Then she remounted and rode away with Crow alongside. Owen watched her for a moment, his weariness gone. Tucking his crutch under his arm, he swung up on the boardwalk and into the jail.